To Sam,
I hope
Boi's story
you to act
dreams.

reading
inspires
test

Lance

# Eleven Miles

Lance Greenfield

Lance Greenfield

20th August 2016

For my darling wife, Joy

First Kindle Edition, December 2014
First Lulu Edition, December 2014
Copyright © Lance Greenfield 2014

Edited by Boikanyo Phenyo
Cover design by Lance Greenfield

ISBN: 978-1-326-10803-8

# Acknowledgements

The inspiration behind this story is a remarkable lady whom I met on a business flight to somewhere. I can't remember the destination, but I remember the conversation. When I discovered how Boikanyo Phenyo had forged her path from poor beginnings in a village in Maun, Botswana, to become a well-qualified, international director of beauty pageants, and heard something of her background, I just had to write this story. To earn the education that would change her own destiny, not only did Boikanyo have to work very hard, but she had to walk eleven miles to school each morning and the same distance home in the afternoon. Now she motivates others to follow in her footsteps. She also runs a number of projects to improve the lot of the people of her homeland. One of these projects is a charity which she set up to buy a bus for the villagers of Sexaxa near Maun, Botswana, to transport the children to and from school, and to be a utility vehicle for the general good of those villages. A portion of the proceeds of this book will go to that charity.

Boikanyo has helped me in the production of this book by collecting little anecdotes for me to enlarge upon, and by providing authentic names for the characters and places in my work of fiction. Some of the names are the closest Setswana translations of English names that I had dreamed up in my own head to suit the circumstances. Others are combinations of names from long lists that she and others provided for me.

The book was also edited by Boikanyo, so I thank her for all her efforts in eliminating silly mistakes and providing authentic fit to life in her homeland.

I also thank my father and step-mother, Tony and Liz Greenfield, who listened to my readings from the book with critical ears, and encouraged me when I needed motivation.

# Characters and Place Names

## *Characters*

| Auntie Koketso | To increase | Boi's Auntie |
|---|---|---|
| Badisa | Herd boy | Boy in Boi's class who is always middle order, but doesn't care |
| Boitoi | To witch itself | Girl in Boi's class who is always near the bottom in history, geography, Setswana and English |
| Boitumelo Hope Tumelo (Boi) | Happiness Hope Faith | A little girl who must travel eleven miles each way to attend her secondary school to gain the education she so strongly desires. |
| Bokang | Praise | Mister van Gils's chauffeur |
| Bonolo Gosego (Bono) | Soft - It's lucky | The Botswana national athletics coach |
| Bontle | Beauty | The girl whom Sergeant Dintwa courts |
| Captain Duncan Odongo | | The Chief of the Marekisokgomo police |
| Gabanakitso | They don't have knowledge | A classmate from primary school who was usually near the bottom of the class |
| Gasenna | It's not me | Thapelo's mischievous friend |
| Gogontle Mooketsi | It's beautiful One who | Moagi's father |

| | increases | |
|---|---|---|
| Gontse | It's enough | Grace's brother |
| Gotweng | What's to be said | Friend of The Fox |
| Kagiso | Peace | Owner of the only car in Itlhomolomo |
| Kedibonye | I have seen them | The school security guard |
| Kefilwe | I have been given | Brainy friend from primary school |
| Kethwaahetse Motsumi | A hunter | Joins Boi's class in Form Three. He has moved from East Ville, and now lives in Nonyane, close to Dinokana and Moagi's farm. |
| Lefoko Dintwa (aka 'The Fox) | Word Wars | Sergeant in the BDF - Botswana Defence Force (the equivalent of Ministry of Defence in Botswana) |
| Mary-Jane Deakin | | American marathon runner |
| Mister Michael Way | | Sports master from England. Olympic triathlete |
| Mma K Agisanyang | Build together | Boi's Form One teacher. Deputy head of the MISS - responsible for the Junior Secondary School |
| Mma Kebonang | What do I see | Setswana teacher |
| Mma Kelebogile | I have thanked | Art teacher |
| Mma Lesedi | Light | Form Five and History teacher |
| Mma | Small person | The kind old lady who |

| Mothoriyana | | lives in Inagolo. Boi greets her on the way to school each day |
|---|---|---|
| Mma Othusitse | She has helped | Home Economics |
| Mma Ratanang | Love each other | Social Studies teacher and Form Three class teacher |
| Mma Reetsang | Listen | Music teacher |
| Mma Tlotlo Mothale | Respect | The head teacher and mathematics teacher at Marekisokgomo Integrated Secondary School |
| Mmama | | Boi's grandmother Full name: Mothusi (helper) Mpho (gift) Lesego (luck) Moved to Gakhibidu when Boi was little |
| Moagi | A builder; a resident | Classmate of Boi Lives on a farm in Dinokana |
| Molathegi | He who is lost | Classmate of Boi and Grace |
| Mompati Tumelo (Ntate) | One who accompanies me Faith | Boi's Dad – known to Boi as Ntate Works in the Orapa mines |
| Moreetsi Mothatego | One who listens | Established female Batswana marathon runner |
| Mosetsanagape | A girl again | Girl in Boi's class who had to leave at the end of Form Two because she was pregnant |
| Ntatemogolo | | Boi's granddad - first |

| | | name is Ofentse |
|---|---|---|
| Nyack Mothusi Tumelo | Helper Faith | Boi's second brother – picks up odd pieces of work at the mines. Always stays in Orapa in the hope that he will get a permanent job as a miner, like his Dad and elder brother. |
| Patience Tumelo (Mme) | Patience Faith | Boi's Mum - known to Boi as Mme |
| Rre Kitso | Knowledge | English teacher - and Form Four class teacher |
| Rre L Tsholofelo | Expectation | The local builder in Marekisokgomo |
| Rre Lekgowa | White man | Integrated Science and head of the senior secondary school |
| Rre Moreri | Preacher | Religious Education teacher |
| Rre Tholego | Nature | Agriculture teacher |
| Rre Tshotlego | Suffering | Form Two teacher |
| Seloilwe | It's been witched | Older boy from Itlhomolomo |
| Sethunya | A flower | A flirty girl in the class above Boi |
| Simisani Mathumo | | Traditional doctor from Setshwano |
| Tabansi Gosego Tumelo | Shining Faith | Boi's eldest brother Works in the Orapa mines |
| Tadelesh Mothibi Tumelo | Lucky Faith | Boi's third brother - helps on the dairy farm between Itlhomolomo and Kintisha. |
| Thapelo Olebile | Prayer | The youngest of Boi's four |

| | | |
|---|---|---|
| Tumelo (Lesilo) | He is looking Faith | brothers - only one year older than herself. Also known to some as Lesilo (naughty one) |
| Tshegofatso Grace Maphenyo (Grace) | Blessing | Boi's class mate and best friend from the days of their earliest memories Runner and netball team player who lives in neighbouring village - Kango |
| Uncle Kgotlhang | Conflict | Boi's uncle Son and daughter - Boi's cousins: Kabo (to give), Phala (whistle) |
| Uncle Tsholofelo Poifo | Expectation Fear | Boi's uncle, who becomes her manager when she shows money-earning potential at running. Lives in Phuthaditšhaba. |

## *Place Names*

| | |
|---|---|
| Bonwakatse | Village that Kefilwe moves to after leaving the school at the end of Form Two |
| Dinokana | Village where Moagi lives |
| East Ville | Town from which Kethwaahetse moved |
| Gaborone | Capital of Botswana |

| | |
|---|---|
| Gakhibidu | Village that Boi's grandparents moved to when she was little |
| Inagolo | Village where Mma Mothoriyana lives |
| Itlhomolomo | Boi's village<br>Eye = Leitlho<br>Mouth = Molomo<br>With combination first 2 letter are missed out so<br>Eyemouth = Itlhomolomo |
| Kango | Village where Grace lives |
| Lephutshe | Town near to Bonwakatse |
| Marekisokgomo | Town of secondary school<br>Cattle-market = Marekisetso-a-Kgomo<br>or in short<br>Marekisokgomo |
| Metsimantsho | The swamp - translates as dark water |
| Nonyane | The village of Kethwaahetse |
| Orapa | Town of the diamond mines where Rre Mompati Tumelo works |
| Phuthaditšhaba | Village of Uncle Tsholofelo Poifo |
| Serowe | Capital of the Central District and location of the national schools athletics competition |
| Setshwano | Next village to Inagolo |
| Tobetsa | Village on the edge of the swamp |

# One - Nngwe

Boi was already awake when the cockerel crowed. In fact, she'd hardly slept all night. She'd been far too excited to sleep. Her mind had been spinning with thoughts of what the daybreak would bring, and how she imagined her future following this momentous day.

At long last, her first day at secondary school had arrived. It seemed to her that an age had passed since she'd celebrated her final day at Itlhomolomo Primary School back in October. That had only been six weeks ago, but the days had dragged by. She had thought of little else but what she would do at her new school. It meant the world to her. She was determined to get herself a full education and move on to university. Not for her was the drudge of child-bearing followed by home-making, alongside two or three mundane jobs, from the age of fourteen until the day she died. With greatest respect to her female ancestors, what was the point of that?

She knew, with absolute certainty, that it was about five to four. Throughout the eleven years and two months of her life to date, the cock had always crowed with unerring accuracy at exactly the same time each morning. Of course, the family's current cockerel was not the first she'd known. It was probably the fourth or fifth. They had eaten the last, named Jeremiah, on the day that she'd graduated from Primary School. She had very happy memories of that wonderful family feast. She had been the guest of honour, sitting on the floor of their house in the place normally occupied by her father, Rre Mompati Tumelo. That day, Ntate had willingly given up his place to his daughter.

Her uncles and aunts and many of her cousins had

come from the surrounding villages to join the celebrations.

Her mother, Mma Patience Tumelo, had spent most of the day preparing and cooking the bird and the fresh vegetables in the small round house adjoining their family house, which was their kitchen.

As Boi lay in her bed, she remembered every detail of that day, including the mouth-watering aroma as Jeremiah roasted on a spit over the cooking fire. It had amazed her that everyone had contributed so much to the meal that there had even been plenty of left-overs. Of course, there had not been anywhere near enough meat on Jeremiah to feed the entire family, so the additional contributions had all been very welcome and essential to the completeness of the celebration.

How happy and proud she had been to receive the congratulations of her entire family on that day. She had felt like a queen for the day as each person had come forward and paid homage to her achievements. From this first school-day forward she would strive to repeat the experience. In just five years she would be sitting in the same place, having attained top grades in her BGCSEs. And then it would not be too long before she would sit with select members of her family, and some yet-to-be-acquired intellectual friends, in a real restaurant in a real city, as they celebrated her graduation, with honours of course, from a university.

During her brief moments of sleep, she had dreamed of many things, but especially of her father. She had clearly seen Ntate, proudly waving to her until she disappeared around the bend on her first walk to school. Sadly, he would not be there this morning.

She loved her father. He was so kind to her. She knew that he spoiled her really, but what girl wouldn't allow herself to be spoiled by a kind father? Ntate would never let her down, and would literally work his fingers to the bone to ensure that his Boitumelo could achieve her academic ambitions.

At last, she heard her mother calling, "Wake up, Boitumelo Hope Tumelo! It is time to get ready for school. Wake up, Thapelo Olebile Tumelo! You must take your little sister along the road to the school. It is a big day for her, and you must look after her. It is your duty."

Boi pretended to stretch and gradually become fully conscious, just as if she had really been sleeping.

"Oh Mme! I am so happy. Today is truly the beginning of my education. Primary school was just a playground. I will learn such a lot!"

"You will, Boi. You are a very good girl."

"Is there any phalishi left over from last night? I am really hungry."

"No. I used up all the maize flour for our supper, and we finished it all. Don't worry. The school will give you some lunch in the middle of the day. But I've got a little bit of bread you can have. Light the fire quickly and I'll make some fresh coffee when the pot boils. Make sure you have a drink of water before you go."

\* \* \* \* \*

As they waited for the pot to heat on the fire, Boitumelo lamented the absence of her father and two elder brothers. She was almost crying. Her mother had to remind her that without the money that Ntate and the eldest of her four brothers, Tabansi Gosego Tumelo, sent home from the diamond mines in far-away Orapa, she would not be going to school today. They wouldn't even have enough money to put food on the table.

3

"Ntate and Tabansi saw your smart school skirt and blouse when they were home two weeks ago. I am sure that they are thinking of you today, Boi."

"Yes. I really appreciate everything that they do for us, Mme, but I really miss them."

"Well, they still come home at least once a month to see us. It is a long journey for them, and they miss three of four days of pay every time they come. Next time they are here, I am sure they will be very interested to hear how you have enjoyed your early days at the big school."

"It is always good to see them, Mme. But we haven't seen Nyack for over a year. It was his sixteenth birthday last week. Surely he could have come home to celebrate it with his family."

"As I have explained it to you many times, Boi, Nyack Mothusi Tumelo cannot afford to leave Orapa for even a single day. He must go to the mine manager's office every day to ..."

"Alright Mme! I know! You have told me a million times before."

Nyack had always harboured strong ambitions to also work in the mines like his brother and father. While he waited for a well-paid, full-time job as a miner, he stayed in Orapa and picked up any work that he could get. Some days he would be washing pots in the miners' canteen. Other days he would be running errands for the shopkeepers. Occasionally, he would be lucky enough to be called upon to make some repairs, or to do some gardening, at the big house that belonged to the owner of the mines, Mister Jako van Gils. On those days he knew that he would at least be well fed. Unfortunately, making himself always available for work, and earning very little money, meant that Boi hardly ever saw him. It just meant that Nyack could never leave Orapa for fear of missing the elusive employment opportunity which he felt sure would eventually come his way.

"How long is that pot going to take to come to the boil, Boi?"

Boi's third brother, Tadelesh Mothibi Tumelo, was impatient. Boi knew that he had to get going soon if he was to get to work on time. He'd left school two years earlier, when he was just thirteen, and he was still living at home. He helped on the dairy farm between Itlhomolomo and Kintisha. It was only two miles from their home to the farm, but he had to be there by five o'clock every morning to round up the cows for milking. He enjoyed the work though, and would often be carrying a pail of fresh milk to share with the family when he returned to the house at nine in the evening. This never failed to make them all very happy.

According to Boi, all of her brothers were naughty in one way or another. But the most mischievous, by far, was Thapelo, who was only one year older than herself. She was sure that he did not study hard, and that he only went to school to get up to no good with his friends. Over the next few days, she would find out her assertion was true. For the moment, she was very pleased that Thapelo was still at school and could escort her on the long walk for her first day. However, if she discovered that what she had been told about his fooling around at school were true, she would be very angry. After all, Ntate and Tabansi were working hard to fund his education too. The least he could do to repay them was to work hard to achieve good results.

\* \* \* \* \*

Having washed and dressed, Boi sat on the ground

5

outside the door of their little house to enjoy the small chunk of bread and the mug of hot coffee that Mma Tumelo had given to her.

Her new shoes felt strange on her normally bare feet. Nyack had made them for her out of rubber tyres and sent them home with Tabansi especially for this day. He'd written her a short letter, which she treasured. He had wished her well at her new school, and asked her to promise to wear the shoes for the long walk to and from the school. They would last her for many years and save her feet from cuts on the stones along the rough track. In her reply, she had made that promise, but she wasn't sure how long she could keep it. She was in no doubt that she would be reverting to her more customary barefoot style within a few weeks.

The sky was already a pale peach colour. She could hear the noises of the surrounding families as they awoke and prepared for the day ahead. Already, Mma Marumo was yelling at the dogs which always plagued her little compound. Would she never learn that throwing the food scraps on the ground outside her house just attracted the dogs from all over the village? Boi wasn't going to tell her again. Her foolishness kept the dogs away from her own family home.

"Come on Boi. You can't sit there all day. It's a long walk to school. We must get going immediately."

Boi jumped to her feet. For a moment, she had been lost in thought and had almost forgotten the adventure of the day ahead. How could she?

"Bye Mme. We'll see you later. I love you."

Mma Patience Tumelo came running out of the house, holding back the tears as she hugged her only daughter tightly.

"Look after her Thapelo. If anything bad happens to this girl, I will never forgive you."

"I will guard her with my life, Mme. You know that you can rely on me," he grinned. "At least, for today," he added cheekily.

His mother met the comment with an attempted light slap to the back of Thapelo's head, which he avoided quite easily.

"You know your duty, boy. Don't fail me, or your father will soon hear about it."

She watched as her two youngest children walked out of the little courtyard. She could not resist the temptation to follow them as far as the edge of the village so that she could keep them in her line of vision until they disappeared from view. It would be many lonely hours before they returned. Her beautiful fledglings had flown the nest. At least they would be back by the time the sun set that evening.

# # # # #

# Two - Pedi

Boitumelo was enjoying her first walk to school. Already, the heat of the Botswana sun was upon them, but she had lived with it all of her short life. This was a very happy day for the young girl.

Thapelo chatted incessantly, but Boi was glad of his company. He was telling her about all the teachers and the pupils, who she should trust and who to watch out for. Although she was very grateful for his advice, she'd decided to make up her own mind. After a while, she didn't take in much of what he said. He had become like a bird chattering in a tree.

As they walked through the village of Inagolo, Thapelo waved to a lady with no legs who was sitting outside her house. He greeted her cheerily. "Dumela Mma Mothoriyana! O tsogile jang? Le kae?"

"I am well, Lesilo. Who is this? Is it your sister?"

"Yes Mma. This is my sister, Boitumelo Hope Tumelo. She is attending her first day at the Marekisokgomo Secondary School. Look at her in her smart uniform!"

"You look very smart, young lady. I am very pleased to meet you."

"It is good to meet you too Mma."

"Call in to see me on your way home. I will bake a cake today and you shall each have a piece of it. We must celebrate your first day at Marekisokgomo Junior Secondary School. It is a big event in your life, Boitumelo."

"We will definitely come to your door this afternoon, Mma," Thapelo replied.

"Mma Mothoriyana's cakes are even better than our own mother's, sister. Don't you dare tell Mme I said so, though," he chuckled.

"We must go quickly now. I promised to meet Gasenna at the crossroads. Goodbye Mma."

For the next mile, Thapelo forced the pace. Boi had never seen his brother in such a rush to get anywhere. Moreover, he was unusually silent.

"Who is Gasenna, brother? You haven't told me about him."

"Weren't you listening to me as we walked along earlier? I told you. He is my best friend, and we will meet him at the crossroads. Hurry! He will be waiting for us."

"Why are you in such a hurry to meet your friend?"

"You will see, Boi. We always have a competition."

They rushed along the dry track. Boi's rubber tyre shoes were weighing heavy on her feet, but something was weighing even more heavily on her mind. Eventually, she had to ask her brother the question that was troubling her.

"Why does Mma Mothoriyana call you Lesilo? Naughty One?"

"Oh, she just thinks I am very cheeky because I always have a smile and a joke for her."

Thapelo was pleased that his answer appeared to satisfy Boi. However, despite her pan face, something was still niggling at her mind. The name seemed to match her brother's reputation.

As they approached the crossroads, Boi could see a boy sitting in the shade of a tree. As soon as the boy saw them approaching, he leapt to his feet and greeted Thapelo as if he had not seen his friend for months.

"Hello Thapelo. We are really lucky this morning. While I was waiting for you, I managed to find SIX

9

cans lying around. People are so careless with their litter, but that works out very well for you and me. I have balanced them on the branch of the tree over there, ready for our competition."

"You have done well Gasenna Karabo. Shall we throw ten stones each?"

"Yes Thapelo. I set them up, so you can throw first."

"What is going on, brother? We must get to school. I can't be late on my first day!"

"Don't worry little sister. We will be there in plenty of time. Tradition is important. This duel is a tradition between me and Gasenna that has been running for many months. Watch us. You will learn something and be proud of your brother's victory."

Thapelo bent down and selected his first stone. He stared towards the tree in which the cans were balanced. Suddenly, he cast the stone at great speed towards the tree, and a can clattered to the ground.

"Yes! It is my day. You are already beaten, my friend."

"We shall see, Thapelo. You still have nine throws, and nothing is certain."

When Thapelo's next four stones missed, it looked as if Gasenna's prediction might come true. His sixth stone knocked another can out of the tree.

"Two hits from six is not good. I am going to beat you this morning."

"C'mon. Hurry up! We are going to be late!"

"Tell your sister to be quiet. This is a serious competition."

"Calm down Boi. I tell you: we have plenty of time to arrive at the school before Mma Tlotlo will make her welcoming speech."

Thapelo cast his seventh stone. It sailed through

the branches of the tree, going nowhere near to any of the cans. His last three stones followed suit.

"Oh Thapelo. Only two hits. You are surely beaten today. Admit defeat, and we can go straight to school."

"No Gasenna. I will replace the two cans that I hit, and we shall soon see if you are as good with your hands as you are with your mouth."

A few seconds later, all ten cans were balanced in the branches of the tree and Gasenna was taking aim with his first stone.

He threw.

A can bounced onto the ground beneath the tree.

"That was very lucky my friend. I could see you were aiming for the middle cans, yet you hit the can on the extreme left."

"Rubbish! I am going to knock them down, one-by-one, from left to right. That was always my plan."

But, contrary to any plan that Gasenna did or did not have, his next nine stones all missed their targets and Thapelo won the contest.

"Tomorrow will be different, Thapelo. I was out of practice this morning, and I was stiff from having to wait so long for you."

"You boys are both pathetic. Even I, a mere girl, could beat you both at this game."

"Don't be silly, Boitumelo Hope Tumelo. Your brother and I have plenty of experience at throwing. Besides, as you say, you are merely a girl. It is very well known in Botswana that girls cannot throw stones."

"If you are so sure of yourself, Gasenna, pick up that can which has fallen, and stand back. I will show you what a MERE girl can do!"

Gasenna did as he was told. He stood, with his

arms folded, watching Boi as she stooped to pick up a stone. She bent her knees and wound up for her first throw. She launched the stone, hard and low, towards the tree. It struck the trunk but came nowhere near any of the cans.

The two boys hooted with laughter. Boi frowned at them and picked up another stone. She held her breath and closed her eyes for a few seconds before spinning on her heals and flinging the stone with all her might at the tree.

Ping!

A can cart-wheeled out of the tree.

"YESSSSS!"

"That was beginner's luck, Boitumelo. Let us see you do that again."

"Don't be too sure, Gasenna. My sister is good at most things. She may yet surprise us."

Boi picked up her third stone, and repeated her previous feat.

"YESSSSS! That is two out of three for me! I have beaten you already, Gasenna, and I am equal with my brother."

"All right. I am impressed, but I still say that it is beginner's luck. We should go to school now."

"No. My brother says that we have plenty of time. I intend to throw all seven of my remaining stones."

As Boi repeatedly picked up her stones, and knocked down cans, the two boys could only watch open-mouthed. She only missed with one throw, so all six cans were lying on the ground by the time she had thrown eight times.

"Now what do you have to say, Gasenna?"

"Well, I have to admit that you are very good, Boi. For a mere GIRL, anyway."

"Six-one was a very big victory for a girl OR a

boy. You should admit that."

"OK. You deserve my respect. You have it. Now let's get to school."

After a few hundred metres walked in silence, Gasenna turned to Thapelo and told him, "Your sister is quite something, Thapelo. I think she is going to do very well at Marekisokgomo Secondary School."

\* \* \* \* \*

Half an hour later they arrived outside the school. Lots of children were milling around, greeting each other excitedly. Boi looked around for anyone that she might know. There was bound to be somebody, but she didn't know if the families of any of her friends from primary school had been able to afford the fees, or even if they would endure the long walk to Marekisokgomo for their education.

Thapelo continued to chatter instructions to his sister, which she only half heard.

"You will go in that door over there, at the end of the building, Boi. All the new Form One pupils will go there. You will sit on the floor in the big room. The head teacher herself will address you. She is very wise. She will tell you a lot of useful information, and you must remember it all. She will ....."

"Aaayeeeee! Boi! It is you!" A scream came from behind them.

Boi turned, and was truly delighted to come face to face with her very best friend from primary school.

They hugged each other tightly.

"Oh Tshegofatso Grace Maphenyo! My dear friend! I am so pleased to see you here at the school. I can't tell you how wonderful it is to have my best friend here today. I hope that we will be in the same class."

13

"You WILL all be in the same class, sister. There will be about forty of you in Form One. All in the same class together."

"Have you seen anyone else we know, Grace?

"Yes. But only that boy, Kefilwe. I am sure that you remember him." She giggled.

Boi's heart fluttered. Of course she remembered him. She really liked him, and it was no secret that Grace really liked him too. Not only was he handsome, but he was very good at every subject at school. Boi, Grace and Kefilwe had always competed for the top three places in class. Boi was already wondering if this would continue into Form One at Marekisokgomo Junior Secondary School. She enjoyed the competition and strongly believed that, if she could prevail, Kefilwe would come to like her enough to ask her to be his girlfriend.

However, she knew that her friend, Grace, would not be her only rival for either the top place in class, or for the attention of Kefilwe. There would now be many more bright girls and boys coming in from all the villages around. Some of the girls might be much prettier than her, and they would surely turn the head of her intended boyfriend.

A very tall and dignified-looking lady appeared at the door which Thapelo had previously indicated. In her hand, she held a brass hand bell. She raised it and rang it several times. The children hushed slightly, not quite to silence, but enough to be able to hear her cry out.

"Would all new students, starting today, please follow me into the school hall?"

It was not really just a request. In obedience, the younger children gravitated towards the doorway into which the teacher had now disappeared.

Inside, Grace and Boi sat together exchanging

14

snippets of news from the past few weeks since they'd last seen each other. Kefilwe sat down behind them and greeted them both with genuine delight.

"That's four of us who have come from Itlhomolomo Primary School together."

The girls looked around for anybody else that they knew.

"Who else came with us, Kefilwe?"

"There! Look! It is Gabanakitso. Over there."

They looked where he was pointing.

Boi couldn't believe her eyes. Gabanakitso had always been near the bottom of the class throughout their primary school years. "She is a lovely girl, and I like her, but I didn't think that she would continue with her education."

"I agree Boi," said Grace. She is very pretty too. I always thought that she would be heading for Gaborone to find herself a rich husband."

"You are both wrong. She spent most of her time at primary school being distracted and having a lot of fun. She could get away with it. Now she is serious, and she is going to work hard."

"How do you know so much, Kefilwe?" asked Boitumelo.

"Didn't you know? Her family moved to my village at the end of last term. We have spent a lot of time together over the summer."

There was no time for further conversation. Silence fell in the large room as Mma Tlotlo stood up to speak.

The two girls turned to face the front, raising their eyebrows at each other as they did so.

*What could he mean?*

\* \* \* \* \*

15

Mma Tlotlo smiled broadly, and took her time to look around her new intake. Forty-two faces shone back at her, reflecting her obvious enthusiasm.

"I am Mma Tlotlo, the head teacher of Marekisokgomo Integrated Secondary School. I warmly welcome you to OUR school. I say OUR school, because for the next five years, this is as much your school as it is mine. I am proud to be a part of this school, and very soon you will all be just as proud as I am.

"We all work together, staff and pupils, to achieve excellent results. We all work very hard, but we ALL enjoy everything that we do here.

"For your first two years, you will be in forms one and two in Marekisokgomo Junior Secondary School, in rooms on this side of the playground. You will then graduate to Marekisokgomo Senior Secondary School, on the far side of the playground, for your final three years at school. Officially, these are two schools, but I think of them as a single, integrated school, sharing many facilities such as the library and the gymnasium. Our school is the first integrated school in Botswana. We are pioneers in many respects. So far, we have been very successful, and there are already three other schools in our country who are following our example.

"We have a deputy head teacher in charge of each of the schools.

"This is Mma K Agisanyang, who is my deputy responsible for the junior secondary school, and who will be your form teacher for the whole of your first year: your foundation year. You know that her name means "build together", and she will be working together with all of you to build the foundations of your secondary education for the years to follow."

Mma K Agisanyang stepped forward and surveyed her new intake of pupils. She was much shorter than Mma Tlotlo, and rather rotund in a cuddly sort of way. Boi thought that she looked very friendly and took an immediate liking to her Form One teacher before she even spoke.

"Good morning children!" she beamed.

About half of the class responded with a polite "Good morning Mma."

"We will soon get to know each other very well. As Mma Tlotlo says, we have a lot of hard work to do in the coming year, but I am sure that we will all enjoy ourselves."

She took a step back to allow the head teacher to continue.

"In a few minutes Mma K Agisanyang will take you all outside and show you around the school. It may seem daunting at first. It was for me when I first arrived. But if there is anything you don't understand, please ask Mma K Agisanyang immediately. She will be happy to inform you. Please pay attention to her when she tells you the places that you can and cannot enter, and especially the places where you should only go if you are accompanied by a teacher.

"Now I am going to tell you something very important. Please pay attention."

She paused.

"The motto of this school is 'There is no prejudice.'"

Again, she paused.

"Allow me to explain what this means to you, to me and to the teaching and administrative staff. I expect everyone in this school to treat everyone else with the utmost respect. It does not matter what their background is, or where they live, or what they believe.

17

It does not matter that different people have different strengths and weaknesses. There is no difference between those who are blind and those who can see. There is no difference between those who can hear and those who cannot. There is no difference between those who are lame and those who are fit and able. Everybody has strengths and weaknesses. We all have some great talent, a gift from God, even if we don't know what it is yet. If you see somebody who is struggling, then you must help them rather than mock them.

"So this school motto, 'There is no prejudice,' is taken very seriously by everyone at Marekisokgomo Secondary School, and observing it is paramount to the success of this school."

Mma Tlotlo looked around as the pupils tried to absorb this message. She knew that some of them would not immediately understand, but it would not be many weeks before almost all of them would be proud, and happy, to live their lives by the school motto.

"Now, please follow Mma K Agisanyang as she shows you around the school and, eventually, to your classroom. Enjoy the rest of your first day."

* * * * *

The rest of the morning was taken up with the tour of the school.

Mma K Agisanyang deliberately took her time so that she could speak to her new class as a whole, and get to know each individual. While she explained the various parts of the school, she observed all of the children and as they connected with old friends and made new acquaintances.

They were all very enthusiastic, as she would have

18

expected, but one child stood out from all of the rest. It was Boi.

Mma K Agisanyang asked the girl where she was from.

When she heard that Boi was from Itlhomolomo, she asked, "You must be the sister of Thapelo Olebile Tumelo?"

"Yes Mma. He is my brother. He is in Form Two now."

"I know him well, Boitumelo. He will be very successful someday." She reflected for a few moments. "He will be very successful someday; IF he takes his unbounded energy in the right direction." Her meaning was obvious to Boi. "He tells me that you like to read a lot."

"Yes Mma. I read every book and newspaper that I am lucky enough to lay my hands on."

"We have a small school library here. I will be showing you this later after we have seen the gymnasium. I have a feeling that you will become very well acquainted with the library during the coming years Boitumelo."

"Yes. So do I, Mma. And the gymnasium too, I hope!"

Mma K Agisanyang pointed towards the classrooms of the Senior Secondary School which they would occupy in their years three to five. She told them that they would soon be able to see inside the classrooms, but first she wanted to show them the two newest buildings in the school grounds. After all of that, they would return to the opposite side of the playground, and their own classroom, at the end of their tour.

"Here is the gymnasium. It has only been built and equipped in the last four years. We are very proud of it."

Mma K Agisanyang opened the double doors of a large, new-looking building and the children filed in. None of them had ever seen anything like the sight before them. The whole of the large hall was constructed of smooth, shiny, light-coloured wood. All around the walls were wooden climbing bars. Strong ropes hung down from the very high ceiling. There were large boxes, full of all sorts of equipment in the four corners of the room.

For the first time since Mma Tlotlo had finished her welcoming speech, the children fell silent. As they looked around them, in wide-eyed awe, some of them allowed their mouths to hang open.

"You will all be spending much time here. The physical education master, Mister Michael Way, is from England. You will meet him tomorrow. He was in the British athletic team in the Sydney Olympic Games in the Form Two - thousand. If you want to be good at sports, Mister Way is the man who can help you.

"Take a look around, but do NOT touch the equipment or try to climb the ropes or wall bars. It is not safe until you have had proper instruction from Mister Way."

The children broke up into small groups, exploring the gym, looking into the boxes, and chattering excitedly.

"Thapelo told me about Mr Way, Grace. He is very strict but he knows a lot about every sport you can imagine."

"I hope that he can take us swimming. Swimming in the river is alright, but I want to learn how to race properly."

"You are a very good swimmer, Grace; better than anybody else our age. I also hope that he will help you

20

to be even better. Perhaps he could even help you to swim for Botswana in the Olympic team. That would change your life."

"Don't be ridiculous, Boi! It is very unlikely."

"Why not Tshegofatso Grace Maphenyo? You are already faster and stronger than all the girls AND boys of our age. And that's with no coaching. If you are still better than all the girls by the time we leave school in five years' time, you will be in the Botswana team for the Olympics. Why not?"

"I suppose you could be right. Let's see what Mr Way has to say to us tomorrow."

Their conversation was interrupted by a shout from Mma K Agisanyang.

"MOAGI! GET DOWN FROM THERE!

"Come here Moagi. Gather round everybody."

When all of the children had assembled around their teacher, she lectured the culprit.

"Did you hear me tell you NOT to climb on the wall bars, Moagi?"

"Yes Mma. You did tell us."

"So you deliberately disobeyed me, didn't you?"

"Yes Mma. I am very sorry."

"I understand your excitement, Moagi, but that is no excuse for your disobedience," she told him sternly. "You must listen to everything that I say to you, and you should do as you are told."

Moagi shuffled awkwardly, but said nothing.

"This time, I am going to let you off with a warning. Consider yourself very lucky. The next time you disobey me you will feel the pain of my cane. Do you understand?"

"Yes Mma. I will listen to you in future, Mma."

"Good! Let that also be a warning to all of you. I

hope that we will all get along very well together, but I will not tolerate disobedience. Do I make myself clear?"

"Yes Mma!" they chorused.

"Now, let us move on to the school library."

The children were a little quieter as they trooped next door into a much smaller building. They were unanimously shocked by Mma K Agisanyang's threat of discipline. Meanwhile, their teacher was secretly satisfied that Moagi had given her such an early opportunity to express her position on discipline. Furthermore, no physical pain had been inflicted upon her unintentional assistant. She really did not like to have to use her cane, and she hardly ever did so.

The library was so small that forty-two children and one comfortably built teacher almost filled the room to capacity. They had just enough room to be able to look around at the sparsely populated shelves which lined all four walls.

"You can see that three-quarters of the shelves are empty. This is not because most of the books are out on loan. It is because we rely on donations to fill the shelves. If you or your families have any books at home that you'd like to bring in, we would be delighted to have them. I will explain how the library works in an English lesson later this week, but if you are keen to borrow any of the books before that lesson, just let me know and I will tell you the rules.

"Now, follow me as we visit the classrooms of the Senior Secondary School before returning to our own side of the playground."

\* \* \* \* \*

By the time that they'd interrupted the classes of

years three to five, walked back to their own side of the school to visit Form Two, and finally arrived in their own classroom, it was almost time for lunch.

They were each given a blank notebook and a pencil and told to take very good care of them. These books were for general notes and to keep a diary of their school activities and assignments. Mma K Agisanyang had written the list of subjects which they were to study up on the blackboard. She told her pupils that they would receive individual notebooks for each of the subjects as they began their studies of each one.

The teacher showed them the blank grids which she had pinned to the walls around the classroom. On these grids, she told them, she would keep records of their scores in each of the subjects, and their grand totals on the grid at the front of the classroom. This way, they could track their own progress and see how they were doing against their classmates. At the end of each term, there would be small awards for the top pupils in each subject and overall. At the end of Form One, which was a long way away, there would be actual prizes for the top performers. She could not say what the prizes would be, or even if they would be awarded for every subject, but the school would do it best with the available funding.

The children were excited, already dreaming of out-achieving their fellows.

"Now it is time for our lunch. We must go into the playground and form orderly queues at the tables which have been set up. You will each receive a small snack and a drink. It is very important that you eat and drink what you are given, and then you must put your litter into the bins provided. Do not give away your snacks and drinks to your friends, and anyone whom I see throwing their litter on the ground WILL be punished.

"Once you have finished your lunch, you can play for a while. Don't wander off into the town, and come back into the classroom immediately when you hear the bell.

"Now go and enjoy your lunch."

All of them did enjoy their lunch. They each had a chunk of bread and butter and a drink of orange juice. Boi was aware that it wasn't really freshly squeezed orange juice, which would have been a rare treat, but had been made up from a powder dissolved in water. However, she was very grateful for the tasty drink.

Moagi, the boy who had been told off for climbing the wall bars, came and sat next to Boi and Grace. Kefilwe and Gabanakitso also joined the little group. Moagi was very excited. All of his life had been spent on his father's small farm in Dinokana, and he had only ever been as far as the two closest villages before coming to Marekisokgomo to begin secondary school. He was almost overwhelmed by the scale of everything.

"I can't wait to start physical education lessons with Mr Way in the huge gym!" he said. "I hope that he will be here tomorrow."

"Until then, you will have to be content with climbing trees on your way home," said Kefilwe.

\* \* \* \* \*

When they got back to their classroom after lunch, Mma K Agisanyang was already there waiting for them with a tall, distinguished-looking man.

"For the rest of the afternoon, your subject teachers are going to come to our classroom to introduce themselves, and to meet you. This gentleman is Rre Kitso, who will be teaching you English in years one and two."

24

Rre Kitso asked two of the children at the front of the class to hand out one exercise book to each pupil. They all had to write their names in the centre of the front cover, and the word "English" on the dotted line next to where the word "Subject" was printed. He then took some time to explain what they would be learning during the next two years, and how this would eventually help them to decide if they wanted to study English Literature in the Senior Secondary School. "Of course," he said, "English Language will continue to be a compulsory subject for you all the way through to the end of Form Five.

"Mma K Agisanyang is very good at keeping track of your progress. You have already seen the score grids that are pinned to the walls of the classroom. I will be giving all your marks to her for the work that you submit to me, and she will record them for you all to see.

"Are there any questions?"

Some of the pupils asked him questions about what he had just told them, but most remained quiet, a little bit shy and afraid to show themselves up in front of the class.

Shortly after Rre Kitso had left the room, the children were surprised when the door opened and Mma Tlotlo walked in. They all stood up respectfully.

"Please sit down children."

They resumed their seats.

"Why am I here? I will tell you. As well as being your headmistress, I will also be your maths teacher for much of your secondary school career. I love maths, and I always have. It relates to everything that we see and do. I can understand if some of you are secretly groaning inside, but I assure you that maths can be very exciting. You may not believe me today, but I hope that you will soon all be as enthusiastic as I am today."

She went on to explain what they might expect to learn in Form One, and, just like Rre Kitso before her, she equipped them all with exercise books for their maths classes and got them to write on the covers accordingly.

She was encouraged when some of the new pupils asked some very insightful questions. One girl was particularly enthusiastic and stood out from the crowd. It was Boitumelo Hope Tumelo.

During the rest of the afternoon, various other teachers were brought into the classroom for similar introductions.

The next two teachers to come into the room were Mma Kebonang, who would be teaching them Setswana, and Rre Lekgowa would teach them Integrated Science.

At this point, Mma K Agisanyang gave them a short break during which they all drank some water. Before more teachers were introduced, she explained to them that all of the subject that had been covered so far would be compulsory for years one and two. Physical Education would also be compulsory for Form One. "As I told you this morning, Mister Way will be your P.E. Teacher, and you will meet him tomorrow in the gym. The rest of the subjects will be taught to you for the first term only. At the end of the first term, we will decide between us which three or four subjects you will continue to learn for the rest of Form One and the whole of Form Two. Once we know which subjects are better for each of you, it will make your options easier."

Next into the classroom came Rre Tholego, the Agriculture teacher, followed by Mma Reetsang, the music teacher. Then came Mma Kelebogile for Art,

Mma Ratanang for Social Studies, Mma Othusitse for Home Economics and Rre Moreri for Religious Education.

By the time Rre Moreri had left the classroom, each of the pupils had an impressive pile of exercise books which Mma K Agisanyang told them to look after and only use for the subjects for which they'd been designated. At the back of the classroom, there were some small shelves. The pupils were given small white cards in which they wrote their names and used to label their personal shelves. Their teacher informed them that they could leave their books on their shelves overnight, or they could take them home in their school bags.

"Whatever you decide, these exercise books are your responsibility. You must take care of them."

At half past three, Mma K Agisanyang told her pupils, who were all very tired by this time that they could go home. Grace stayed with Boi as they waited for Thapelo to come out of his classroom at four o'clock. She grew impatient. She wanted to get home to tell Mme all about her first day at the school. It had been wonderful. It had been everything that she had dreamed. The two friends agreed that the next five years would shape their lives. Working hard for a good education, and gaining BGCSE results which would take them to university, would give them their passports to get away from the typical lives of village girls which generations before them had suffered. They didn't want to start producing children in their mid-teens and die at a young age. That was not for them. This day was truly the first day of the rest of their lives. They knew that was a cliché, but they really felt that it was true.

Thapelo and Gasenna burst out of the Form Two classroom door and raced past the waiting girls.

"Hey! Thapelo! Have you forgotten your little sister who you promised Mme you protect with your life?"

Thapelo skidded to a halt.

"Sorry Boi. I was in a hurry. Gasenna and I intend to go fishing."

"No Thapelo. Not today. You can go tomorrow. You made a promise to Mme. She will beat you if you break it."

"But you can walk nearly all the way home with Tshegofatso Grace Maphenyo. Your journeys home only split about half a mile before you get to Itlhomolomo. She only lives in Kango. You have walked there many times to see your precious friend. It takes you less than ten minutes."

"OK Thapelo. I will do that. Do you want me to tell Mme that you have gone fishing with Gasenna, and you will be home later?"

Thapelo paused for thought. Boi was right. Mme would be very angry. He could take a beating, but Mme's displeasure was hard to bear.

"Sorry Gasenna. I will come with you tomorrow after school. Today I must walk home with my sister and her friend."

"Will you definitely come fishing tomorrow Thapelo? Make a promise."

"I promise. And we will meet at the usual place on the way to school. Tomorrow I will beat you."

On the way home, the girls chatted non-stop, despite attempts by Thapelo to interrupt them.

Eventually, they reached the village of Inagolo where Mma Mothoriyana was watching out for them. She came hopping out of the shade of her little house and greeted them.

"Thapelo! Boitumelo! I have been waiting for you.

Come! Come! I have made a cake. Bring your friend too."

She hopped back into her house.

Boi was a little shocked. Only now did she realise that, as they had talked in the morning Mma Mothoriyana had been seated outside her house. Boi had not noticed that the old lady's left leg was missing from the knee down.

They sat down on the floor inside the little single-room house, happy to be out of the heat of the late afternoon. Mma Mothoriyana gave them each a cold drink of something which Boi suspected had been made from boiled leaves of some sort. She didn't really care. She was confident that this kind old lady would not be trying to poison them. And besides, it was very refreshing. Then they were each handed a chunk of delicious light sponge cake. It tasted of lemon, and Mma Mothoriyana confirmed that she had used some lemons that her nephew had kindly brought to her that morning.

"Will you please introduce me to you friend, Boitumelo?"

"Certainly Mma. This is Tshegofatso Grace Maphenyo. She is from Kango. We have been friends since we were babies, just as our mothers and grandmothers before us."

"Oh! I know your Mmama very well Boitumelo. Mothusi Mpho Lesego is very well known and respected. She is a few years younger than me of course. I haven't seen her since she moved away to Gakhibidu about five years ago."

"It was eight years ago Mma. I was only three. We travel to see her occasionally, and she came with my uncle when we had a big feast to celebrate my graduation from primary school."

"Yes. That would be right. How the years fly by!"

"This is delicious cake, Mma," said Thapelo. "Didn't I tell you, Boi?"

"Yes it is. Thank you very much, Mma. It is very tasty!"

Grace enthusiastically echoed Boi's thanks.

"I think I know your family too, Grace. Is your mother known as Botshelo Kelebogile, and your grandmother known as Itumeleng Kelebogile?"

"Yes Mma! You truly know my family!"

"Yes. I know them very well, Grace."

Mma Mothoriyana was very happy to see that the children had finished the cake that she had given them and had obviously enjoyed it very much.

"Would anyone like another piece of cake?"

"Yes please Mma!" the three chorused in unison.

As they eagerly devoured their second pieces of her delicious cake, Mma Mothoriyana noticed Boi glancing at her stump.

"You are probably wondering what happened to my leg, Boitumelo."

"Oh no, Mma! I don't mean to be rude."

"Don't worry child. You are just being curious, and I don't mind telling you at all. It saves you the bother of believing all the stories that people like to make up about it. I will tell you.

"Some people say it was blown off by a mine. It wasn't. Some say that a crocodile or a hippopotamus bit it off. That didn't happen either. Some people even say that I was shot by the police as I was trying to rob a bank!" She laughed loudly. "I can tell you that I am no gangster!

"It is a much more boring story than any of those, I am sorry to tell you.

"When I was a child, younger than you, I was

running along at the back of the village here. I was very careless about where I put my feet. I stepped on a fallen branch and a big thorn went into my foot. It went almost all of the way through. As you can imagine, it was very painful. My mother washed it thoroughly, but it became infected. She rubbed aloe vera on the wound several times a day, but it got worse. She even mashed aloe vera plants up, and wrapped them around my foot with cloths during the night when I slept.

"After two weeks, it was still deteriorating badly, and the infection was spreading up my leg. I had a fever and I fainted every time she changed the dressing. The pain, and the smell, and the sight of it, was just too much for me. I still remember it well to this day.

"Eventually, she decided to take me to hospital. In those days, you had to go all the way to Gaborone, as there were no hospitals any closer. It took three days to get there, and you can imagine how ill I was by the time we arrived.

"The surgeon took one look at it and immediately decided to amputate. My mother was horrified, but I was begging for them to chop it off. I just wanted to get rid of the pain and the horrible mess that it had become.

"So, you see, it was nothing as dramatic as the people around here would have you believe. They love to make up big stories around the most trivial of events."

The children sat, open-mouthed, for some time before Boi quietly said, "I don't think that having part of one's leg cut off is 'trivial', Mma, no matter what led to that happening."

"Oh Boi. You are such a sweet girl. I can assure you that much worse things happen in life. And look at me now. Many, many years later, I am very well, and fit enough to bake a cake for you to eat on the way home from your first day at secondary school."

"I am glad, Mma. And it is a very tasty cake. Thank you."

She glared at her brother.

"Yes Mma. As Boi says, it is a very tasty cake. I told her it would be. Thank you."

"Thank you Mma," added Grace, quickly.

"You must be on your way now, children. Your mothers will be looking out for you and wanting to hear all you news. I don't want to keep you."

"You are right Mma. We will go home, but I will come to see you again soon."

"Please do. It is a pleasure to chat with you. I can't promise you a cake every day, but I will make another one in a week or so."

\* \* \* \* \*

By the time Boi and Thapelo arrived home, Boi was very tired. Walking twenty-two miles on top of a full day at school would be enough to make any young girl or boy very tired.

Mme was sympathetic, but she still expected Boi to gather some wood for the fire and fetch some water from the river.

As she completed her chores and tucked in to the stew that her mother had prepared for her, she told Mme of all the exciting events of the day.

How she had met all her Form One teachers, and would meet the P.E. teacher, Mister Way, tomorrow, and that he was a real Olympic athlete! How she now had a shelf in the classroom with her own name on it, and that it was full of exercise books which she couldn't wait to put to use. All about the visit to Mma Mothoriyana in Inagolo, and how she had baked them a special cake. Finally, she told her mother she was going to study very hard for the next five years, at all subjects, so that she could go to university and become one of Botswana's top doctors.

She was still buzzing with excitement when the family's mood was further lightened as Tadelesh arrived bearing a pail of fresh milk from the dairy farm.

Boi's first day at Marekisokgomo Junior Secondary School could hardly have been better. She went to bed very happy, and slept like the proverbial log.

# # # # #

# Three - Tharo

The cock crowed. It was five to four. Boi sprang to her feet and ran across to hug Mma Patience Tumelo, her mother, whom she loved dearly. She had never been happier in her life.

Boi lit the fire and put the water on to boil. While it heated, she put a little cold water in a bowl and went outside to wash her hands and face. Then she savoured the chunk of bread that Mme had saved for her, and enjoyed a mug of hot coffee. She couldn't wait to get to school, and hoped that she would meet her best friend, Tshegofatso Grace Maphenyo, along the way.

Once more, Mme instructed Thapelo to take very good care of his sister. He promised that he would do so, but Boi could see that he was eager to race ahead and meet Gasenna for another silly competition. When they arrived in Inagolo, Boi told Thapelo that he could run on ahead as she would like to spend a few minutes chatting with Mma Mothoriyana. She had already formed a close bond with the old lady and they enjoyed listening to her stories of old.

A few minutes after she'd sat down on the ground outside Mma Mothoriyana's little house, Grace appeared. The two girls hugged each other in delight.

The rest of the walk passed quickly as Boi and Grace talked about their ambitions and about the day ahead. They were both excited about meeting Mr Way, and they didn't have long to wait. After Mma K Agisanyang had called the register, he walked into the classroom and told the pupils to follow him to the gym.

Mister Way was very tall, about one metre eighty-eight, Boi thought. He wore shorts and a tight, red running vest which showed off his well-defined muscles. Around his neck was a piece of chord with a whistle attached. On his feet he wore the most amazing shoes that Boi had ever seen. Although they were covered in dust, she could see that they were bright blue and must have been very expensive. She looked down at her own shoes. They had been lovingly crafted out of rubber tyre by Nyack, but she couldn't help envying the teacher.

They filed into the gym. Mister Way told them to take their shoes off and leave them near the door. He explained that, if they had shorts and t-shirts that they could bring especially for P.E. lessons in future, then that would be better than having to wear the same, sweaty clothes for the rest of their classes. But today he was just going to give them a taste of what lay ahead.

His soft English accent captured them all. They had never heard somebody speak like that before, and most of them liked it.

All the equipment was laid out in sections. In one corner of the gym, some cones were laid out in a zig-zag pattern. In another part of the gym, four medicine balls were spaced evenly along a yellow line painted on the floor. Other sections contained wooden poles and ropes and rubber balls and bean bags.

The teacher led them around from section to section and showed them the correct way to exercise with each piece of equipment. He chose four children to repeat the demonstration of the exercise at each station to make sure that it had sunk in.

When they had completed a circuit, he divided the children evenly between the sections. When he blew his whistle they had to commence the exercise and keep going till he blew again. Then they'd skip across to the next piece of equipment and start on the next whistle blast.

He only gave them a minute on each section, because he wanted to take them outside. On the way, he asked if anyone had any questions.

Moagi's hand shot into the air.

"Tell me your name, and ask your question."

"I am Moagi, Rra." He paused. The teacher smiled.

"Yes, Moagi. What would you like to know?"

"Will we be allowed to climb on the wall bars and ropes, Rra?"

"Yes, Moagi, but that is for a future lesson. Do you like climbing?"

"Oh yes, Rra! I have climbed all the trees on the farm, and some of the trees on the way to school. I love to climb. Maybe I will climb the rocks in the mountains some day."

"I like your enthusiasm, Moagi. Perhaps you will climb the rocks one day. In the meantime, please only climb the wall bars and ropes in the gym when I am there to supervise you. Any more questions?"

Grace slowly raised her hand.

"What is your name?"

"My name is Tshegofatso Grace Maphenyo, Rra, but my friends all call me Grace."

"Then I shall also call you Grace. What is on your mind Grace?"

"Mma K Agisanyang told us that you competed in the Olympics, Rra. Is that true?"

"Yes Grace. I represented Great Britain in the Sydney Olympics at triathlon. Do you like athletics Grace?"

"Yes Rra, but I like to swim more. Did you win the triathlon at the Olympics, Rra?" she asked eagerly.

"Well, I didn't win the gold medal, but I managed to come third and get the bronze."

Many of the children gasped in admiration. One of

them blurted out, "We are very lucky to have such a teacher."

Mr Way heard the comment.

"I hope that you will still feel the same after you have had a few P.E. lessons. We are all lucky that we have such a well-built and equipped gymnasium, and look at this field in which we can run and play games of football and hockey."

They were in a big field which was dry and dusty, but was marked out with a running track and a football pitch.

"Follow me!"

Mister Way led them across the field to the edge of the river. At this point it was wide and placid and slow-moving.

"This is where you will have your swimming lessons. I know that is going to please at least one of you," he said, glancing at Grace. "Once again, I warn you that you must not swim in the river without supervision. Sometimes, crocodiles wander in here during the night, and I wouldn't want any of you to be eaten! Also, there are times when there are dangerous undercurrents. I can recognise them, and I will teach you how to spot them too. But don't swim unless a teacher is here. Is that clear?"

"Yes Rra," muttered most of the class.

As they made their way back across the playing field, some of the children chased each other. Some gathered around Mister Way, asking him questions about what they would do in their future lessons, and about his Olympics experience. There wasn't a single child in the whole class who wasn't bubbling over with enthusiasm.

When they got back to their classroom, they were surprised to find that Mma K Agisanyang had been replaced by their esteemed head teacher, Mma Tlotlo. Perhaps something was wrong.

Mma Tlotlo recognised the worry on their faces.

"Don't worry. There is nothing wrong. It is just time for your first maths class, and I am pleased to be your maths teacher.

"Who would like to go outside for their first maths lesson?"

A forest of hands shot into the air.

"Alright. We will do that. We are going to measure the height of the big tree by the school gate. Kefilwe, please bring that tape measure which is on my desk."

Kefilwe picked up the tape measure, which was the size of a dinner plate, and followed Mma Tlotlo out of the classroom. The rest of the class followed on.

A few seconds later, they gathered around the foot of the tall tree.

"Now! Who is good at climbing trees?"

Only three children raised their hand, and one of them looked very nervous.

Kefilwe said, "Moagi SAYS he is very good at climbing, Mma."

"Oh yes. I have heard this already."

*She must be referring to the incident in the gym yesterday,* thought Boi.

Kefilwe was thrusting the tape measure into the hands of Moagi who was already eyeing up the tree and picking out his route to the top.

"No. You keep the tape, Kefilwe."

"But..." retorted Kefilwe with trembling voice.

"Nobody is going to be climbing this tree. We don't want any accidents today. No. We are going to use simple geometry.

"All of you: make an angle of forty-five degrees between your arms."

They all obeyed. Most of them got it right first time, but a few of them only made the correct angle once they copied what the majority were doing.

"Good! Now look at this."

The children crowed round as Mma Tlotlo picked up a stick and drew a triangle in the sand.

"These two angles are forty-five degrees. What do you notice about the other two sides?" She paused and looked around the intent faces. "Grace?"

"They are the same length, Mma."

"Exactly, Grace! Well done."

Some of the children were already making the connection before Mma Tlotlo told them to move to a place where they could point one arm at the base of the tree and the other at the top of the tree, forming a forty-five degree angle.

"Now you can all see that you are standing roughly the same distance from the tree, and that distance is equal to the height of the tree."

They all understood now, and they were quite excited about the lesson that they'd just learned.

"Kefilwe. Take the tape measure and put one end under Grace's foot." He did so.

"Stand firmly on the tape, Grace, so that it doesn't move while Kefilwe rolls it out to the base of the tree."

The class watched as Kefilwe measured the distance to the foot of the tall tree.

"Sixty-three metres and twenty-five centimetres, Mma."

"Good Kefilwe. Now roll up the tape and we'll all go back into the classroom."

Once they were back at their desks with their maths exercise books in front of them, their teacher instructed them to write "Measuring the height of a tree," at the top of the page. Then they had to draw a forty-five

39

degree, right-angled triangle with a tree on the vertical side and a stick figure at the opposite base angle. Underneath the diagram, she wanted them to write a brief account of how they had measured the tree.

It only took about fifteen minutes before they were all finished. As they drew and wrote, Mma Tlotlo walked around the classroom observing the variety of standards that the children were setting themselves and offering a few words of encouragement and advice.

When they had all finished, Mma Tlotlo said, "I am very pleased with you all. You have learned something this morning. You can now measure the height of anything without the trouble, and risk, of climbing the object. You don't even need a tape measure, as you can get a good estimate by simply counting the number of paces that it takes you to walk to its base from where you measure the forty-five degree angle. You don't have to do this, but you might like to take the time to work out the length of your own pace. An easy way to do this is to go out to the sports field and count how many paces it takes you to walk from one end of the 100 metres track to the other, and then do a simple division. Perhaps we'll do this together in a future lesson.

"Finally, there is one more lesson to learn this morning. There is a slight error in our calculation. You may have spotted it when you made your drawings. Anyone?"

Boi's arm shot up.

"Yes Boi?"

"When I drew the triangle, I noticed that we hadn't taken into account the height of Grace's shoulder above the ground. If you project that line back, it makes the base of the triangle longer than the distance that Kefilwe measured. So the height of the tree is really sixty-three twenty-five PLUS the height of Grace's shoulder."

"That is very good, Boi."

To illustrate the point, Mma Tlotlo drew the diagram on the blackboard, and projected the longest side back onto the ground behind her stick figure. She wrote in the distance from the feet to the tree.

"There is another possible error, because we all only guessed the angle of forty-five degrees. But we have discovered a very good method of finding a close estimate of the height of anything we choose to measure, and, as long as we always understand the size of possible errors, we won't go too far wrong.

"Our next maths lesson together is on Thursday. It's time for your morning break now. When the bell sounds, I think that you are back in the classroom for your English lesson with Rre Kitso. I hope that you all enjoyed your first maths lesson with me, and that you have learned something this morning."

Minutes later, as she walked back across the playground to her office, Mma Tlotlo was thrilled to see her Form One students walking around, holding their arms at forty-five degrees, and pointing at the tops of surrounding trees and buildings and telegraph poles.

Boi didn't think that the rest of her school day could be as enjoyable as her first two lessons, but she was wrong. Every class just was as interesting and exciting. She couldn't wait to get home to tell Mme. And on the way, she would make a brief stop to tell her new friend, Mma Mothoriyana, about her experiences.

As it turned out, though, as she walked home with Thapelo, Gasenna and Grace, her brother persuaded them all that they should interrupt their journey with a swim in the river. The hot Botswana sun reinforced Thapelo's case. A swim would be quite refreshing.

The river flowed close to the crossroads where they had met Gasenna on Boi's first day at the school. The children stripped off to their underwear and had great fun splashing around in the water. Grace challenged Boi to a race across to the far bank and back again. The total distance was probably less than a hundred metres, but Grace was back on dry land before Boi had half completed her return crossing.

"You are a really good swimmer, Grace. I think that you could beat anyone our age."

"I don't know why I am so fast. I have always just loved swimming. I hope Mister Way can coach me to be even better. He certainly knows what he's talking about."

The boys were standing in the shallow water, staring intensively at the bottom of the river. The girls went closer to see what they were looking at.

"Shush! Keep away Boi!" Thapelo urged.

"Why? What are you doing?"

"Just stay there a minute and you'll see for yourself."

Boi and Grace sat down on the ground. It suddenly dawned upon Boi that her brother was doing something that they had often done together in the past. He was trying to catch some fish.

The technique was to place a mayonnaise bottle containing a small piece of porridge into the shallow water. When a small fish swam into the bottle to nibble the porridge, Thapelo would be ready to quickly place his hand over the opening and lift it out of the river. The fish would go into his bag and be taken home for supper.

They didn't have long to wait before Thapelo jumped out of the water with his bottle and added another fish to the three that were already flapping around in his school bag.

He placed another piece of porridge in the jar and rested it gently back in the shallows.

"Hurry up, Thapelo. It is going to get dark before we get home. Mme will kill us!"

"No she won't, little sister. You know how pleased she always is when I bring home a few small fish for the table."

"Yes. But surely four will be enough?"

"Five will be better. Besides, you can't expect Gasenna to go home empty-handed. You can see that he has been helping me with my fishing. We must catch at least…"

Suddenly, he grabbed the bottle again and sprang back to the bank with yet another fish.

"See! It won't take long. We have five for us. Now we must catch five for Gasenna's family."

"Oh, alright. We'll wait a bit longer. But you must tell me, where did you get that jar? And the porridge?"

"That was easy. I chatted up that young cook at the school. She fell for my charm!" Thapelo grinned back at his sister as he carefully replaced his fish trap. "The hardest part was smuggling it past old Kedibonye."

"Who is Kedibonye?"

"I forgot. You haven't met him yet, but you will. He is the school security guard. He sees everything that goes on. You cannot get away with anything in that school!"

"Well, you seem to have got away with a jar and some porridge, brother."

"Yes. But I know a few tricks to fool him now. I am always sending him off in the wrong direction in search of trouble."

Splash! Yet another fish was caught. This time it was thrown into Gasenna's school bag.

43

The girls sat and chatted about their second wonderful day at school and their expectations for the future, while the boys continued with their fishing. They forgot about the time until Boi noticed that the sun was getting very low in the sky.

"Thapelo! It's going to get dark very soon. We must go."

"Just one more and we'll be...."

Splash!

"There! We each have five! Now we can go. We will be late home and Mme will worry. Why did you let us stay here so long Boi?" he teased.

Boi threw him a glare and grunted. She didn't need to say a word.

They said goodbye to Gasenna at the crossroads, and rushed along towards Inagolo, almost running. It was still hot, and Boi's rubber shoes felt heavy on her feet. She took them off and put them into her bag. Her feet were hard from years of running around barefoot, and she could move more quickly, more comfortably, when she wasn't wearing any shoes.

Mma Mothoriyana was sitting outside her house, waiting for them to pass. She waved and called to them.

"You're very late, children. It will be dark soon."

"Yes Mma. We know. Sorry. We cannot stop today. My mother will be anxious already. See you tomorrow."

They moved on quickly. Boi and Grace hugged each other as Grace took the track towards Kango.

Their mother greeted them with, "Where have you been? It is dark! It is many hours since school finished. Did you get lost? I can't believe you could get lost."

"I am sorry Mme. It is all my fault. It was so hot on the way home. Grace and I went swimming in the river and lost all track of time. Thapelo told us that we'd be late, but we were enjoying the water too much. I'm really sorry, Mme."

"Well you should be careful, Boi. And you should pay attention to your brother sometimes. He…"

"No Mme. It is not Boi's fault. We ALL went swimming, and then Boi wanted to come home. But I insisted that she wait for me while I did some fishing with Gasenna."

"That is a version of the truth that I can believe more. You are a good boy for taking the blame, Thapelo, but you were still wrong to delay your journey home. You both were. You must always try to get home before the sun goes down. I worry about you."

"Look Mme" He showed her the five fish. It brought a broad grin to their mother's face.

"Oh. This is good. I will cook them for our supper. I have some fresh vegetables to go with the fishes. Well done Thapelo Olebile Tumelo. You can be naughty sometimes, but you are a good boy at heart."

She took the fish and put them on the table.

"We need some wood for the fire. You can both go and find some, but don't be long. Tadelesh has already gone to fetch some water."

By the time they got back to the house, laden with the branches that they had gathered from under the trees near to the village, the smell of the fish and vegetables cooking was filling the room. They were a very happy family as they sat down together to enjoy a rare feast.

"Where did you go swimming Boi?"

"Where the river comes close to the crossroads just the other side of Inagolo Mme."

"That's alright. I think that you are safe there. But don't ever go swimming in the Metsimantsho swamps. Auntie Koketso visited today, and she told me that the rogue hippo, Menomagolo, has struck again. A boy

45

from Tobetsa is in hospital, lucky to be alive. Menomagolo is said to have bitten his arm off."

"How terrible Mme! That hippo is a killer. He's already killed two people and I don't know how many legs and arms he has chomped in the last few years. Couldn't the police, or the Army, come and kill him?"

"That's exactly what Auntie Koketso said, Boi. But Menomagolo is a cunning one. He seems to hide in around Metsimantsho. The police have tried several times to find him, but they can't."

"That's stupid, Mme," declared Thapelo. "How can a beast as big as a hippo hide amongst the rushes?"

"It is a very big area to search Thapelo. Two police officers in a boat would have to be lucky, or maybe very unlucky, to find him there. As I said, Menomagolo is a cunning beast."

"I know who can find him, Mme!" said Thapelo excitedly. "Sergeant Lefoko Dintwa! He has captured poachers who come down from Angola and Zambia. I heard that he killed a water buffalo with his bare hands when it ran amok in his soldiers' camp. Menomagolo wouldn't stand a chance against the brave sergeant!"

"You may be right. A lot of people are saying that. Ntatemogolo is going to ask him next time he comes home on leave from the Army."

"I will volunteer to help him, Mme."

"That you won't, Thapelo. That you definitely won't! Do you hear me?

"Yes Mme," Thapelo replied meekly. *That I definitely WILL,* he thought. *Sergeant Dintwa already knows that I am the bravest, strongest boy in Itlhomolomo. He will choose me as his assistant to hunt and kill Menomagolo.*

That night, they all went to bed with different dreams. Thapelo dreamed of being cheered by villagers

46

from all around Metsimantsho. Mma Patience Boitumelo dreamed about watching her beautiful daughter, Boitumelo Hope Tumelo, graduating from the University of Botswana. Boi had a very similar dream, but even more advanced than that of her mother. She was presenting from the stage of an international medical conference in Capetown: eminent doctors and professors from all around the world, hanging on her every word. Tadelesh's dreams were much more modest, and slightly scary. He dreamed of a bloat of wide-mouthed hippos chasing him and his herd of dairy cattle across the plain. He woke up, in a cold sweat, before the fearsome animals caught up with him.

Full bellies lead to the most wonderful dreams.

# # # # #

# Four - Nne

With only two weeks to go until the end of her first term, and Boi was becoming obsessed with the charts on her classroom wall. Just as it had been when they were at Itlhomolomo Primary School together, the first three places were being closely fought by Boi, Grace and Kefilwe.

The rivalry between the three was friendly, and Boi still strove to impress Kefilwe, believing that he might ask her to be his girlfriend. Grace harboured exactly the same thoughts about her chances with Kefilwe. But it was obvious that he only had eyes for Gabanakitso. This baffled Boi and Grace. How could he fancy a girl who was so thick? She was bottom of the class in every subject, even though she scored an occasional very high mark in one subject or another. Suspiciously, these odd results almost exactly coincided with Kefilwe's scores for those homework assignments.

Boi calculated that, overall, she was one point ahead of Kefilwe, and five points clear of Grace. The next in line was Khumo, who was about thirty marks behind Grace and didn't stand a chance of catching up before the end of the term.

Boi was determined to finish first. She realised that she needed to put in some extra work, so she decided to extend her school day by arriving earlier and leaving later. As it was, it was impossible to do extra work at home in the evenings as there were no electric lights in her village, and candlelight was too much of a strain on her eyes. Staying at school would give her the benefit of proper lighting. Mma K Agisanyang had no objections to any pupils staying late. In fact, she positively encouraged it.

So that she could arrive earlier, Boi started to run to school. The rubber tyre shoes that her brother, Nyack, had kindly made for her were far too heavy and cumbersome to run in, so she ran barefoot with the shoes in her school bag. At first, the eleven mile journey was too much for her. She often had to slow down to a walk. By the time she got to the end of her first year, she would be able to run all of the way to school and home again without walking. Of course, she'd frequently gain a rest by stopping to talk to her friend, Mma Mothoriyana in Inagolo.

Her efforts paid off. The extra hours allowed her to submit more work, of better quality, in every subject. By the end of the term, she was twenty marks ahead of Grace and Kefilwe, who were second equal in the class. She basked in the praise that she received from both Mma K Agisanyang and Mma Tlotlo.

Both Grace and Kefilwe seemed pleased for Boi, and praised the amount of extra work that she had put in to come top of the class. But they both vowed that they would beat her in the second term.

In the short holiday between terms, Boi was delighted that Ntate and Tabansi could return from the mines for a few days. They brought news that Nyack was getting more work up at the house of Mister van Gils. He hoped to be able to come home with them next time they returned.

Boi told them, excitedly, about her school experiences and achievements.

"It fills my heart with joy to hear how well you are doing and how much you are enjoying your education, Boi."

"I realise that it wouldn't be possible without the money that you and Tabansi send to fund my schooling, Ntate. I will always be grateful, and I will never forget.

49

When I am a famous doctor, you will receive free medical attention, whatever your ailment. I will have friends in high places."

Mompati laughed. "It is wonderful to hear your ambition, Boi. You are so young, and yet you have such high dreams. You are bound to be successful and make your old father very proud."

"I hope so, Ntate."

\* \* \* \* \*

The school holiday, and their time together as an almost complete family was far too brief, but Boi was pleased to return to school to start her second term. Some days, Grace would be waiting for her where the track from Kango joined Boi's path from Itlhomolomo. They would run together. Although Grace was also very fit, she found it difficult to keep up with Boi's effortless pace. Boi usually slowed down to stay with her friend, but sometimes Grace would encourage her to run on ahead. They both always arrived at the school long before the first class.

One day, when they had eaten their lunchtime snack and found a quiet spot to chat by the river, Boi told Grace how she wished she had a bicycle.

"Wouldn't it be so much easier, and quicker, than running to school, Grace?"

"But you like running, don't you?"

"Yes. I do. But I keep seeing that man on the edge of Marekisokgomo, cycling around, carrying shopping for his neighbours. You've seen him too, Grace. I confess that I am envious. It would be lovely to own a bike."

Grace grinned at her friend. "You are in luck, Boi. My brother has some special magic dust that he hides

50

under his bed. I know where it is."

"What do you mean? Magic dust? What is that?"

"You believe in the power of magic, don't you?"

"Yes. Of course. But that is for only a few very gifted people, like traditional doctors. Your brother hasn't got that gift, Grace."

"Oh yes he has! Well, at least he has obtained this special magic dust from somewhere. And he has a bike to prove it."

"He has a bike? I didn't know that. Has he let you ride it?"

"Yes. Of course. But only around the village. That's why you've never seen it."

"So what does this magic dust do?"

"It is simple. He has told me all about it. All you do is wait for sunset, dip your wet finger into the dust, circle it three times above your head, and wish for what you want. Within three days, you will have your wish."

"That can't be true, Grace. If it were, you would have a bike too."

"It is true, Boi. Where do you think my netball ball came from?"

That made Boi think long and hard. She knew that Grace's family couldn't easily afford to buy a ball like that, but her friend always proudly brought her own ball in when Mister Way was coaching netball, or they had a match. Grace was a very good netball player as she was so tall for her age. She easily fitted into the school team with the older girls. Having her own ball made her all the more popular.

"OK. I believe you. But couldn't you have a ball AND a bike."

"No. You only get one wish each with Gontse's magic dust. He doesn't even know that I used it. He might wonder where I got the ball from, but he doesn't know for sure."

"Do you think he'd let me have some?"

"No. Not a chance, but if you come to my house this evening, I'll see if I can smuggle his jar of magic dust out to you."

"That would be brilliant! I can't believe that I'll have my own bike in a few days' time. I love you Grace. You are such a good friend."

They hugged.

\* \* \* \* \*

After school that day, Boi told Thapelo to tell Mme that she was going over to Grace's house, and might be a little bit late home.

The two girls ran all the way back to Kango. They treated it as a race, and Boi was sitting under a tree, waiting, when Grace came puffing up the hill.

"I have been here a long time, my friend. What kept you?"

"We will have another swimming race soon. Since Mister Way has been coaching me, I have got even faster. You haven't seen me recently, but I can tell you that I will be across the river and back again before you have even reached the other side!"

"Let's do it tomorrow. I am quite fast myself, you know."

"OK. On our way home. There is a wide, calm stretch of water on the edge of Metsimantsho, near to the road. We can race there."

Even the mention of the swamp sent a shiver down Boi's back, despite the heat of the day.

"No. I cannot swim there, Grace. I promised Mme that I would not go near the swamp. It is very dangerous. Menomagolo will emerge from the swamp and eat us."

"Don't talk rubbish! I am far too fast in the water for a hippo to catch me. Besides, he hasn't been seen for weeks. I think he may have gone elsewhere. Or he may have died."

"I don't want to risk it. Let's go to the spot where Thapelo and Gasenna go fishing. It is quite safe there."

"Alright Boi. But you will lose wherever we swim."

They laughed as they looked forward to their race.

"Are you going to stand here chatting all day, or are you going to get your brother's magic dust for me?"

"I'll go inside now. But I'll have to wait for an opportunity to sneak it out. I'll be in terrible trouble if anybody sees me. My mother doesn't even know about the magic dust, and Gontse will probably be in even more trouble if she finds out. Wait here."

Boi waited. She waited a long time. She could see Grace's mother peering out of the shadows of the doorway at her from time to time. She felt uncomfortable.

With the prize of a magic bike in her sights, Boi had almost limitless patience. Even after almost two hours sitting under the tree, she was still excited about the thoughts of the magic dust and her new bike.

Gontse and Grace came out of the house and walked off towards the edge of the village. A few minutes later they came back with some firewood that they had gathered.

"Go home Boi. I'll see you at school in the morning," Grace called across to her as she ducked back inside.

Boi ignored her. She knew if she waited long enough, her friend would emerge with the jar of dust.

Another hour passed and it was getting dark.

Eventually, Grace's mother came across to her.

"Why are you sitting here, Boitumelo Hope Tumelo? Your mother will be waiting for you to arrive home."

"I am just waiting for Grace to come back out, Mma. She said she would be allowed out to play after her supper."

"Don't you girls spend enough time together at school? Now, be a good girl and get home before it becomes pitch black."

Boi had little choice but to obey.

Sure enough, when she got home, her mother was worried and a little bit annoyed.

"Where have you been? You should be home long before this."

"I was in Kango, Mme, playing with Grace. Didn't Thapelo tell you? He is such an idiot!"

"Don't speak about your brother like that! Of course he told me. I still expect you to be home earlier than this."

"Oh, it's alright for him to be off playing with his friends until it gets dark, even when he's supposed to be at school. You never tell him off, Mme."

"That is simply not true, and you know it. Now get your bowl and help yourself to some phališhi from the pot there. I don't want to hear another word from you this evening. You are getting far too cheeky."

Boi ate her food in silence. The truth was that she was frustrated because the expected magic had not come her way. *Perhaps tomorrow I will have more luck,* she thought.

\* \* \* \* \*

The next day, Boi was up very early and had run to

school by just after seven o'clock. She was sitting at her desk writing up her latest Integrated Science project for Rre Lekgowa, when the head mistress walked into the classroom.

She stood up.

"Good morning, Boi. You are here very early."

"Good morning, Mma Tlotlo. Yes. It is very quiet at this time. I find that I can concentrate more on my studies when there is nobody else around."

"I have noticed that you study late after school too. Your maths results are always excellent, and I hear from the other teachers that you excel at their subjects too, without exception. As I tell all of the pupils and staff, hard work pays off. You are a good example to the whole, Boitumelo Hope Tumelo."

"Thank you Mma."

"Don't burn yourself out though. Make sure that you have some fun in your life too."

"Oh, I certainly have some fun, Mma."

With a huge smile of satisfaction, Mma Tlotlo left the classroom and headed for her office.

What seemed like only a few minutes later, the rest of the class started to arrive. First through the door was Moagi.

"Yeuch! Moagi! What's that smell?"

"I'm sorry, Boi. One of our cows is very ill, and my father made me sleep with her the whole night last night. I didn't have time to wash properly in the river before I came to school. You know if I am late, Mma K Agisanyang sends me home. I get behind if I miss a day at school."

"We can't have that smell in the classroom all day. Why don't you go across the sports field and wash in the river before everybody else arrives?"

It was already too late. Kefilwe, Grace and

Gabanakitso sauntered into the classroom together, laughing.

They soon stopped their merriment when the smell of Moagi hit them.

"You stink, Moagi! Get out!" Gabanakitso exclaimed.

"I'm sorry everyone. It's a sick cow."

"YOU'RE a sick cow, Moagi! Please go and wash."

"You know I can't go in the river unless Mister Way or another teacher is there."

"You're allowed to go in if Kedibonye is around, Moagi," Grace suggested. "I've often been swimming myself with just him keeping watch. It's OK."

"Alright. I'll go and find him. I'm really sorry about the smell. It's just that when a cow gets sick, you can't …"

"Yes, yes. Just go and get washed!"

When he'd left the room, the remaining children just looked at each other and burst out laughing. It was hilarious.

Grace sat down next to Boi.

"Sorry about last night," she whispered. "I just couldn't get the magic dust from under Gontse's bed without him noticing me. It was as if he suspected that I was up to something."

"That's alright Grace. I am prepared to wait. The prize is too great for me to start getting impatient. Maybe we can try again this evening, instead of our swimming race."

"You're not scared of losing, are you? You realise that you'll lose whenever we race in the water."

"Maybe I will, but you'll never beat me at running."

More classmates had arrived. Ten minutes later, a

rather wet looking Moagi came back into the classroom, smelling much better.

Rre Moreri entered and placed a pile of books on the front desk. They were ready to start the first class of the day, Religious Education.

\* \* \* \* \*

Throughout the day, Boi found it very difficult to concentrate on her studies, and was continually brought out of her reverie by the call of a teacher or a classmate. All she could think about was Gontse's magic dust and the amazing bike which was bound to come her way in the next few days. She had heard tales of such magic throughout her life, so she knew them to be true. But she had never imagined that she would be lucky enough to be on the receiving end.

As soon as school was finished, she took off for Kango and had been sitting under the tree opposite Grace's house for almost an hour before her friend strolled up.

"Where have you been?" she asked under her breath. "Gontse is not home. Only your mother is in there. Now is the perfect time to steal his magic dust. Or, I should say, borrow. Hurry up!"

"I will try, Boi. Wait here." Grace went inside. A few minutes later, she emerged carrying a large plastic bucket. She shrugged in the direction of Boi.

"I can't get it yet. I have to do my chores. Mme is watching me." She made off towards the river.

Boi waited patiently for more than two hours. Once again, Grace's mother came out and told her to get home before it got dark.

"I don't know why you wait here, girl. Grace cannot come out to play on school days. She has chores

57

to complete, and her homework too. You must have the same. Come to play with her on Saturday. You can go swimming together."

"Alright Mma. See you tomorrow."

"No. Not tomorrow Boi. You will be wasting your time again. Come on Saturday, as I told you."

Despite the warning, Boi returned on her fruitless mission day after day. Each time, Grace failed to steal Gontse's jar and her mother came out to tell Boi to go home.

By the middle of the following week, even Boi's patience was wearing thin. When she saw Gontse heading off down the track leading away from the village, she decided to follow him. Perhaps she could bribe him into letting her try a finger-full of his secret dust.

When they were about a mile down the track, Gontse turned round and challenged her.

"Why are you following me Boitumelo? And why do you sit under the tree outside our house every evening?"

Boi hesitated.

"It is very awkward, Gontse, but I think that you can help me a great deal. I will do anything in return to repay you. Anything."

"What do you mean? I don't know how I can help you. You'll have to tell me."

Gontse stood with his mouth hanging increasingly open as Boi told him about how she wanted just one try with his magic dust, and how much she desired a bicycle to ride to school.

"You are crazy! What makes you think that I have magical powers? Do you think that I would be hanging around here if I were really so powerful?"

Boi was confused. She couldn't imagine for one

minute that her friend would have lied to her. Gontse must be the liar. She explained how Grace had told her all about his magic dust, which was hidden in a jar under his bed.

"I know all about it, so there is no need to try to hide it from me. PLEASE let me have some Gontse. Just one finger-full. You won't miss it, and I will find a way to repay you for your kindness."

He could see that she was serious and that she honestly believed that he owned a jar of magic dust.

"I swear on my mother's life that I do not have any such dust, Boi. I think that my sister has played a trick on you. It is her idea of a joke. She has a wicked sense of humour sometimes."

It dawned upon Boi that he was right. She had known Grace all her life. Indeed, they had occasionally worked together to play tricks on their friends and their brothers.

She started to cry.

"Don't cry, little one. It is not that bad. You surely couldn't have believed that a bike would appear out of thin air."

"Yes, I did," she sobbed. "Magic happens. Dreams do come true."

"Yes, but not for people like us. Not very often, anyway."

"I can't believe that Grace would be so cruel to me."

"She wasn't really being cruel to you. She obviously thought it would be a very funny joke. Go home now. By the morning, you will be laughing about it too."

"No I won't. When I see Grace tomorrow at school, she will be in big trouble. I will think of a way of gaining my revenge on her. Tell her that she had better look out. Nobody crosses Boitumelo Hope Tumelo, and gets away with it. Nobody!"

"I don't think I will tell her anything about our conversation, Boi. It is up to you to tell her. But I promise that you will be seeing the funny side by the morning. Sleep on it."

Boi trudged home, deep in thought. As usual, it was a hot day, but she felt as if her blood was boiling. That night, she hardly slept at all as she reflected on the trick that her best friend had played on her, and plotted her revenge.

The next morning, Boi was waiting in the playground when Grace arrived. As Gontse had predicted, she had cooled down, and she had come around to thinking that it really was a funny trick. In fact, she wished that she had thought of such a clever ploy herself. She would think of something to get her own back on Grace, but it may take some time.

Although her ire had completely evaporated, she feigned passionate anger as she told Grace how cruel her trick had been.

"I really believed you, Grace. You will pay for this. If it takes me a year, I will have my revenge. We will be quits, no matter how long it takes"

"It was meant as a joke. I just wanted to see how long I could string you along. I'm amazed that you came back after the first evening. But SIX evenings sitting outside my house. You're hilarious!"

Boi could feel her cheeks beginning to flush. How could her friend show no remorse whatsoever?

"Well, you'd better watch out. That's all."

She spun around and strode off towards their classroom.

By the end of the day, they were best of friends again, as if nothing had happened. But the memory would linger on in the back of Boi's mind for many months to come. She was sure that she would think of a clever trick to play on Grace eventually.

# # # # #

# Five - Tlhano

Although her number one passion in life was her school and her schoolwork, Boi always looked forward to the weekends. She and Thapelo would work very hard at the chores that Mma Patience Tumelo would set for her children to complete before they were allowed to go and play with their friends. Tadelesh, of course, couldn't help around the house, as being a dairyman is a seven day a week job.

Boi was happy to help with any work that her mother asked her to do. She was so very grateful to her parents and her eldest brother for funding her education. The fact that her education was going to be her passport out of the typical cycle of village life for village girls in Botswana was never far from her thoughts. She had observed it all her life. There were not many women who managed to live to the ripe old age of her friend, Mma Mothoriyana, or her Mmama, Mothusi Mpho Lesego.

She hoped that Mme would never die, but she had seen lots of women who were not much older than her mother, and some who were even younger, just pass away in their thirties. It was frustrating to Boi that people just seemed to accept this state of affairs as "the will of God." *Surely, our benevolent God would not want this to happen. It is not good.*

No matter what happened to others, Boi was determined to make something of herself. She would make her parents proud of her. She would repay them, double, for everything that they did for her. She would work hard, at home and at school, to fulfil her dreams.

Usually, there were routine duties to complete, such as sweeping the floors of the huts and the yard, washing up, taking care of the laundry, and so on. Of course, there were always daily tasks to complete, whether it was a school day or not. She would fetch water from the river, which was nearly a mile away, at least once. Carrying a full bucket balanced on her head had become second nature to her since she was very small. She played a game with herself to see how full she could fill the bucket and still get it home without spilling a drop. Very occasionally, this challenge backfired on her. She would drop the bucket on the ground, spilling the entire contents, about a hundred metres from home, and have to repeat her journey. But this was fun.

Her favourite task, which she didn't mind at all, was when Mme asked her to cook a meal for the family. If they were lucky enough to have been able to buy a few ingredients, she could cook a tasty stew from a recipe of her grandmother, and accompany it with fresh vegetables. Desserts were a rare treat. She loved to make fruit parcels, wrapped in pastry, and add a sauce made from the milk that Tadelesh brought home from the farm.

Once the routine tasks were complete, both Boi and Thapelo were required to go with their mother to the field by the river to help with the crops. Weeding by hand or with the shared hoe was very hard labour in the hot Botswana sun.

Mma Tumelo watched her children carefully. She made them drink lots of water as they worked. If they looked as if they were getting tired she would call across to one of them.

"Thapelo! It is your turn for scaring duty."

It was her way of giving them a legitimate break. Wandering around the field, scaring off any birds or small animals that were helping themselves to the plants was much easier than any of the other work, and it was a lot of fun too. Once Thapelo was sufficiently rested, she would call him back and send Boi off for her turn to shoo off the birds.

There was always a lot of joking and laughing amongst the children of the village as they toiled amongst the crops. Occasionally, one of the women would strike up a song, and others would join in, including the children. It made the time pass more quickly. Most of them enjoyed the work.

Their hard work was worth the effort. Not only did they have food for themselves, but they were able to sell some of the maize, pumpkins and sugar cane that they grew to pay for what Mme called necessities.

"You must be dressed correctly for school, in a uniform, Boi," she told her daughter. You cannot expect to learn your lessons if you are not correctly dressed. Look at that girl, Gabanakitso, for example. She is not as clever as you. She is bottom of the class. That is because she is a very scruffy girl."

"That's not true, Mme. She just struggles to learn. Some children find it difficult."

"Don't argue with me, Boi. See for yourself. Name me one child who is scruffy who can achieve better results than you."

Boi just frowned. She didn't like to tell her mother that this might be more down to her own hard work than her smart skirt. But she knew what sacrifices the whole family made for her, and she didn't want them to think she was being ungrateful, because she certainly wasn't.

"See! You can't. That just proves my point."

"Yes Mme. You are right, of course."

"I know that I am right. And don't go thinking that I haven't seen you put your rubber shoes that your brother kindly made for you into your school bag as soon as you think I am not watching you. I hope you put them back on your feet when you get to school. I'll find out if you don't."

"I do Mme. I promise. Those shoes are very precious to me. It's just that I like to run, and that is much easier with bare feet than wearing rubber tyres on my feet."

"Good. We'll say no more about it then. Now cut that pumpkin there, and we'll take it home."

Boi longed for the day when she would be able to send money home from the hospital where she would be earning lots of money as a top doctor. Her mother wouldn't have to slave in the fields then. She would just go and buy what she needed from other people.

Despite all the household and agricultural chores that were put their way, there was always enough time at the weekends for other, less arduous activities.

Thapelo was never happier than when he was down by the river. Boi loved to play too, especially when Grace could make it across to join her.

Fishing was always fun, and it never failed to bring the reward of at least a small pile of fish for their supper. God provided a never-ending supply.

Although fishing with a mayonnaise bottle and some porridge was a good way of catching the smaller fish, they all knew a much better method, which yielded more fish and bigger fish. It took a bit more work than the bottle and porridge method though.

When they'd been dismissed from their duties at home and in the field, they would collect lots of river-weed and long grasses, and twist them together to form a thick rope. It would take a couple of hours to make one that was long enough to be useful. The technique required teamwork. The children would then wade into the water with their rope until they were knee-deep. Then they would drag the rope back towards the shore. With any luck, there would be a few fish attached to the rope when they approached dry land. It usually took a few attempts before there were enough fish lying on the bank to share amongst their families.

Sometimes, if they were really lucky, they would trap a much larger fish between themselves and the shore that had been scared by their splashing and their rope. It could be a catfish or a tiger-fish.

One of the boys, usually Thapelo, would take a lunging dive at the big fish and toss it out of the water onto the river bank. He would lose it more often than he would be successful, but it caused enormous joy and celebration when he managed to win the slippery fight.

On one such occasion, they formed a noisy semi-circle around Thapelo and a really big catfish as he wrestled with it. He managed to plant his feet firmly on the bottom and stand up with his arms wrapped around the fish. It was very heavy. And it was very slippery too. It wriggled from his grip. He made a couple of grabs at it before it escaped back into the water.

Then the fish seemed to panic. Instead of looking for an escape route through the dancing children to the open river, he made for the shore. Thapelo dived on him again and got his hands underneath the fish's body.

Through the screams he heard somebody clearly shout, "Throw him on the shore, Thapelo!"

He knew what he was going to do.

He planted his feet on the river bed once more, and used all of the strength of his legs, his body and his arms to launch the fish high into the air. It flew like a rocket.

For a brief moment, they all fell silent as they watched the silvery fish spinning towards the shore. It landed on the dusty ground with a thump. Thapelo was not far behind it. There was no way he was going to allow his catch to squirm its way back down into the water. He pounced on it, snatching up a small rock off the ground as he did so.

One quick blow dispatched the fish. Thapelo stood back to admire his prize. He was panting with the exertion, but his face wore a broad grin. His friends gathered around, laughing and patting him on the back.

"Mme is going to be so pleased with you, Thapelo," Boi yelled into his ear as she hugged her brother tightly. "You are my hero!"

She looked down at the fish which lay at their feet.

"It must be almost a metre long!"

She knew it was probably just under than 80 centimetres, but it was certainly very big, and 'almost a metre long' was the description that she thought it richly deserved.

As Thapelo proudly picked up the huge fish, urged on by Boi, the rest of the children shared the remainder of the day's catch between them. Even though none of them had the big fish to take home, they couldn't wait to tell their families about the amazing adventure. In their heads, and in their stories, Thapelo's fish had already grown to be bigger than a grown man.

Of course, Mme was absolutely delighted to see the pair of them with, what to her, represented a massive feast.

"I will cook this tomorrow. It will make a very good Sunday lunch, with the pumpkin and the vegetables. There will be far too much for the four of us. We'll invite Auntie Koketso and Uncle Kgotlhang, and your cousins, Kabo and Phala."

"Mme?"

"Yes Boi."

"Could we invite Ntatemogolo and Mmama too? They do so much for us, and I know that my grandfather pays more than half of my school fees out of the pay he gets at the lodge."

"It would be lovely to have them Boi, but it is eight kilometres to Gakhibidu. How will we get word to them in time?"

"That's easy, Mme. I run more than four times that distance every day to get to school and back. I'll go now and be back by dark."

"I know, but you have worked all day, and helped Thapelo to catch this fish. You must have a day off from running."

"I don't care, Mme. I want my grandparents to share our joy, and to see this magnificent fish."

"Oh yes, Mme. Please let her go and tell them. They would be very happy to see this fish, and to eat their share. Please let her go, Mme!"

"Oh alright then. But have a good drink of water before you go."

"Thanks Mme. I won't be long."

\* \* \* \* \*

The next morning, they were all up early. The yard had to be swept again as Mme Patience Tumelo wanted everything to be neat and tidy for the visit of her parents. She knew that they wouldn't really care if the compound was littered with the family's belongings, but she just wouldn't feel comfortable.

Boi helped with the preparation and cooking of the vegetables.

Thapelo disappeared somewhere, no doubt to play with his friends. When he came back several hours later, his mother was very angry.

"You wanted your grandparents here today to see your great fish, but you disappear and leave all the work to me and your sister. How dare you!"

"I am sorry Mme. We were having such fun, and I just forgot the time."

"I don't know why I beat you, Thapelo, but it is the only way you will learn. Now bend over."

She had her cane ready and gave him six hard lashes with it across his backside. He squealed, and there were tears in his eyes, but he took his punishment bravely. He knew he deserved it for letting them down.

Boi watched, and she flinched with each strike on her brother's bottom. She had often been on the receiving end of a beating from both of her parents when she had been naughty. In a way, her mother's cane hurt her more than her father's heavy hand. The physical marks certainly stayed longer.

"I won't be late again, Mme. I promise."

"You have promised me before, Thapelo. That is why I am disappointed in you. Now go and smarten yourself up. Ntatemogolo and Mmama will be here soon."

"Shall I get some more firewood before I wash?"

"No. You are too late. Boi already got all we need. Put on that clean white shirt when you're washed."

When their grandparents, auntie and uncle and cousins turned up, everything was ready. Thapelo and Boi were looking really smart. Boi's hair was plaited. Thapelo's bum still stung from his beating, but his pain didn't show. As predicted, everyone was impressed by the fish, which was still whole and steaming away in a big pot.

"You are so clever, Thapelo Olebile Tumelo," said his proud grandfather. "How did you catch such a fish? It is almost as big as you!"

"Oh, it was nothing Ntatemogolo," replied Thapelo with transparently false modesty. "My friends helped me, and I suppose I was just lucky."

He was actually telling the truth, but in the hope that his relatives would tell him that he was speaking nonsense, and continue to heap praise on him.

He was not disappointed, his grandmother did exactly that.

As the family tucked in to the delicious feast, the level of approval that he was receiving from every direction so inflated Thapelo's ego that he eventually promised his grandparents that he would catch another fish of similar size and bring it to Gakhibidu the following Saturday.

Boi was becoming bored with the focus of attention on her naughty brother, and was astounded by his bragging. She knew that it was an absolute fluke that they had trapped such a fish with their rope. Yes, she could admit to herself that Thapelo had done really well to be able to toss it onto the shore, but it was the first time that they'd ever even seen a big fish like this when fishing with a rope. It was very unlikely that they'd repeat the act a few days later.

* * * * *

The following Saturday, Thapelo couldn't wait to get his chores finished and assemble his friends down by the river again. They were enthusiastic and many of them believed that they could repeat the feat of the previous week. The rope that they'd made was still there. They picked it up and paddled out into the water.

For three hours, they walked the rope in towards the shore, and caught a few small fish each time. There was no sign of any fish that was bigger than about fifteen centimetres long.

Eventually, most of the children drifted away and went home.

Boi and Thapelo sat on the bank, staring at the river.

"It's the opposite of last week when we had too much food. Mme's only got a few vegetables and corn that we picked this morning. And she won't have any money until we get some more from Ntate at the end of next week. It's all my fault. I promised that I'd catch another big fish for our grandparents."

"It's not your fault brother. Although you really should learn to keep that mouth of yours shut from time to time."

They sat in silence for a few minutes. Thapelo wished that a big fish would jump out of the river into his hands. It was not going to happen. For a change, he was deep in thought. *What are the options?*

"I know, Boi!"

"What do you know?"

"We will go hunting. I've still got the bow that Ntate helped me to make when he was home in July. I've practised with it. If we can get close enough to a hare, or some other small animal, I could kill it with an arrow." Thapelo's excitement rose. "Imagine if we could shoot a lechwe, or an impala!"

"Don't be ridiculous, Thapelo. You went hunting several times with Ntate. How many animals did YOU actually shoot?"

"Well, none, but I helped Ntate to kill quite a few, as you know."

"What did you do? Did you fire a single arrow?"

"Yes. But I admit that I missed. I came very close though, and I helped Ntate to stalk his prey. He said I was a natural tracker."

"Alright. Maybe we can try a bit of hunting tomorrow. Have you got any better ideas for today?"

Thapelo paused for a full minute before he replied. His eyes lit up.

"Yes! I know what to do. Ntate has taught us both to forage. There's plenty around here to supplement our larder."

Now it was Boi's time to think.

"You are right brother. For once in your life you have come

71

up with a brilliant idea!"

Thapelo's chest swelled with pride. To receive such a complement from his clever little sister made him feel fantastic.

"Do you really think that we could find enough food amongst the scrub to put a smile on Mme's face?"

"Yes. I do. Come on. I'll show you."

They'd only walked a very short distance when Thapelo pointed to a group of mushrooms.

"I saw some growing here last week, and I was going to pick some, but I forgot all about them when we caught the big fish. These ones will be fresh. New ones grow every day."

"How do you know so much?"

"Well, I know what Ntate taught us, but I also know a lot from exploring the bush with the older boys."

"These ones are beautiful, and they look very tasty. But are you sure they're safe to eat?"

"Yes. Of course. Seloilwe told me about these ones. He knows everything. Look. You can eat them raw."

Thapelo picked two and gave one to Boi. He finished his off in three mouthfuls. Boi hesitated.

"I am not sure. I heard that if they were colourful, you should be careful."

Before he could answer, Thapelo started choking. Boi was alarmed. His eyes rolled back and he fell down on the ground, unconscious. Boi was really scared by this time. She had to get help.

They hadn't got dressed since they'd emerged from the river, so Boi quickly put on her shorts and shirt and ran the short distance to Kango. She knew that Grace's neighbour had a telephone, and they could call an ambulance if it was working. Luckily, it was.

Boi called to Grace on the way past, and they rushed back

to Thapelo. Orange mucus was coming out of his mouth, which made the girls even more worried.

Boi was crying, fearing that her brother was going to die. She sat in the shade of a tree with him and held him close. Grace fetched some water and tried to pour some into his mouth, but he couldn't swallow as he was still unconscious. At least it washed the horrible mucus away. His breathing was shallow and rapid.

The ambulance arrived, and the paramedics put him on a stretcher inside. They told Boi that they would take him to the hospital in Marekisokgomo and that she should go home and tell her mother.

Naturally, when Mme heard the news, she wanted to get to the hospital as quickly as possible. Kagiso, who owned the only car in Itlhomolomo, was only too happy to take her. He knew that, although she had no money to pay for his diesel at that moment, she would repay him in good time. The whole village was worried about Thapelo.

When Boi and her mother arrived at Marekisokgomo District Hospital, Thapelo was sitting on a bench outside. He jumped up and waved at them. It was a miraculous recovery!

Boi burst out laughing. Partly that was due to the relief she felt to see her brother alive and, apparently, in good health. But mostly because he just had a scarf around his waist and hanging down in front to cover his modesty. In the panic, she had forgotten all about his clothes, which must still be lying beside the river. The sight of Thapelo, almost naked, outside the hospital, was hilarious.

Thapelo became angry with her. Boys don't like being laughed at by their little sisters.

"Thapelo," Mme cautioned, "You should be grateful to Boitumelo. She has saved your life today."

"Yes Mme. But she could have saved my clothes as well."

This had been a day that Boi would remember for many years to come.

# # # # #

# Six - Thataro

It was just two weeks before the end of term, and that meant only two weeks to the end of Form One.

As always, the top three places in most subjects were being contested between Kefilwe, Grace and Boi. The same went for the top three places overall. There was no antagonism, but all three of them were very competitive and desperately wanted to come out on top.

Boi was arriving at school as early as possible. After almost a year of running and walking to and from school, she was finding it very easy to run all of the way without a pause. Eleven miles there, and eleven miles back. Eighteen kilometres there, and eighteen kilometres back. The numbers played in her mind like a recording of poetry. She calculated as she ran: her time, her distance.

One hundred and ten miles in a week. One hundred and seventy-seven kilometres! She rounded it up to one hundred and eighty. That sounded amazing. It was the same as the maximum score with three darts on a dart board. Since Sergeant Lefoko Dintwa had brought the dartboard and some darts to the village when he had been home on leave from the Army, everyone had been playing the game. Boi was proud that Tadelesh was one of the best. And she was able to help him with her quick brain for arithmetic. They made a formidable pair.

Although Boi, Grace and Kefilwe were rivals, they had been friends for most of their lives. So they helped each other to improve. But the girls were still mystified as to why Kefilwe should wish to spend so much with Gabanakitso. After all, her name was most appropriate. The English translation of Gabanakitso is "they don't have knowledge."

*How true,* thought Boi.

One day, they were sitting together, sharing a history book, when Boi could contain her curiosity no longer.

"Kefilwe? May I ask you a very personal question?"

"Of course you may, Boi. But I may not answer. It depends what you ask."

"Fair enough. Why do you spend so much time with Gabanakitso?"

"Are you joking? How long have you been wondering about that?"

"Since we were at primary school together. But it's not just me. Grace has been wondering about it too. Haven't you Grace?"

"Yes. I confess that I have. Boi and I have often talked about it."

"And, when you two have been talking about it, what conclusion did you reach?"

Both girls were rather embarrassed by the direct question. They could hardly admit that they'd speculated that perhaps Gabanakitso had been granting Kefilwe favours that good girls shouldn't grant.

"Erm, well, er..."

Boi interrupted Grace's stumbling response. "Well, we didn't come to any real conclusion, Kefilwe. We have to admit that we are completely baffled. That's why I'm asking you."

"I would have thought it was obvious. Gabanakitso is far from the cleverest. If she is ever to get through school, and she really wants to, then she needs some help. I am lucky enough to be good at schoolwork, so I can help her. I get a lot of pleasure out of any improvement that she makes when I know that it is due to my help. You two like helping people too, don't you?"

The two girls were silenced by his response. Now that the reason had been revealed, it was so obvious. Kefilwe was such a kind boy. Simultaneously, they thought that perhaps they ought to be helping their classmates a bit more. He had set them an example, and they would follow it.

"You are a very good boy Kefilwe," said Boi. She meant it.

"Yes. I wish that we'd asked before now. If we'd known that, we might have helped too."

Kefilwe laughed. "Besides, she is an extremely pretty girl."

A second later, he took a well-deserved punch on each arm.

They all fell about laughing. Spirits were high.

The conversation gave Boi food for thought. As she ran home after school that day, she thought about her classmates and wondered who she could help. Running time was always good thinking time. It was like meditation. Very often, by the time she got home, Boi was completely relaxed.

Badisa was always in the middle order in every subject. He could probably do a lot better. But then he didn't seem to care too much. Boi didn't think that she would have the patience to help somebody who wouldn't work hard.

Despite being fairly good at science and maths, Boitoi was always near the bottom of the class over all. That was because she wasn't much good at English, Setswana, Geography and History. Maybe there would be some room for coaching in that direction.

Then there was Moagi. He'd been doing quite well in the final term of Form One, and it looked like he might finish in the top ten. And at least he was trying. He hadn't been late for school for several weeks, and he was always clean and relatively smart. Boi chuckled to herself. *Mme would say that it was only natural that a boy would show an improvement in his schoolwork since he smartened himself up!*

Boi could see true potential in Moagi. If he worked hard, he could do really well with some of her guidance. It could be her challenge to herself, and it would benefit Moagi. Boi thought that it might even benefit herself. If she was thinking about ways to help Moagi in all subjects, it might help her to do even better at those subjects. Of course, it was already too late for this term, this year, but she made herself a promise to speak to Moagi before the beginning of Form Two. She hoped that he would accept her proposal.

The next day, Boi was feeling rather pleased with herself as she scrutinised the marks on Mma K Agisanyang's charts. She calculated that just three more marks in every subject for Moagi, would move him up from tenth to seventh. Maybe next term, such improvement would see Moagi move up to sixth, or even fifth.

Just as Boi was dreaming of her ambitions for Moagi as she scanned the charts, when there was a sudden, major setback.

"MOAGI!" the teacher shouted. "Come here!"

Moagi moved meekly across the classroom.

"Yes Mma?"

He felt flushed, because he knew that he had just made a big mistake. Mma K Agisanyang had overheard what he had just said. His teacher already had her cane in her hand. She looked very angry and Moagi was trembling with fear.

"What did you just say to Gabanakitso?"

Moagi shuffled from foot to foot and mumbled an answer.

"Speak up! Tell us all what you just said to Gabanakitso."

"I didn't mean it Mma."

"I didn't ask if you meant it. I want you to tell me what you said to her."

"It was nothing Mma," declared Gabanakitso.

"Don't try to cover for him girl. I heard what he said, and it was very spiteful. I want to hear it from his own lips. Admit it Moagi. NOW!"

Moagi jumped backwards.

"I called her 'thick' Mma."

"WHAT?"

"I called her 'thick' Mma. I am very sorry."

"You are sorry? Apologise to Gabanakitso."

Moagi turned towards the girl, who appeared to be suffering as much as he was.

"I am very sorry Gabanakitso. Truly. I did not mean what I said."

His remorse seemed genuine.

"I know Moagi. You just said that by mistake. You didn't mean it. I forgive you. It is alright."

"It is NOT alright. It is good that you apologise, and that Gabanakitso accepts your apology. But you should not say such hurtful things to anyone. Do you understand?"

"Yes Mma. I understand."

"Everyone has their own talent. These are the gifts of God. We must be grateful for those gifts, and we must learn to admire others for their own given talents. Do you understand that, Moagi?"

"Yes Mma. I do understand. Everyone is gifted in some way."

He stood awkwardly in front of his teacher, and in

front of his classmates. He was a very popular boy, and they all felt his shame.

*Perhaps I have escaped a beating, but I feel terrible. I should not have said that to Gabanakitso.*

He was wrong.

"I believe that you do understand now. But I will make sure that you do not forget this lesson. Bend over the desk."

Reluctantly, Moagi did as he was told.

Mma K Agisanyang drew back the cane and brought it down hard on Moagi's backside. He squeaked as he felt the pain.

The blows continued to strike his bottom. He lost count, but the flinching spectators did not. Ten!

As Moagi rose gingerly to stand before the class, Mma K Agisanyang addressed them all.

"None of you should forget what Mma Tlotlo said to you on your first day at this school and has repeated to you many times since. What did she say about prejudice?"

"There is no prejudice," they answered in unison.

"Precisely! Moagi forgot that this morning for a brief moment. Mma Tlotlo also says that everybody has strengths and weaknesses. We all have some great talent, a gift from God, even if we don't know what it is yet. If you see somebody who is struggling, then you must help them rather than mock them.

"So I want you to help each other to make the best of yourselves. You will feel better for it, I promise."

Boi knew, at that moment, that this was a message for her. It just reinforced the thoughts that she had been having about helping Moagi, the farm boy.

\* \* \* \* \*

Everyone was excited. The last day of the school year was always the best day of the whole year. It was sports day, and it was prize-giving day too. In every year, there were small prizes for the top pupils in each subject, and the winners already knew who they were. There were also bigger prizes for the top pupils in each year. But the sports prizes were mostly decided on the day. It was a big competition.

The children spent the morning tidying up the school grounds and taking all of the chairs from the classrooms and laying them out around the sports field for the families to sit on. Under the supervision of Mister Way, some of the senior pupils built a small stage out of wooden crates at the end of the field.

After they'd had their lunch, they started to welcome their families as they arrived at the school. Boi was on the lookout for her mother, who had promised to come along. Tadelesh had also managed to get a day off from the dairy farm. She knew how proud Mme would be to see her walk up to receive at least four subject prizes. Perhaps she would win the Form One academic prize too. Nobody knew the final result, but it was obvious that it would be one of three. What Boi wanted even more, was to win at least one of the sports prizes.

Eventually, she saw her mother and Tadelesh amongst the crowd walking in through the gate. But it was who else she saw that had her screaming with joy. Her father! Her brother, Tabansi! But, even better than that, her brother, Nyack! Her whole family were there. Even the dear brother who she had not seen for well over a year. She hugged them all. She could not remember when she had last felt so happy. Yes she could. It was the day that she had graduated from primary school.

When the welcomes were over, Thapelo and Boitumelo went back to their class groups and the rest of their family found themselves seats with a good view.

Thapelo was in the junior high jump and discus throwing, but wasn't too bothered about winning. In fact, he was so disinterested in the high jump that he was playing with his friends down by the river when his turn to jump came up, and he missed it. He was disqualified.

The focus switched to the river as the swimming events commenced. There weren't many races. All the races were from one bank of the river to the other and back. Boi entered only one: the breast stroke. She came fifth. As expected, Grace won, beating the Form Two pupils in the junior race. She also won the butterfly and front crawl and came third in the back-stroke.

Back on the field, Boi came into her element. She had been entered into the junior 800 metres, 1,500 metres and 5,000 metres. Mister Way had worked on race tactics with Boi. The distance that she had covered running to and from school was good for her fitness and stamina, but being able to plan each race made her almost unbeatable. Almost. She came second in the 800m, won the 1,500 metres by about two metres, and the 5,000 metres by more than ten seconds over her nearest rival. The longer the distance, the more dominance she showed.

When the sports were over, Mma Tlotlo made a speech and introduced Captain Duncan Odongo, the Chief of the Marekisokgomo police, who had been invited to present the prizes.

The sports prizes were handed out first, and there were no surprises as the events were still fresh in everyone's minds. Nevertheless, there was still plenty of cheering. In the true spirit of Marekisokgomo Integrated Secondary School, even those who had not won a prize were delighted for the winners.

Grace won the Form One prizes for Geography, Music, Home Economics and Setswana. Boi won the Form One prizes for History, English and PE. Kefilwe won the prizes for Maths, Integrated Science, Agriculture and Religious Education.

The subject prizes were presented to all of the winners in each of the five years. Then came the biggest awards of all: the overall year prizes.

Boi could not hide her disappointed as Mma Tlotlo announced that the Form One winner was Kefilwe. She squeezed Grace's hand. They shared their disappointment. But, after a few brief moments of despair, they both felt genuine happiness for their old friend, Kefilwe. He deserved it.

*Next year will be different!*

That evening, was a celebration in the Tumelo household. The family was together for the first time in almost two years. Ntatemogolo and Mmama had come over from Gakhibidu. They rejoiced in Boi's great success, but they didn't forget to encourage Thapelo.

Boi became very emotional as she thanked her family. Without them, her dreams of getting her education and becoming a doctor could not possibly be fulfilled. Ntatemogolo only kept going with his job as security guard at the lodge to help with Boi's school fees. Most of Ntate's pay and Tabansi's pay went into the household expenses, but they also helped out with her fees. She appreciated everything that they did to support her.

Of all her brothers, she loved Nyack the most, so she was delighted to hear how well he was doing. It seemed that his hard work had paid off. He was a real favourite with Mister and Missus van Gils, the mine owners. Mister van Gils had agreed to provide Nyack with driving lessons. The idea was that her brother would become his personal chauffeur. Nyack was naturally excited by the prospect.

"He has a beautiful gold Bentley, Boi. A very big, British car. You should see it!"

"I don't know what a Bentley looks like. I only know Kagiso's old Chevrolet, and the few bashed up cars that I see around Itlhomolomo."

"Believe me. It is the most perfect, BEAUTIFUL, English car you could ever see. One day, Mister van Gils will allow me to take you for a ride in it."

"Oh! I will look forward to that day, Nyack."

Nyack explained to the family how he would not only have to learn to drive, but he would have to learn to service it, and he would be responsible for cleaning it and keeping it in immaculate condition. The van Gils family all treated him very well and it seemed that they liked him.

"I am sure that is true, Nyack," confirmed Ntate. "I have seen them with you. And do you think that Mister van Gils would have offered you this big opportunity if he wasn't certain that you were good for his whole family?"

"That is true, Ntate. That is very true."

"What is happening to his current chauffeur?"

"Oh. He is quite old and will be retiring in about six months from now. Mister van Gils wants somebody to be totally ready to replace him. Of course, Bokang's uniform is not going to fit me. Missus van Gils says that he is 'of comfortable build', whereas I am 'a little too skinny.'"

They all laughed at this.

"I have already been to the tailor in Orapa to be

fitted for my uniform. They are having two made up for me, and I will have a smart cap to go with the uniform. It has shiny buttons, and I will have to wear a fresh white shirt and tie every day. They have bought me three shirts. I will look very elegant in my uniform."

"Then you will be excellent at your job, according to Mme," snorted Boi.

Her mother guffawed. "You are a VERY cheeky girl, Boi. I don't know where you get it from," she said, winking in the direction of her husband and grinning broadly.

# # # # #

# Seven - Supa

Rre Mompati Tumelo and his two eldest sons were able to stay for the first three days of the school holiday before they had to head back to Orapa. Boi loved having them around, despite the amount of communal family work that they had to do, and the fact that the living conditions were a bit cramped with all seven of them in the huts and compound. Nyack and Tabansi slept in the kitchen hut. Boi was able to sleep in the main hut with her parents. Tadelesh and Thapelo could have slept in the store, but they preferred to sleep outside, under the stars.

During those days, they were able to carry out some much-needed maintenance on the walls of the huts. The whole family worked together as a team to carry mud from the edge of river, which seemed like a very long way with a heavy load in the hot Botswana sunshine. They added cow dung to the mud to make the mixture much stronger over the repaired area. Although there were a small number of cows nearby that belonged to the Itlhomolomo villagers, the best supply of material came from the dairy farm where Tadelesh worked. That was even further away than the river.

As they worked, and as they ate together in the evenings, Boi spoke to her father and elder brothers incessantly about her school activities and adventures, and her teachers and her classmates. She even told them about that first memorable maths lesson with Mma Tlotlo, when they had learnt how to measure the height of a tree without climbing it. Despite her continuous chatter, they never got tired of hearing her stories. She was so enthusiastic, and they were all thrilled that she was enjoying her education so much. After all, they were all chipping in to provide her schooling.

There were a few tears when Ntate, Tabansi and Nyack returned to Orapa, but their visit had provided a few very happy, family days together.

Sometimes, when Grace had completed similar tasks at her own home, her mother allowed her to come across to be with Boi, who was always delighted to see her best friend. The short period that they had spent apart made them both realise how strong the bond was between them. Neither girl had any sisters, just an abundance of brothers, so they loved each other as sisters would. They had grown up together and had hardly ever quarrelled, as blood sisters probably would.

If Boi had not finished her work when Grace turned up, the latter would happily muck in and help the Tumelo family until Mme was satisfied enough to allow Boi some leisure time.

Almost always, they would head straight for the river. Thapelo would come too, and Tadelesh if he wasn't working up at the dairy farm. When they got to the river, Thapelo's friend Gasenna was usually already there with quite a crowd of other children from the surrounding villages. They would often go further afield to discover new bends in the river and good places to swim and fish.

It was Grace who first suggested that the two of them have a combined running and swimming race. She had taken the idea from something that Mister Way had said at school one day. He had been talking about his triathlon days, and some of the great international triathletes against whom he had competed when he was at his peak. He just happened to mention something that was new to Grace: aquathon.

"What is aquathon Rra?"

"It is a combined running and swimming race,

Grace. Usually, it is over shorter distances than a triathlon. Perhaps a five hundred metre swim in open water followed by a five kilometre road run. There was one that I participated in, in France that was even more interesting. The swim was in the middle. So we ran two-an-a-half kilometres to reach the side of a lake, swam five hundred metres around a course that was marked out with little buoys, and then put out running shoes on before running back to where we started. Everyone enjoyed it."

"That sounds like fun Rra. Perhaps we could have such a race at school?"

"Now that you say so, Grace, I think that is a very good idea. I will think about how it can be arranged and speak with Mma Tlotlo about it. We could even invite pupils from other schools to come to our event."

Grace told Boi about this conversation as they sat by the side of the river.

"It sounds great, Grace! And, if you think about it, this is the perfect race to even things out between the two of us. Your superiority at swimming might be cancelled out by my slightly better running."

"Well, you are much better at running than me, Boi, but it would be interesting to discover how close we would be at the finish. We'll find a good place and do it next week sometime."

"Why wait until next week. Let's do it now!" exclaimed Boi with rising excitement. "Look at that lone tree on the hill in the distance."

Grace peered at the little hill at which Boi was pointing. It was easy to see. There aren't too many hills in the Okavango Delta. There are many ant hills but real hills are a rarity and are never more than a few metres high.

"I can see it, but it looks like it is miles away."

"Rubbish! I would be willing to bet that it is almost the perfect distance for Mister Way's so-called aquathon. It is just over two kilometres away."

"Okay. I am up for a race if you are."

"Come on then. Let's walk to the tree and start and finish with a touch of the tree. The river here is just over a hundred meters wide, so if we swim across and back twice, and you have to get out at the far side, that will be close to five hundred metres."

"Perfect!"

And so it happened; the first of many running and swimming races between the pair. And it led to a very close finish. As expected, Boi reached the river's edge well ahead of her friend. Looking over her shoulder, she thought that Grace would not stand a chance of catching her in the water, but she was very wrong.

Grace carved a path through the water like a speeding canoe. By the time they were half way back on the first leg of the swim, she was passing Boi. When she reached the near shore for the second time and got into her running stride, Boi was only just emerging from the water on the far side of the river with another width yet to swim.

Boi naturally made up the ground, but didn't catch Grace until the point where the ground started to rise at the foot of the hill. The strength of her legs told as she sprinted up the final two hundred metres. Grace arrived about ten seconds later, gasping for breath. Boi was hardly breathing.

They threw their arms around each other and collapsed to the ground.

"That was brilliant, Grace! What a fantastic idea. I've never heard of aquathon before today."

"You are right. It WAS brilliant! Loved it, even though you beat me." She paused for breath, "THIS time."

"We will do it again. I am sure that you will beat me, but I will make it hard for you."

"Shall we keep a score? It is one-nil to you. Next time, I will draw level."

"Yes. That is a good idea."

Boi found a sharp-edged rock and slashed a mark on the side of the tree.

"I will keep my score on this side of the tree, and you can keep your score on the other side."

"That's a good idea, but my side of the tree will soon have no bark left and your side will be very healthy."

They fell about laughing at the idea.

As they approached the spot where they'd left Thapelo and all their friends, they could see that the children had gone.

"Perhaps they've gone home."

"No. It's too early. I'll bet that my brother and Gasenna are at the heart of whatever they're up to now."

"You are probably right, Boi. It will be some mischief, for sure."

They decided to go home and meet again the next day.

* * * * *

When Boi got home, she was very surprised to see Thapelo already there. He was unusually quiet, and looking rather miserable.

"What are you doing here? We thought you'd all gone somewhere else."

"Everybody else did," Thapelo mumbled.

"For once in his life, your brother has done as I told him, Boi. He has been a very good boy this afternoon."

"Why? What has he done? What has he done that is so good?"

"The other children have gone swimming in the swamp. They have gone to Metsimantsho. I hope that they'll be alright."

"They will Mme. I wish I'd gone with them."

"You were right not to go, Thapelo. Please don't go there. Both of you. I don't want either of you to go near that swamp. You remember what happened to that boy from Tobetsa. He was lucky to escape with his life. As it is, he is going to have to live the rest of his life with only one arm. Menomagolo is dangerous, and he is cunning. He is a killer."

"But nobody has seen him for months, Mme. Gasenna believes that he must be dead. His body has been consumed by the fish in the swamp."

"There are plenty of other good places to swim. Please promise me that you will never go swimming in Metsimantsho."

"Okay Mme. I promise you that I will never go swimming in Metsimantsho."

"You too Boitumelo."

"Yes Mme. I also promise that I will NEVER go swimming in Metsimantsho."

"Good. Now go and fetch some water please. Thapelo. Go and fetch some more wood for the fire."

# # # # #

# Eight - Robedi

On their first day back at school, Boi and Grace agreed to walk the distance together. They had a lot to discuss.

Boi confessed that she had been mulling over her disappointment at the discovery that any chance of a romance with Kefilwe was off. That was the same for both of them. To think that her belief that being top of class would draw Kefilwe to her had driven Boi through primary school. That drive had helped her to achieve her Junior School Certificate, with Special Commendation, so she felt that she really ought to be grateful for that.

"It wasn't just that, Boi. You are very brainy, and you have always worked hard. You would have achieved good results without trying to impress that boy."

"Yes. You may be right, Grace. But I know you worked harder to come top for exactly the same reason. He makes me so angry!"

"Well, we both did well. It doesn't matter what our motivation was."

"I know. But I am determined to do even better now. I must go to university. I am going to be very successful. You will see."

"I believe you. I hope that I can be as successful as you are going to be."

"You will be, Grace."

Boi told Grace about how she had been inspired by Kefilwe's desire to help Gabanakitso, a less gifted pupil, to do better with her schoolwork. She was going to do the same for Moagi.

"Have you told him?"

"No. Not yet. I shall tell him today."

"It's a great idea, Boi. I am going to do the same. I'll have to think about who I will help."

"If I hadn't chosen Moagi, I was thinking of Boitoi or Badisa."

"Hmmm. I'll think about that. Perhaps Molathegi would appreciate some help. I have seen him crying when he gets low marks. He really tries hard. With some guidance, he could probably do a lot better."

"Yes. The reason that I chose Moagi is because I know that he will work hard. Nobody gets anywhere without putting in the effort."

They walked for a while in silence as Grace mulled over her options. She came to the conclusion that she would help Molathegi.

Eventually, Boi broke into Grace's reverie with, "Have you heard much about Rre Tshotlego? Thapelo is so happy that he is now in Form Three. He hated being in Rre Tshotlego's class. He is so strict."

"Form Two might be very tough for us. But he is only the class teacher. We won't have him for every subject."

"Thapelo told me that he often received beatings from Rre Tshotlego. I find him a bit scary. He's very tall, and he looks strong. I don't want him to beat me."

They walked a bit further before Grace suggested, "I am sorry to say this about your brother, Boi, but perhaps Thapelo deserved his beatings. You know how mischievous he is. Many would say naughty."

"I suppose it's possible."

"Mma Mothoriyana calls him Lesilo; the naughty one. You have to consider where she got that from."

"Yes. You are right. She is not the only one who calls him that. There's no smoke without fire."

"He's not really bad, Boi. He just likes to mess

around. All his friends think it is fun. He is very popular."

"I love him to bits, but I am not happy that my Dad and Granddad, and even Tabansi, are paying for his education, and all he does is fool around. He should be earning money too."

"They all pay for you to attend school too, Boi."

"I know. It is nearly five hundred Pula per term, each. That's a thousand Pula. And Ntatemogolo pays for our uniforms too. But you know very well that the difference is that I work hard, and that I will make them proud of my accomplishments. Thapelo is just coming to school to play. He is having fun and avoiding work."

"Will you tell your father?"

"No. I think that my family will understand what he is eventually. Anyway, we must wait to see how Rre Tshotlego will treat us, Grace. I hope that we can avoid trouble."

When they arrived in the classroom, Boi's hopes were immediately dashed.

"Ah! Boitumelo Hope Tumelo. The sister of Thapelo Olebile Tumelo. I hope that you are going to behave better in my class than your brother. He was very lucky that he made it through Form Two unscathed and is now the problem of the Senior Secondary School. I warn you now, that if you put one foot out of line madam, you will feel the pain of my cello bow. Has he told you about that?"

"Yes Rra. He has told me," replied Boi, meekly. "I will behave. I promise."

"If you know what is good for you, you will."

Rre Tshotlego helped his new pupils to settle into their new classroom, showing them the shelves which had been prepared for them, just as they had had in Form One."

Boi was happy when the familiar sight of their head teacher, Mma Tlotlo, appeared in the doorway for their first maths lesson. Her day suddenly got better.

* * * * *

As Boi ran to school the next day, she did a double-take as she ran past Mma Mothoriyana's house. It was very strange that the old lady wasn't sitting outside her house, waving, as Boi ran past. She stopped and entered the house.

Mma Mothoriyana was lying on her bed, groaning.

"What's wrong, Mma? Are you ill?"

"Yes, Boitumelo. I have a very bad stomach. You must fetch Simisani Mathumo from Setshwano. He will soon make me better."

"Are you sure, Mma? I know that he is a traditional doctor, but shouldn't you try a modern remedy?"

"No, Boitumelo. Simisani Mathumo knows exactly what he is doing. I will be very well by the time you come home from school this evening."

"Alright Mma. I will fetch him."

Boi ran the short distance to the neighbouring village, and soon found Simisani Mathumo.

"You must come quickly to Inagolo, Rra. Mma Mothoriyana is very ill. She is doubled up on her bed, and groaning loudly. She needs your help, urgently."

"I will go to her house immediately. Will you come with me?"

"No Rra. I am sorry. I am already late for school. I must go."

"Don't worry. I know Mma Mothoriyana's house. I will soon make her better."

By the time Boi arrived at school, classes had started. Rre Tshotlego was waiting for her.

"You are LATE Boitumelo Hope Tumelo. You must return home and miss today's classes. That is the rule."

"But, I can explain Rra," Boi pleaded.

"No excuse is acceptable. And you will feel my cello bow before you go home. Bend over and lift your skirt."

Boi was horrified. So were most of her classmates, especially Grace. But she did as she was told.

Rre Tshotlego seemed to take great pleasure in thrashing Boi's backside in front of the class. He liked to administer pain.

Over the coming weeks, Boi wouldn't be the only one to suffer painful weals on her bottom as Rre Tshotlego thrashed the Form Two pupils for the most trivial of reasons. Grace and Boi soon discovered that Thapelo had been telling the truth. He was indeed a horrible teacher, but it was also well known that his pupils tended to achieve good academic results. Perhaps it would be a case of getting through the year relatively unscathed.

By the end of her beating, she was crying. Rre Tshotlego had no sympathy.

"Go home now. And let that be a lesson to all of you. There is no excuse for being late for your classes in Form Two. You will receive your punishment and then be sent home for the whole day. Now get out of my classroom Boitumelo Hope Tumelo, and don't come back until tomorrow morning. You won't be late again, will you?"

"No Rra," she sobbed, "but I was only late because..."

"Didn't you hear me?" he interrupted. "I just said that there were no excuses. Now go!"

She shuffled out of the classroom and made her

way towards the school gate. Her spirits rose when she saw the headmistress approaching.

"Good morning Boitumelo. Why aren't you in your classroom? What is wrong? Have you been crying?"

"Good morning Mma. Yes, I have been crying. Rre Tshotlego beat me for being late for school, and now he has sent me home. I am not allowed to attend any lessons today."

"It is most unlike you to be late for school. You are usually here very early. Did something happen to delay you today?"

"Yes Mma. An old lady, who is my friend, was very ill. I had to go and find somebody to help her."

"You are a kind girl Boitumelo Hope Tumelo. And you did the right thing."

Boi's expectations improved. *Perhaps Mma Tlotlo will reprieve me and tell my teacher to allow me back into the classroom. That would show him!*

Her hopes were immediately dashed.

"But Rre Tshotlego has very clear rules. He will not tolerate tardiness. He is consistent in his punishment too. Anyone who is late will receive six strokes of his cello bow and be sent home with no lessons for that day. It doesn't matter who you are, or what has happened to make you late. You have been unfortunate to become his first example of this school year. I can safely say that there won't be many more Form Two pupils who will be late. Now go home and we'll see you tomorrow."

It was a long trudge back, as Boi walked the eleven miles back to her home in Itlhomolomo. She cried most of the way. It wasn't the stinging pain of her bottom that made her cry. It wasn't even the humiliation of having to lift her skirt in front of the entire class to receive her beating. She cried because she was utterly miserable.

She walked slowly because she was too miserable to run. She thought that perhaps running would make her feel slightly better, but, when she broke into a slow jog, she found that she just wasn't in the mood for running.

The sun was high in the sky, and felt unusually hot, even for Botswana, as she approached Inagolo. The sight that met her eyes cheered her up somewhat.

Mma Mothoriyana was sitting on the stool outside her house, smiling and waving at Boi.

"You are here very early Boi. Is something wrong? Are you ill?"

"I have been sent home for being late for school Mma. I don't like to miss my lessons."

"Oh dear. This is my fault. Come in. I shall make you a cup of tea. I haven't got any cake, but I have some bananas. Would you like a banana?"

Boi entered Mma Mothoriyana's house and sat on the edge of the bed as the old lady put a pot of water on the stove to boil for the tea.

"It is not your fault Mma. I just think that my teacher is mean. He is very strict. He wouldn't even listen to my reason for being late. I am sure that he takes pleasure from beating his pupils."

"He BEAT you too?!"

"Yes Mma. His standard punishment for being late is six strokes on the backside with his cello bow."

"Is it painful?"

"Yes Mma. Very. It stings a lot."

"I will help you. Lay face down on my bed."

Boi did as she was told. Mma Mothoriyana went outside and came back with a piece of aloe vera plant. She sliced it with a sharp knife to expose the juicy flesh inside.

She pulled Boi's dress up to her waist to reveal the nasty-looking weals on her bottom. They were raised up in six straight bumps.

"I am sorry, but you will have to take off your pants to allow me to treat the whole of your injuries."

Boi reached down and slid he pants down her thighs.

Mma Mothoriyana gently rubbed Boi's bottom directly with the aloe vera plant. It felt cool and immediately soothed the burning sensation that she'd been feeling. When enough of the sap of the plant had been applied, Mma Mothoriyana put it to one side and softly massaged the area with her fingers. Boi started to feel good for the first time that day.

As she relaxed, her thoughts wandered back to her morning discovery of the old lady curled up in pain on this very bed. She had been so wrapped up in her own misery and pain that her friend's seemingly miraculous recovery had passed her by.

As she lay there enjoying the continuation of the wonderful treatment that her bum was receiving, she asked, "Are you feeling better now Mma? I was very worried about you this morning."

"Oh yes. Of course I am feeling better. Simisani was able to remove the *koko* that was running around in my stomach. I no longer feel any pain, and he didn't leave a mark on my old skin"

"WHAT! You had a chicken running around inside your tummy?" laughed Boi. "I do not believe it."

"You should believe it," said Mma Mothoriyana quite seriously. "I can tell you that I saw it with my own eyes and the pain disappeared immediately."

"Well, I apologise for doubting you, but I find that hard to believe Mma. You saw the chicken? Was it still wearing its feathers? OUCH!"

Mma Mothoriyana had touched a raw wound a little too harshly.

99

"No. It was not wearing its feathers, but it was definitely a small chicken. It was just like messy meat, but I could see its chicken feet. There was no doubt."

"Whatever he did, you are certainly much better than you were this morning."

When the treatment was finished, Boi pulled up her pants and sat up to enjoy her tea and the banana. She was much happier, even though she was still upset that she had missed a day of her precious education. They were both happy. That morning, they had both helped each other.

* * * * *

Back at home, Mme was initially angry when she heard what had happened to her daughter. She was soon offering words of advice though.

"In future, if something like this happens, you must find somebody who doesn't need to get to school to help your friends in times of trouble. I am sure that there were plenty of people around who could have gone to fetch Simisani Mathumo from Setshwano.

"Now that you are here, there is plenty for you to do today. You can start by fetching some more water from the river. Then you can sweep the floors of the huts and outside in the compound too.

"While you are doing your chores, you can think about how you will avoid the wrath of Rre Tshotlego in the coming year. I didn't think that you would have the same trouble as your brother. He has always had a naughty streak. You are usually such a good girl."

"It wasn't my fault, Mme!"

"No. You are right, Boi. I don't like the idea of Rre Tshotlego handing out so many beatings, but he's been doing it for years, and it's not going to change. But you will know how to stay out of the way of his stick in future."

* * * * *

As the term wore on, Boi managed to stay mostly on the right side of her Form Two teacher, although, like most of the children in the class, she couldn't escape the beatings entirely. He was always looking for the slightest reason to dish out a punishment. Even if he saw litter blowing across the playground, which may have come from the nearby streets, he would find somebody in his class who was responsible for the crime.

Their subject teachers were much the same as they had been in Form One. The healthy competition between the top three pupils continued too, but with added spice. Now that Boi and Grace had followed Kefilwe's example, and all three of them were openly mentoring a chosen friend in their class, they were keen that their own choice would beat the others.

At the end of term, Grace finished top of the class with Kefilwe and Boi only three marks behind in second equal position. Boi, however, gained some satisfaction as Moagi finished seventh, several places ahead of both Gabanakitso and Molathegi, the latter being Grace's choice.

Even Rre Tshotlego was obliged heaped praise on the top three in his class, pointing out that he was doubly pleased with them, as they had been tutoring other members of the class.

It was still fairly evident that he disliked Boitumelo. She thought that his harsh treatment of her was grossly unfair as his feelings towards her were really based upon the misdemeanours of her brother during the previous year. She was a strong-willed girl

101

though, and his unfair conduct made her even more determined to do well. There was no doubt in her mind that she would succeed.

Her ambitions were changing direction. Following her achievements with Moagi's education, she was beginning to think that she might make a better teacher, or even a university professor, than a doctor. She decided to keep her options open.

Almost every weekend, Boi and Grace had continued to compete in their new-found event: aquathon. They'd moved further afield to find better courses, but their first course remained their favourite. Their scoring tree was evenly cut on both sides. The race was a perfect choice for the close friends. Pushing each other was also good for their performances. They were both getting much faster and this was reflected at school too. They easily outclassed the rest of Form Two at running and at swimming.

\* \* \* \* \*

In the second term of Form Two, Moagi was continuing to benefit from Boi's coaching. He had his eyes on a top five finish by the end of the year. He was so pleased that he would often bring his mentor some produce from his farm. Mme was always happy when Boi brought something home with her. They were very poor, and every little supplement helped.

Moagi also offered to help Boi to climb trees. Although athletic, her climbing skills were sadly lacking.

Boi's hunger to be best at everything made her think that it wasn't such a bad idea. Moagi had been climbing all his life, and could scale a tree as quickly and as balanced a monkey. To be fair to Boi, the trees

102

around her village were not exactly made for climbing. They were mostly very thorny. Moagi had a variety of good climbing trees on his farm, he said, more like the ones to be found in Marekisokgomo.

So Boi soon became quite proficient and had the confidence to climb even the tallest trees near to the river by the school. She had long since realised that she'd never be as good at tree-climbing as Moagi, but he would probably never be as good as her at maths or English.

Towards the end of term, Moagi and Boi had been in the shade of a large tree, after school, as they often did, to go through their maths homework together. Boi was a natural coach. She made Moagi work for his results. She would suggest ways to approach a problem and then ask Moagi to show her how he would solve it, correcting him if he went wrong. This way, he would arrive at the correct answer through his own efforts, and would eventually learn how he had done it. Sometimes it would take several goes at a similar problem before he grasped a concept. Boi was very good at making up similar problems, with different numbers, so that Moagi could practice.

Moagi also learnt how to coach from Boi. They would look at a complex tree from the ground, and Moagi would ask her, "If you were trying to get up to that branch, which route would you take?" His mimicking amused them both.

On that particular day, Moagi had finished his homework to hand in to Mma Tlotlo the following day. The tree that they had been sitting under was about twenty metres outside of the school gate. They could see Rre Tshotlego staring at them from the door of their classroom. No doubt he was just waiting to pounce on any wrong move that they might make. His gaze made them nervous.

"Shall we climb this tree Boi? He won't be able to see us up there. Then I will go home."

"Yes. That's a good idea. I don't think we have ever been up this one, even though it is close to the school."

"I have been up it, but you have yet to climb it. I think it is quite tricky, but there is a very good view of the whole town from near the top. Which way will you go?"

Boi stood away from the tree and looked up at it, frowning. She walked around it. Twice.

"It looks like there is only one way to get to that place, but from there it is hard to see from here. I think I will have to decide when I get there."

"Alright. I will stay here and watch you till you get to that point, and then I will come and join you."

Boi started climbing. She had only got about three metres from the ground when she slipped, but she managed to grab a hold on a small branch to stop herself from tumbling to the ground.

"Be careful Boi!"

"I am being careful. But this tree seems a bit awkward."

"Yes. It is. That's why you must be careful to get a good hold."

Boi was trembling.

"He is still watching us you know."

"He can't do anything. There is no law, or even a school rule, against climbing trees."

"I know, but you know what he is like. He can always find some excuse to beat us. Especially me."

"Just ignore him and climb. You don't have far to go before you will reach the point where you have to decide."

She reached up for the next solid branch which was at full stretch for her. She got a good grip on it before she placed her foot in what looked like a strong fork in the tree.

As soon as she lifted her other foot and put her weight on the first, it cracked and broke. The full weight of her whole body was too much for one hand to bare, and she fell.

As she dived towards the ground, she made a big mistake. She put her arm out to break her fall.

CRACK!

She screamed. The pain was horrendous.

Moagi could see immediately that his friend's lower arm had snapped. It was broken and bent, unnaturally, at almost ninety degrees. Poor Boi was lying on the ground crying with the pain.

Moagi looked across at the school. Rre Tshotlego was still standing there, calmly watching them as if nothing out of the ordinary were happening. Moagi could swear that he was actually smiling.

"Help Rra! Boitumelo has broken her arm. Please come and help."

Rre Tshotlego turned and walked into the shade of the classroom.

Moagi looked around. The only other people he could see were Gabanakitso and Boitoi, who didn't seem to have even noticed Boitumelo's accident despite the noise she was making.

He ran across to them.

"Come quickly. Boi needs our help."

They followed him back to where Boi was writhing on the ground.

"Oh! That is horrible! What has she done?"

"She's broken her arm Gabanakitso. What do you think? Isn't it obvious?"

"Well, I can see that. But how?"

"Never mind that. Just help me to get her comfortable. Then you must stay with her until I can fetch her mother."

"You must be joking, Moagi. Just go and tell the teacher. Boi lives in Itlhomolomo. It's miles away. It will take you ages to get there. Just go and find Rre Tshotlego."

"He won't help. I already called him and he turned his back."

"Typical! He doesn't care about us. I think he likes to see us in pain."

They moved Boi so that her back was against the trunk of the tree, and gently moved her arm so that it rested in her lap and was fairly straight.

"I must run to get Mma Tumelo now. She would do the same for any of us. See if you can find some straight sticks to make a splint while I am gone. Her arm needs to be straight."

They nodded and looked around.

"Just stay as still as you can Boi. I will be back as soon as I can. Boitoi, get her some water to drink."

The two girls looked as if they were finding it difficult to cope with the situation. Moagi was used to dealing with emergencies on his farm, but that was mostly with goats and cows, not with humans. Nevertheless, it gave him a calmness that was not shared by Boitoi and Gabanakitso.

"Make sure you stay with her till I get back. I will never forgive you if you leave her."

"Alright Moagi. Stop nagging. Just go!"

As he ran, and walked, the eleven miles to Itlhomolomo, Moagi had a lot of time to think. He wondered what had happened to the school security guard, Kedibonye. It was very unusual for him not to be on the scene for even the most minor event. He would have to ask the guard next time he saw him.

He also became angry as he thought about Rre Tshotlego's strange behaviour. Of course, he would not be held to account. The accident happened outside the school grounds. But any decent person, indeed, any other teacher at their school would have come charging to Boi's aid.

*Why is he even a teacher if he hates children so much?* he mused.

And he thought about Boi. She was such a caring girl. She loved her family, and it was obvious that she loved her best friend, Grace, but she was always willing to help absolutely anybody out if she could. It made him even angrier to think that their teacher could just ignore Boi lying on the ground, screaming, with a broken arm.

*One day, God will strike him down where he stands. And I won't pick him up.*

Moagi felt bad about himself for a few seconds. He had never had such bad thoughts about anybody in his entire life. But then he shook his head and recovered his senses.

*Rre Tshotlego will deserve his punishment from God, when it comes!*

\* \* \* \* \*

When Kasigo's old Chevrolet rattled up to the scene of the accident, with only a single headlight glowing, Boitoi and Gabanakitso were still sitting with Boi under the tree. Gabanakitso, who lived nearby, had gone home to fetch some blankets to keep all three of them warm in the chilly evening air. Her mother had come back with her to help them tend to Boi.

They had managed to put a makeshift splint on the broken arm, and Boi was in quite good spirits, considering her predicament.

Of course, Moagi had told Mma Tumelo all about Rre Tshotlego's behaviour as Kagiso had been driving them back to Marekisokgomo.

Boi's mother was fuming.

After checking on how her daughter was, and giving her some motherly comfort, she said, "Just wait here a few minutes, my darling. I must speak with your teacher."

She had noticed that the lights were still on in the school, so there was a good chance that Rre Tshotlego was still there. Mma Tlotlo certainly would be, as she never seemed to leave the premises.

"No Mma. Please don't. He will only take it out on me."

"I don't think so. Just leave him to me. I will sort him out!"

Boi groaned.

"Come with me boy," she commanded Moagi. "He knows that he cannot argue with me when I have an eye-witness."

The idea of testifying against his teacher terrified Moagi. Mma Patience Tumelo could see his fear rising.

"Don't worry. I don't think you will need to say anything. Just being there will be enough."

As they approached the Form Two classroom, Rre Tshotlego emerged from the doorway.

"Good evening Mma Tumelo. I saw the car and heard the commotion. Is there anything that I can do to help?"

It was obvious to Boi's mother that he was pretending that he had only just become aware of the situation.

She laid into him with the greatest tongue-lashing that the man had probably ever received in his life. She screamed and shouted at him.

At first he appeared shocked and, when she paused for breath, he indignantly appealed to her.

"I am sorry, Mma Tumelo. I am unaccustomed to being spoken to in such..."

She shouted him down. Unwilling to listen to his protestations.

In the end, she terminated the conversation with a promise to return to the school the following day, when she would have calmed down, to speak with the headmistress about his appalling behaviour.

He started to reply, but she had turned on her heel and was already making her way back towards the tree, dragging Moagi along with her.

They got Boi, who was moving very gingerly, into the back of Kagiso's car. Mma Tumelo turned and hugged Moagi warmly.

"Thank you very much for all your help today Moagi. I will not forget this, and I will reward you someday soon. You are such a very good boy."

She also thanked Boitoi and Gabanakitso, and Gabanakitso's mother, before Kagiso drove them off to the hospital.

The next day, despite the big plaster on her arm, or perhaps because she wanted to show it off to all of her friends, Boi insisted on attending school as normal. Mme also insisted on walking all the way to the school too. She would have a meeting with Mma Tlotlo.

As it happened, Mma Tlotlo was already well aware of the events of the previous evening and Rre Tshotlego was in her office when Mma Tumelo arrived. He apologised profusely, and promised that he would take very special care of Boitumelo Hope Tumelo for

| | |
|---|---|
| Title | Eleven Miles |
| Author | Lance Greenfield |
| Price | £10.00 |

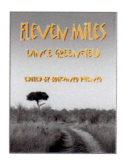

Also written by Lance:

| | |
|---|---|
| Title | Knitting Can Walk! |
| Price | £10.00 |

| | |
|---|---|
| Email: | lance@greenfieldresearch.co.uk |
| Blog: | lancegreenfield.wordpress.com |

## *Lance Greenfield Mitchell*

I was born in the St Pancras borough of London in December, 1955. My father is from Yorkshire, and my mother is from Scotland. I've spent most of my life trying to work out if I'm a Londoner, a Yorkshireman or a Scotsman. I've come to the conclusion that I'm half Yorkshire and half Scots. The place of your birth doesn't really count.

I am married to Joy and currently live in North West Hampshire. My home city is probably Perth, although it could be Sheffield.

I love to travel. I have visited about 80 countries in my life, and I love to immerse myself in different cultures, languages and cuisines.

The greatest passion in my life is the way that people treat people. Witnessing a great act of kindness brings as many tears to my eyes as witnessing horrible cruelty. Hence my personal motto:

### **One world, one people – Care about them all**

*email:* **lance.greenfield@greenfieldresearch.co.uk**
*Blog:* **lancegreenfield.wordpress.com**
*Mobile:* **+44 7825 784 713**
*Twitter:* **@lancegmitchell**          *Telegram:* **@lancegmitchell**

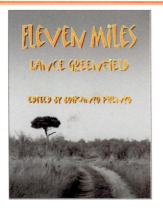

**Two inspiring stories by Lance Greenfield**

**Eleven Miles** is about the amazing achievements of a Botswana girl who walks eleven miles every day for five years to gain her education

**Knitting Can Walk!** is about a disabled orphan whose nickname is "Knitting". Despite expert opinion that she will never walk, she learns to walk by her own determination and with the help of a British teenager

**Please review on Amazon and Goodreads**

the remaining few days of the term. He then accompanied Mma Tumelo and Mma Tlotlo back to the Form Two classroom.

There, in front of the entire class, he made a public apology to Boi and wished her a speedy recovery. His humility was painful. Moagi hoped that it felt as painful to the teacher as was one of his beatings to his pupils.

Boi, of course, did not think along the same lines. She was rather embarrassed by the apology, and wondered if Rre Tshotlego would treat her so nicely once her mother and head teacher had left. As it turned out, not only was he nice to her for the rest of that term, but he treated her with respect, and even uncustomary kindness, for the rest of that school year.

The terrible teacher had learnt a tough lesson!

* * * * *

Although the individual subject prizes went much the same way at the end of Form Two as they had the previous year, Grace maintained her lead for the whole of the year and took the prize for overall first place in class. The sports prizes also went much the same way. Boi had justly gained a reputation for being one of the best runners the school had ever known.

One of the biggest surprises was when Moagi was awarded the prize for 'Most Improved Student in Form Two.' Boi was almost as delighted as Moagi himself. Moagi's parents and elder brother had made a rare trip to the school for the sports day and prize-giving. They were amazed at their son's progress and immensely proud of him.

When the parents, teachers and pupils were milling around after the presentations, they made a point of thanking Rre Tshotlego.

"We are so grateful to you Rra. Moagi has done so well this year compared to last. You must be a very good teacher," complimented Moagi's father.

"Thank you Rra Gogontle Mooketsi. I am well-known for producing good results even from the less talented pupils. It is all a question of discipline. Other teachers should follow my example."

Moagi was horrified. As soon as they were out of the earshot of his teacher, he put his father right.

"Ntate; he is the WORST teacher ever! He is horrible. I scored high marks in subjects that he does not teach. It was other teachers who helped me. Most of all, it was Boitumelo Hope Tumelo who helped me to get good marks."

"What? Are you saying that you have been copying her schoolwork?"

"No Ntate. She has been coaching me and showing me how to work things out for myself. SHE is the one who has helped me to gain good results."

"Really? Are you telling the truth Moagi?" asked his mother. "We will find out if you are fibbing to us."

"Yes Mme. I swear! She is the one who has been teaching me to solve problems and to write good answers. Rre Tshotlego is cruel. All he does is beat us for breathing the same air as him. I could tell you some tales, but I am not one for telling tales, as you know."

"We believe you," said Rre Mooketsi. A smile broke out on his face. His mood changed. "You have done very well, whoever helped you."

"It WAS Boitumelo, Ntate."

"Yes. We believe you. Even so, YOU are the one who has put the work in to achieve such wonderful results. Well done!"

They made their way over to Mma Tumelo, who was standing talking with Grace's parents. Grace and

Boi were listening dutifully to their mothers' conversation. Thapelo was nowhere to be seen.

"Mma Patience Tumelo, you must be very proud of your daughter. Not only is she a brilliant athlete, and a top scholar, but Moagi tells us that she has been his tutor for the past two terms, and is responsible for his success."

"Yes. I am proud of Boi, Rra. And I am happy that she has helped Moagi."

"It is good that he is doing so well. We work very hard to pay his fees, and all the time he is at school, we are one worker down on the farm. But he has the chance of an education that I never had, and he may be able to go to Agriculture College in Gaborone when he graduates from the senior secondary school. He will make our farm much more productive and profitable with all his education."

"We feel much the same about Boi, Rra. Our family all work hard to pay for her education. She is going to be a famous doctor, you know!" boasted Mma Tumelo.

"I don't think that there can be much doubt about that, Mma."

"I haven't decided for certain Mme. I might become a professor at the university instead."

The adults laughed.

"She'll probably change her mind a dozen times before she leaves school, Rra Mooketsi, but I am sure that she will be successful, whatever she does. She works hard."

"I agree. Hard work and determination usually reap rewards. That's what we find on the farm."

"Anyway, I should be the one who must thank you for the courage of your son, Rra."

"What do you mean?"

112

"Don't you know what he did to help Boi last term?"

"No. I haven't heard. What did he do?"

"You must ask him for the whole story, but when Boi broke her arm, he came all the way to Itlhomolomo to fetch me. Boi would not have recovered so well if it had not been for your Moagi."

His mother squealed. "Moagi! You did not say anything of this. Why didn't you tell us?"

"You always told me not to boast, Mme. I didn't think you would want me to tell you."

"Oh Moagi! Of course I would have wanted to hear about this. From what Mma Tumelo says, it sounds like you are a hero. You will tell us ALL about it, THIS evening."

The events of the day were not quite over.

Just as Boi and Grace and their families started to walk down the road away from the school, Kefilwe came running after them.

Panting, he said, "I've got something important to tell you. I didn't know until my father just told me." He looked distressed.

"Oh Boi. Grace. I don't know how to tell you this."

"What is it, Kefilwe?"

"My family is moving to Bonwakatse. It is the home of my grandparents."

"I have never heard of Bonwakatse, Kefilwe. Where is it?" asked Boi.

"It is near to the town of Lephutshe. That is where I will go to school. Do you know where that is, Boi?"

"I know it," replied Grace. I have an aunt and uncle living there. It is MILES away! It is on the edge of the desert. Do you HAVE to go, Kefilwe?"

"Yes. I must go with my family. I cannot stay here."

The two girls were close to tears. At the same moment, they realised that the three of them had been inseparable friends for most of their lives. They had both fancied Kefilwe for a while, but had given up on that line at the end of Form One. However, the bond between the three was strong.

"We are going to miss you very much."

"Yes, we are. That is the truth."

"I am going to miss you too. And I won't know anyone in Bonwakatse or Lephutshe."

They hugged each other and the two girls cried. Kefilwe, himself, only just managed to contain his emotions. They only separated when Grace's mother urged her daughter to come along. It was a sad moment.

# # # # #

# Nine - Robongwe

Boitumelo had very mixed feelings, as she ran to school on the first day of her third year at Marekisokgomo Integrated Secondary School. She was very happy that she had graduated from the Junior Secondary School, and was about to take the symbolic walk across the playground to begin her three years at the Senior Secondary School. It was a significant event.

She was also very happy that she had made it, relatively unscathed, through her year under the guardianship of the cruel Rre Tshotlego. Apart from several beatings for the most trivial of misdemeanours, and a broken arm which had mended very quickly, it had been plain sailing.

On the other hand, she couldn't help wondering how Kefilwe would fare in his new school. If he would make new friends very easily and forget his old ones. She felt sure that he would continue to do well at his academic subjects. But she knew that she would miss him.

She would also miss seeing her naughty brother, Thapelo, around the school. He had completed his Form Three, but with dismal results in most subjects. When their father had returned home during the school holidays, he had had a serious discussion with Thapelo.

Thapelo had admitted that his academic failings had been because he spent most of his time "just having a bit of fun with my friends," and not concentrating on his studies. Ntate had pointed out that it made no sense for members of the family to use their hard-earned cash to pay for his schooling if there were going to be no worthwhile results. He would have to leave school and get a job.

Being a very practical boy, he'd had no trouble in finding work as a labourer working for Rre L Tshireletso, the builder, in Marekisokgomo. There was a lot of development of new tourist hotels going on, so there would be plenty of work for him.

She had no fears regarding her Form Three class teacher, Mma Ratanang. Over the past two years, Mma Ratanang had been Boi's Social Studies teacher, and Boi had been a big favourite for the plump, friendly lady, who was always smiling. She looked forward to a beating-free year.

When she arrived at the school, early as usual, the children were already gathering. There were many young ones there, who would be starting their Form One on that day. Boi recalled her first day. It brought back pleasant memories. She knew that these children would be very nervous, but would soon be put at their ease by Mma Tlotlo and Mma K Agisanyang.

As was the custom, the Form Three pupils gathered on the junior school side of the playground, and awaited the arrival of Rre Lekgowa. As well as being the Integrated Science teacher, Rre Lekgowa had the responsibility of being Mma Tlotlo's Deputy Head, responsible for leading the Senior Secondary School.

Grace and Boi held hands and talked about their holidays. Their free time had been mainly occupied by a continuation of their aquathon races, which had continued to be closely fought. Of course, they'd had plenty of time to fish and to swim.

Grace told Boi about the great excitement in Kango the previous evening. Snakes usually kept away from the village, but their next door neighbour had found a cobra hiding in his wood pile. Everyone in the village had come to look, but most were too scared to do anything about it. Eventually, Gontse had volunteered, against their mother's wishes, to catch the snake. He had watched somebody else catch a snake with a forked stick about a year ago.

Gontse cut a stick to the required, snake-catching

requirements. It was long and straight, with a fork at the end.

"The longer the better!" said Gontse to the admiring and fearful crowd.

He had crept up on the cobra, with the stick extended before him.

The cobra reared up, with its hood extended, ready to strike.

Gontse had lunged at the snake, which dodged out of the way and made a dash for freedom. The crowd split, leaping out of its way, as Gontse semi-courageously, chased it out of the village into the bushes.

"It was all a bit of an anti-climax in the end, Boi. I thought that my brother was going to have a snake-skin trophy to nail to the wall of our hut, and he would be the local hero. He still is a bit of a hero though. The whole village are talking about him, and the size of the cobra increases with every telling."

"It's quite a story, Grace. It's a shame he didn't have any magic dust to sprinkle on its tail."

"You are never going to let me forget that, are you Boi?"

"No. I am not. And you will live to regret that trick you played on me. I will get my own back, so you had better not forget it either," she chuckled.

A deep voice behind them startled the two girls.

"Excuse me. Is this the Form Three group?"

They turned to find themselves staring up at the smiling face of a boy who was a full head taller than both of them.

"Erm... Yes, it is. Are you joining us today?"

"Yes. My name is Kethwaahetse. Kethwaahetse Motsumi. My family have just moved into the area from East Ville. This is my first day at this school. What are your names?"

"I am Boitumelo Hope Tumelo. My friends call me Boi. Welcome to Marekisokgomo, Kethwaahetse."

"Thank you Boitumelo."

"Boi. Please!"

"Thank you Boi. And you are...?"

"My name is Tshegofatso Grace Maphenyo, but you may call me Mma Maphenyo."

She grinned.

"No. I am only joking. Please call me Grace."

"OK Grace. Pleased to meet you both. I am sure that I'll meet the rest of the class as the day wears on. A lot of people call me Keith."

"May I call you Kethwaahetse?" asked Boi. "It is such a poetic name. I like it."

"Yes please. After all, it IS my given name."

"Where do you live, Kethwaahetse?"

Before he could answer, they were called to order by Rre Lekgowa.

"Form Three students! Please listen to me."

They fell silent and looked towards their new class teacher, who was familiar to them all, except Kethwaahetse of course.

"Today is a very big milestone in your young lives. We will now cross the playground and enter the Marekisokgomo SENIOR Secondary School. Please follow me."

The other children around the playground, who had also fallen silent as Rre Lekgowa made his announcement, burst into loud applause and cheering as the new Form Three students marched proudly towards their new classroom.

It was certainly a big occasion. Boi's happiness at the moment made her feel so emotional that she felt she might shed some tears. She managed to control herself, but only just.

They entered their new classroom, where Mma Ratanang was already waiting for them.

Rre Lekgowa formally handed over the students of

118

"the new intake."

"Please sit down at any desk you like," invited their Form Three class teacher.

The children looked around the classroom as they found themselves a place each. It was very similar to the classrooms that they had occupied in years one and two. Even the shelves, labelled for each individual pupil were exactly the same.

The room smelt of fresh paint which had obviously been applied during the holiday.

The biggest difference, which many of the pupils felt, although they dare not say, was the kindly teacher who stood before them in the shape of Mma Ratanang.

*Such a wonderful change from horrible Rre Tshotlego,* thought Boi. *Form Three is going to be enjoyable, even if it will be hard work.*

They quickly settled in to their new surroundings.

When it came to the morning break, the new boy, Kethwaahetsė, proved to be very sociable, circulating amongst his classmates and quickly making friends.

At Mma Ratanang's request, he had stood up and briefly introduced himself to the rest of the class. His father was a surveyor, who mostly worked on road construction and was often away from home. His mother stayed at home, tending to the house and a small plot of land that they'd acquired, but she took in laundry and tailoring to earn a little extra cash. They lived in Nonyane, which was near to Dinokana, and Moagi's farm.

He had previously attended East Ville Junior Secondary School, which was miles away from Marekisokgomo. He was very happy when his family had moved to this town, as the nearest senior secondary school to East Ville would have been too far for him to travel. He had never known of an integrated secondary school before arriving in Marekisokgomo, but thought that it was a great idea.

119

"Perhaps it will catch on throughout Botswana some day," he declared.

During the rest of the day, they received their timetables for the first term and met some of their subject teachers. Kethwaahetse became instantly popular with all of his new classmates, but one in particular. Boi was totally spellbound by the tall, muscular boy who was proving to be rather intelligent as well.

In the first three weeks of term, the newcomer had replaced Kefilwe as the main competition in all subjects for Boi and Grace. Unlike Kefilwe, he was also exceptional at most sports. His stature gave him an added advantage, and he was even able to compete with Form Five pupils. Despite his apparent all-round superiority, Kethwaahetse was extremely modest, never bragging about his unquestionable talent. He thought nothing of his achievements, and he was very generous with his assistance to all around him. He was just so natural. These attributes made him all the more attractive to Boi. However, he seemed not to notice her attention. He devoted equal amounts of time to all his new friends.

She began to challenge herself to attract his attention without being too blatant. Some of the other girls were playing the same game. Most of the girls in the class fancied Kethwaahetse, and would have liked to be is girlfriend. Every time Boi caught him looking at her, she could feel herself blushing. She was sure that he would notice, but he said nothing.

Boi would often stay late after school so that she could take advantage of the electric lighting to complete her homework. At home, the best light she could expect came from tallow candles, which would strain her eyes. One or two other children would also stay from time to time, but Boi was the only regular.

Kethwaahetse, who also liked to work hard, began to get into the same habit.

One evening, when only the two of them remained and both had completed their set homework, they got into a deep conversation. They talked to each other about the members of their own families and backgrounds.

The boy asked her if she had ever had a serious boyfriend. She said that she hadn't, but she'd once had a crush on a boy who never knew about her feelings for him.

"So you've never kissed a boy?"

"No. I haven't." She felt slightly embarrassed.

He fell silent for a moment, then he leaned forward and kissed her firmly on the lips; just like that!

Boi was very excited by her first kiss, but she was also very confused by how it made her feel. She just stood still, like a statue, totally shocked.

This time it was Kethwaahetse's turn to blush. He didn't quite know what to do. After a few seconds, he decided to run off before Boi could hit him.

Boi packed up her bag and set off on her run home. As usual, she found that her journey was a time for deep thought. She remembered what she had learned in biology lessons about how babies are made, and she didn't want to make THAT kind of mistake at her early stage of life! That was exactly what she was trying to avoid by getting a good education. She wanted to go to university and make a good career for herself.

Mosetsanagape, one of her class mates up to the end of Form Two, had failed to turn up for the new school year. They had only just discovered the reason for her absence. She'd had to leave school because she had become pregnant. The suspected father of the child was a boy who had been in

Thapelo's class. He had also failed to turn up at the beginning of term. Boi thanked the Lord that, for once, the miscreant hadn't turned out to be her brother.

By the time she arrived home in Itlhomolomo, she had decided to manufacture the same situation again, but next time she would make sure that she had some condoms with her in case things got out of hand.

One evening, two weeks later, she found herself alone in the classroom with Kethwaahetse. She'd been increasingly aware of him looking at her during classes, especially during P.E. lessons. She felt the warm tingling of excitement in her tummy as she brought the conversation around to girlfriends and boyfriends. They talked in the abstract about who, amongst their friends, would make good couples, and why. They speculated about who might already be "an item."

Eventually, she plucked up enough courage to shyly ask him if there were any girls in the class whom he particularly liked.

Kethwaahetse confessed that he had always liked Boi's best friend, Grace, since the moment he'd first met the pair of them in the school playground on his first day.

"You really are close, aren't you?"

Boi tried to hide her disappointment and answered his direct question.

"Yes. We grew up together. I have known her all of my life. We love each other even more than sisters ever could."

Kethwaahetse was shocked.

"You're not ... um ... You don't mean that you and Grace ... Are you ...?"

Boi laughed loudly.

"No! We're not lesbians, if that's what you mean!"

"Oh. I thought for a moment..."

He felt really awkward about his mistake.

"On the contrary. I know for a fact that I have no feelings in that direction at all. All I was saying is that she is the dearest friend possible. She is such a lovely girl. I would be devastated if we were separated. I hope that her family never move away from here. I don't think that they will. Nor will mine.

"She would make a wonderful girlfriend for you. If you like, I'll tell her that you fancy her. I am sure that she'll be delighted."

"I'd rather you didn't, Boi. You see, it is YOU that I really fancy."

"Me?"

It was very difficult to remain calm. She could feel the heat rising in her belly and in her cheeks. It felt like her irrepressible joy was going to explode like a volcano from within her core.

"Yes Boi. I am sorry that I shocked you when I kissed you a couple of weeks ago. I just couldn't stop myself. You are so gorgeous."

"Would you like to kiss me again, Kethwaahetse?"

"Oh yes. Yes please!"

"Go on then. Kiss me."

He stepped forward and kissed her on the lips. She kissed him back. Immediately, their kissing got very heated and they soon found themselves rolling around on the floor, pulling each other's pants off.

At almost the last moment, Boi realised that she couldn't give him the condom, because he would want to know why she had one in her bag. At the height of their passion, just as he was trying to enter her and she was trying to avoid the inevitable, he ejaculated all over her dress.

Embarrassed, he jumped to his feet, pulled up his pants, grabbed his schoolbag, and ran out of the classroom. Over his shoulder, he called, "I'm really sorry Boi. See you tomorrow."

When Kethwaahetse had gone, Boi sat at her desk in stunned silence. Once again, she had mixed feelings. She had never experienced such strong sexual feelings in her life. She had no regrets whatsoever, and couldn't wait for their next intimate encounter. Perhaps they could find somewhere private, away from the school, and take more time to get to know each other's bodies and desires.

She cursed herself as she realised, far too late, that she could have said that the school nurse had given condoms to all the girls as an "insurance policy." This was the truth. Both under-age pregnancy and sexually transmitted diseases, especially HIV, were far too common in Botswana. This was a national problem which, for once, the government had taken seriously. Some parents objected, saying that giving condoms to young girls was just encouraging under-age sex. But, as Boi had just discovered, once the urge overpowers you, there is very little you can do to resist it, whatever your age. She was only fourteen, but her boyfriend had made her feel like a woman.

How strange that sounded in her mind: her BOYFRIEND!

The next day, during the first break, Kethwaahetse shuffled up to her and quietly asked if she was alright.

"Yes Kethwaahetse. I am VERY alright, thank you. How about you."

"I am also VERY alright Boi. I was worried that you would be upset with me. Now that you tell me that you are not, I am even more VERY alright."

"What are you thinking?"

"I am thinking that what we did last evening makes us officially boyfriend and girlfriend." He hesitated to take in the look on her face. "That is, if you WANT to be my girlfriend."

Boi liked to be in control. Despite her urge to blurt out an immediate answer, she kept a dead pan face and silently stared him out.

He cracked.

"Oh. I am sorry. I didn't mean to pressure you. If you don't want to be my girlfriend, I'll understand. We can still be friends, can't we?"

She made him wait a few more second, enjoying his

discomfort. With her index finger, she beckoned him to lean down so that his ear was close to her mouth.

She whispered, "There is nothing I want more right now, Kethwaahetse, than to be your girlfriend."

He let out a big breath. He was so relieved.

"Oh. That is good, Boi. That is very good!"

"Well, there is actually something else that I DO want more."

"What is that? If I can get it for you, I shall do so."

"You can't get it for me. But you can give it to me. I want to make love with you."

"I would like that very much, but it would be very inadvisable to make love here in the playground."

She laughed.

"No, silly! After school. I know the perfect spot. It is secluded. Not many people know of it, but I go there sometimes to think on my own."

"Where is it? Where shall we meet?"

"Behind the lemon tree in the school garden."

"I didn't even know there was a lemon tree in the school garden."

"See! It is the world's best kept secret. It is right down in the far corner. Stay in the classroom for a whole hour, until all the others have gone. Pretend to work, and then come to the garden. I will be waiting and watching for you. If you can't find my hiding place, I will wave to you."

"I can't wait!"

"I know. You couldn't wait yesterday either," she teased.

"Yes. I am very sorry about that."

"It was not entirely your fault. I did not want you to do it without a condom. I have got some now, from the school nurse. She gives them to all the girls to keep us safe."

"We will take it much more slowly this time. We need to be careful."

"Yes. That is what I thought. See you at five o'clock."

For the rest of the school day, the couple could hardly concentrate on their lessons. They kept stealing sideways glances at each other, and they both felt hotter than usual.

Naturally, Grace noticed how unusually distracted her friend had been. It was very obvious that she wasn't paying much attention to her teachers, and she was hardly writing any notes.

"What is wrong with you Boi? Are you unwell?" she whispered.

"No Grace. I am VERY well, than thank you. Something has happened. Something very good has happened."

"What has happened?"

"Will you two girls stop whispering to each other while I am speaking?" asked Mma Othusitse, more as a command than a question.

"Sorry Mma," chorused Boi and Grace in unison.

Moments later, Boi slipped a note to Grace: *"I'll tell you all about it tomorrow on the way to school. I promise. XxX"*

When school finished for the day, Boi told her friends that she was going to see her brother at the site of the hotel that Rre L Tshireletso was building in the centre of town.

She started off in that direction, but, when she was sure that nobody was watching her, she doubled back and made her way along the side of the river to the back of the school. Hiding behind a hedge, she watched to see if Kedibonye was on the prowl. There was no sign of him.

By quarter to five, she was in position, concealed behind the lemon tree. She had a good view of the entrance to the garden from her vantage point, but was sure that nobody could see her. The entrance was just a gap in the thorn bushes which formed a barrier between the neatly maintained garden and the playground. It did a good job of both blocking the view and keeping any stray animals, which shouldn't really be in the school grounds, away from the precious plants.

Boi felt the tension. It was unlike her to feel impatient, but the seconds were ticking away far too slowly.

She had only waited five, long minutes when Kethwaahetse appeared at the gap in the hedge. *Ten minutes early! He must be as eager as me!*

He was looking around the garden, nervously.

*It is good that he cannot see me. We will be well hidden should anyone else come into the garden.*

Boi peeked out from behind the lemon tree and waved frantically.

"Over here you idiot!" she whispered loudly.

Kethwaahetse joined her in her hiding place, dropping his bag on the ground.

"You are correct. This is the perfect place to make love, where nobody can see us. There is a nice fragrance too."

Boi was surprised. Boys didn't usually notice such things.

"Yes. It is a very special place for a very special occasion."
She kissed him.

"This is my first time, Kethwaahetse," she confessed.
"That is why it is so special to me. I expect that you have done it before with several girls."

"No. It is my first time too, Boi. It is a special occasion for me too. Especially as my first time will be with such a gorgeous girl."

She ran her hand across his chest as they kissed, and undid a button. They undressed each other slowly, caressing each other sensually and intimately as they did so. They were both extremely aroused.

When they were both naked, Boi produced the condom that she had placed under her bag before Kethwaahetse had arrived. She tore open the foil packet and took it out. The school nurse had shown them how to put them on, using a banana, and they had all practised. The nurse had warned them to be very careful as it was very easy for condoms to split, or to come off at the crucial moment, if they were not rolled on properly, squeezing all the air out from the little bulb at the end.

Boi took her time. She didn't want to make a terrible mistake.

Unfortunately, as soon as he entered her, he could contain himself no longer and he came immediately. But, this time, they were much more relaxed about it and collapsed in a giggling heap. When they recovered somewhat, they just started to get dressed and promised each other that they would do it better next time.

"One way of looking at it is that, as with anything, practice makes perfect!"

"Are you saying that we should keep doing this until we do it perfectly?"

"Yes, Boi. That is EXACTLY what I am saying. The more we do it, the better we'll be."

"I agree. Let's do it again tomorrow." They were both laughing together, which made them feel good.

As they made their way out across the playground, Boi suddenly got quite serious.

"You mustn't tell anyone that we are girlfriend and boyfriend, Kethwaahetse. My father has banned me from having a boyfriend until I go to university. I must at least pretend to do as he says. He IS my father, and he IS paying for my education. Well, along with my grandfather and my eldest brother. I don't know what he would do if he found out about us."

"Our secret is safe with me, Boi. I really want to keep you as my girlfriend, so I won't do anything that might lose you. But I am sure that you will tell your best friend."

Boi frowned.

"Yes. You already know us too well. Of course I will tell Grace. We have absolutely no secrets between us. But she is different. There is no way that she would ever give me away. No way!"

"I know. You are very close, and I believe you."

They had reached the road outside the school, and went their separate ways. They deliberately resisted the temptation of a public, parting kiss. Anybody could have been watching.

"See you tomorrow."

* * * * *

Grace was waiting at the junction of the tracks when Boi came running along in the morning. She was eager to hear what had been distracting her friend so much from her studies.

Boi told Grace almost everything. She was now Kethwaahetse's girlfriend.

"But only you know that. You mustn't tell anyone. Not even your mother. Nobody else must know. I will be in serious trouble with my father if he ever finds out."

"You can trust me, Boi. But did he kiss you?"

She continued to question Boi as they walked along. She found out about their assignation behind the lemon tree, but Boi kept back that she had lost her virginity. She was really bursting to tell her friend, but felt that it was far too early to confess. Perhaps, later, she might reluctantly let Grace squeeze the information out of her. If she were to be completely honest with herself, it wouldn't take too much squeezing.

They soon arrived at Inagolo. Mma Mothoriyana was sitting in her usual place outside her house. She was delighted to see the girls.

"Do you know what today is? It is a very special day for me."

Boi giggled. She was remembering the conversation that she'd had with Kethwaahetse the previous evening: a "special day" of both of them.

"Please tell us why it is a special day for you Mma."

129

"Because today is my birthday!"

"Oh! Happy birthday Mma!"

"Yes. Happy birthday!"

They clapped their hands with glee.

"Thank you. It is indeed a very happy birthday. I am eighty years old today. It is a big birthday."

"Congratulations Mma. I hope I look as fit as you when I am eighty years old," said Boi.

"Well, I don't want to delay you on your way to school. I remember what happened when you were late for school because I had a *koko* in my stomach. You must run along now. But, when you come back this evening, I will have a piece of very delicious cake waiting for you."

"How wonderful! That will be something for us to look forward to all day."

It wasn't until they'd walked another two miles down the road, and were a long way past the crossroads where Gasenna and Thapelo used to play out their challenges, that Boi realised that she'd had something else to look forward to after school. The thought of the conflict between the two promised delights made her head hurt. *Oh no!*

By the time, they reached the school, Boi had decided that she could not possibly let the old lady down. There would never be another eightieth birthday cake, but she hoped that she would have many more opportunities to make love to her boyfriend behind the lemon tree.

Kethwaahetse was naturally disappointed, but he was soon persuaded that Boi was right. There would be plenty of chances for them to get together. The only difference was that he would not be getting a piece of the delicious birthday cake.

And so it proved. Boi and Kethwaahetse would meet behind their lemon tree two or three times a week. And, as they hoped, they did get it right most of the time. Sometimes, they'd get carried away, and it would go slightly wrong. Even on those occasions, they would end up laughing about it. They were such a perfect match, and they enjoyed every minute of the time that they shared together.

During the school holiday, they managed to arrange to meet up occasionally.

At the beginning of the second term, they continued to meet in the usual place. The third time they met, they were in the middle of making love when they heard a man's voice close by.

"And what do you think you two are doing?"

It was Kedibonye, the old school security guard!

They scrambled for their clothes, and quickly got dressed. Boi couldn't believe how stupid she had been to forget about him. Thapelo had warned her about him from the very beginning. He was usually everywhere. Nothing escaped his attention. *How have we avoided his attention for so long?*

They were extremely surprised by his attitude. He was very kind, and told them that he wouldn't tell anybody, as long as they promised never to do it again!

They scuttled away, thinking how lucky they had been to escape with just a caution.

Kedibonye's motives soon became clear though. For the rest of the term, every time Boi passed him in the school grounds, he would wink at her in a way that sent shivers up and down her spine. It worried her as she couldn't be completely sure he was going to keep her mouth shut.

After about three weeks, when nobody else was within earshot, he whispered in her ear, "See you behind that lemon tree at five o'clock this evening!"

She became really worried. She'd heard about older men liking young girls, and suddenly realised he must be one of those "dirty old men!" He was going to insist on sexual favours from her to keep his mouth shut.

*What should I do?*

She didn't make the rendezvous that evening.

For the next week, she did her best to avoid Kedibonye, and she also made every excuse she could think of to avoid meeting her boyfriend out of school hours.

Eventually, Kethwaahetse managed to corner Boi alone.

"What's wrong Boi? Have you gone off me?"

"No. Of course not. I'm just scared that we'll get caught again. That's all."

"I think there's more to it than that."

After a bit of evasion, Boi told Kethwaahetse the truth.

"I'll kill him!"

"Don't be silly."

"OK. It was just an expression. But I'll go and speak to him. He promised he wouldn't tell anyone as long as we didn't do it again. He's threatening to break his promise. I'll just scare him. I'm a lot bigger than him."

"Are you serious?"

"Well, what else can we do?"

"I think that the answer is simple. We'll just keep out of his way, and we won't make love in the school grounds ever again. He'll give up in the end."

For the rest of that term, they did just that. It was almost impossible to avoid him completely, but Kedibonye managed to brush past Boi whenever he saw an opportunity. He would fondle her bottom and whisper in her ear. Boi was strong though. She resolved to put up with a little groping to maintain their secret. In the meantime, the couple found plenty of secret places where they could continue their love affair.

# # # # #

# Ten - Lesome

When they all returned to school for their final term in Form Three, the competition for top place in all subjects continued to be between Boi, Grace and Kethwaahetse. Moagi was just about maintaining fourth place in class, but was facing some stiff challenges from about six other pupils. All of them were some way behind the top three.

Boi was very relieved that Kedibonye was turning his attention elsewhere and almost ignoring her presence altogether. It appeared that a very tall, pretty girl in Form Four, Sethunya, was catching the security guard's eye. She flirted at every opportunity, deliberately walking past his hut during break times, and willingly accepting his offers of tea and chocolate. When she sat down near to him, her skirt would magically ride up to reveal a lot of leg. Sometimes, the door to the hut would be closed when Boi was certain the girl was inside.

*Well good luck to the bean pole and the dirty old man,* Boi thought to herself. *At least while he is occupied with her, he is not harassing me!*

Her romance with Kethwaahetse continued. When it came to P.E. lessons, they had a lot in common. Being so tall, he was a natural sprinter, but over longer distances he was no match at all for Boi. In fact, there was nobody in the school, male or female, who could beat Boi over ten thousand metres. Mister Way was very proud of his star, and he took her, in his car, to events at other schools around the north of Botswana.

She would always return as a winner, never second or third, and Mma Tlotlo would always announce her success to the entire school at assembly.

Grace was experiencing similar success at swimming. Although the lessons with Mister Way were still in the river at the side of the school, the council had paid Rre L Tshireletso's company, to build a brand new community pool in the town centre. At the opening event in the pool, attended by many people from all around the district, fourteen year-old Grace won both the two-hundred and three-hundred metre freestyle events. This was a quite remarkable achievement for several reasons. Firstly, she was competing against women of all ages, even people in their twenties. Secondly, she had never had the opportunity to swim in a man-made swimming pool before the day of the event.

Boi was immensely proud of her friend.

"See! I remember telling you, on our very first day at Marekisokgomo Integrated Secondary School that you would be a national champion and swim for Botswana."

Although she was clearly delighted, Grace was keeping her feet firmly on the ground.

"I am NOT champion of all Botswana, sister. I just won a couple of races. Probably, the best swimmers haven't even heard of Marekisokgomo. I just beat a few women from round about the villages."

"You are too modest, Grace. You are the best. I, Boitumelo Hope Tumelo, am telling you!"

They hugged each other warmly. They were so happy.

On the way home that evening, they stopped at their favourite aquathon course. Grace wanted to race, but Boi told her that she should be satisfied with her achievements for one day.

"Losing to me after your two great victories will put a bad end to your wonderful day. Let's just go for a nice swim in the river."

And so they did. It was a beautiful, sunny evening, as was usually the case at that time of year. They relaxed and enjoyed the moment.

When Boi got home, her mother was very anxious.

"Oh! Thanks goodness you are home safely Boitumelo. Where have you been?"

"It is still light, Mme. What is the problem? I come home much later than this when I have homework to do before I leave school for the day." *Or when I am making love to my gorgeous boyfriend,* she thought.

"I know, but I have been worried because of the news. Tell me where you have been."

"I have just been swimming with Grace, Mme. What news?"

"Oh no. It is as I feared. Where did you go swimming?"

"In our usual place, Mme. Near to the crossroads the other side of Inagolo. It is perfectly safe there. It only gets a little dangerous in the rainy season, when it floods, but we don't swim there at that time of year. Bur WHAT news?"

"That is alright then. The news is that a boy has been killed by Menomagolo whilst swimming in Metsimantsho. We all thought that killer hippopotamus had died and been eaten by the crocodiles. He hasn't been seen or heard of for almost two years. He must have been hiding in the swamp all this time, and keeping out of the way of humans."

"That is terrible Mma. Who is the boy? Do I know him?"

"No. I don't think so. It is another boy from Tobetsa. His name is Tebego Pepukani. He is the cousin of the boy who had his arm bitten off by Menomagolo some time ago. That village is very

135

unlucky. Do not go there. And do not go to the swamp."

"I won't Mme."

Boi hadn't seen Thapelo sitting in the dark corner of the hut until he spoke.

"Somebody needs to kill that beast before he causes any more trouble. We are lucky. I have heard that The Fox is coming home to the village on annual leave from the Botswana Defence Force, Sergeant Lefoko Dintwa is the man to kill Menomagolo. And I will volunteer to help him."

Boi and her mother gave each other a meaningful look.

"Don't be ridiculous, Thapelo. Sergeant Dintwa is a highly trained and very experienced soldier. You are a builder's apprentice. Besides, I have told you repeatedly, you are NOT to go anywhere near Metsimantsho."

Boi felt the need to add to her mother's argument.

"And do you really think that the Sergeant will seriously wish to spend his valuable holiday time hunting a hippo? If he has lain low for two years, how do you think a single man, no matter how good a soldier he is, will find him and kill him in just two weeks."

"Alright!" shouted Thapelo in response to both of them, "I won't be able to help him. But I can tell you that he is the man who can save us from Menomagolo. And I can also tell you that I am not the only one who thinks so. Ntatemogolo agrees with me. He is over in the bar at Inagolo right now, asking Sergeant Lefoko Dintwa to get rid of the rogue hippopotamus."

This news put a surprising thought into Boi's mind.

"What would you like us to do Mme? Fetch some water? Sweep the yard?"

136

"Thank you Boi. We have enough water, but we could do with a bit more wood for the fire for the morning. If you and Thapelo each collect as much as you can carry in one load, that will be sufficient."

As they walked across to the trees outside the village, Boi suggested to Thapelo that they should go across to Inagolo to see what was happening with the Sergeant. Thapelo was quick to agree.

When they got back to their house, Boi asked Mme if it would be alright if they went across to see their grandfather.

She smiled.

"Yes. Of course it is alright with me for you to go over to that village to see..." She paused for a moment. "...the heroic sergeant!"

They realised that their ruse had been easily spotted. They were actually the stupid ones, to believe that their mother would be too stupid to see through the ploy.

"Thank you Mma. We won't stay long."

\* \* \* \* \*

The little bar was very crowded when they arrived. It was easy to see where the sergeant was sitting, even though he was not immediately visible. There was a table which was surrounded by young women. He would be there. The girls were flocking around the huge man like vultures around the carcass of a cow.

Boi and Thapelo struggled to get through the throng until they were spotted by their grandfather.

"Thapelo! Boitumelo! Come and join us here. Have a beer!"

The girls had no choice but to make way. Rre

Ofentse was one of the most respected members of the local community. Boi sat next to her grandfather. Thapelo took his seat next to Sergeant Dintwa. His heart was almost bursting out of his chest as he got so close to his hero.

The girls scowled at Boi, even though she really posed no threat to their intentions to win the attention of the soldier.

"Have you asked him yet Ntatemogolo?"

The sergeant answered for him.

"Yes. He has asked me if I could possibly hunt down and kill this notorious hippo, Thapelo."

"And? Will you?"

"Listen to me. All of you. I am a trained killer! Nothing scares me. I am one of the strongest men in the whole of the Botswana Defence Force. And I am definitely the best marksman. Look at this badge on my shoulder to prove it."

Thapelo stared in open admiration at the crossed rifles, marksman's badge on the sergeant's khaki shirt.

"I also have many trophies that I could show you some other time.

"In the past year alone, I have personally killed six poachers coming in to our lands from the north. They would be the death of our country if Sergeant Lefoko Dintwa, The Fox, did not destroy them first!"

Some of the girls gasped. Others sighed. Thapelo said, "Wow!"

Sergeant Dintwa luxuriated in the attention. He loved it.

"I will tell you something. The Fox does not need his rifle to kill a hippopotamus. Oh no!"

He held up raised his fist and displayed his upwardly turned thumb to the admiring crowd.

"I will kill that Menomagolo with my killer

thumb!"

This time the gasps were unanimous, and loud.

"Yes! I tell you! This thumb has already killed a crocodile. That hippo will know no mercy from Sergeant Lefoko Dintwa. He is as good as dead. You will have nothing to fear when I have killed him."

People started to thank him as if he had already done the deed. Boi seemed to be the only sceptical one in the whole crowd, but she kept quiet.

"And when I have killed him, we will have the biggest feast in your living memory. There is enough meat on that hippo to fill all of our bellies and leave plenty for the dogs."

More beers had magically arrived on the table. Boi had not touched the bottle that her grandfather had pushed towards her. She did not like beer.

The party continued long after Boi and Thapelo had kissed their grandfather goodbye and shaken the hand of the community hero. As they made their way back to Itlhomolomo, Thapelo could not stop talking about the glorious gladiator who would slay the monster of the swamp.

Boi occasionally managed to intervene with a "Hmm," or a "Yes brother." She would only believe it when she saw the beast lying dead on the ground. Or roasting on the fire.

\* \* \* \* \*

Boi and Kethwaahetse continued their romance, trying to be discreet but becoming more obvious amongst most of their friends. Grace was still the only friend who knew the truth about their love-making, and Boi wanted to keep it that way.

Boi was continuing to successfully tutor Moagi,

who was clinging on to fourth place in class. It may have helped that he was receiving a little bit of extra tuition from Grace, who was showing him some romantic interest. Moagi was nervously returning her advances, but he was obviously worried about taking things too fast. They had kissed, but, when Grace had invited him to freely explore her body, he had said that, although he thought she was gorgeous, he would rather postpone that experience until "the right time." She accepted that, but hoped that "the right time" would come soon.

Grace continued to help Molathegi. He was doing quite well to maintain a position in the middle of the class.

Sergeant Lefoko Dintwa was visiting a different village, and a different bar, every evening. Boi had not had any difficulty tracking his progress, Thapelo was the sergeant's biggest fan, and always knew where his hero was, and where he would be next. He provided regular reports of the soldier's progress.

Boi told Kethwaahetse all about the local character. She told him about her brother's "rather disturbing hero-worship", and about how the local girls swooned in his presence.

"You have never seen anyone brag so much about how wonderful they are. And he is not in the least attractive. He looks like a bull with his thick neck and his great, flat nose."

"Are you the only one person in the whole of Botswana who is not excited by the achievements of the sergeant? He is obviously the local hero, and he must surely be celebrated."

"I suppose you are right, but I am sure that he exaggerates about his feats of strength and marksmanship. I will celebrate with the masses when he has actually killed Menomagolo and shown us the body."

"You are too harsh. Perhaps you are slightly jealous."

She laughed at that.

"You should be happy that I believe that you are much more handsome and attractive than that great monster of a man."

"Do you know where he will be this evening? I would like to see him with my own eyes, and hear his stories with my own ears."

"Seriously?"

"Yes. It is only fair that I judge for myself. You may be biased."

"Alright. He will be in Tobetsa tonight. We can go there together."

\* \* \* \* \*

That evening, they went straight from school to Tobetsa. Sergeant Lefoko Dintwa was already well settled in at the bar, surrounded by local women as usual. Thapelo was also already there and welcomed his sister and the boy whom he suspected was her boyfriend. He liked Kethwaahetse very much, but his attention was fully focused on his hero. Boi thought that it was pathetic.

Boi's grandfather was also there. He was delighted to see her, and to meet Kethwaahetse.

"Is this your boyfriend, Boitumelo Hope?"

"No Ntatemogolo. He is a very good friend from school, and he IS a boy, as you can clearly see."

"Yes. I can see that he is a VERY good friend," he chuckled. He winked at her and grinned.

Boi silently cursed. *Ntatemogolo knows everything!*

141

*How can I keep anything secret from him? I love him though.*

"Anyway. I have some exciting news. Sergeant Lefoko Dintwa has agreed to hunt down Menomagolo, and save the community from further tragedy."

"Well that's great news, Ntatemogolo. Well done for persuading him. But he is going to have to find the beast in that huge swamp before he can kill him. He is good at keeping out of the way until the next time he wants to attack."

"You have to believe, Boi. Just believe that anything is possible. People have dreams in their lives, and sometimes they come true."

"He is telling you the truth, Boi," said Kethwaahetse. "What is your middle name?"

"You know it. Hope."

"Yes. I do know it. And you should live by it. Have hope. It will be wonderful if the sergeant can really kill this killer hippo, won't it."

"Yes. I suppose you are right. We can all dream. And we can all hope."

The two of them left the party and went home, pausing for a bit of private enjoyment along the way.

\* \* \* \* \*

When the crowds started drifting away from the bar that evening, Sergeant Dintwa took the hand of a local girl, Bontle, and asked her if she'd like to go for a walk.

"Perhaps we could do more than walk, sergeant," she answered suggestively.

So they walked into the bush near to the village and found a very comfortable spot to lie down on the ground together.

For almost two hours they feasted on the delights

142

of each other's bodies. Bontle enjoyed the strength and the roughness and strength of the seasoned veteran of the Botswana Defence Force. She knew that she would be the envy of every other girl in the village, and for many surrounding miles. Foolishly, she didn't allow him to wear a condom. She wanted to fall pregnant, and have his baby. She didn't care about the risk of a possibly fatal disease.

He, on the other hand, didn't care about anything. He risked his life almost every day. If he died from AIDS, then he would at least have enjoyed a wonderful life to the full. It was irresponsible, but why should he care?

*I've had a thousand women. One of them was probably infected. The rest might suffer when I pass the disease on, but at least they'll have enjoyed the best sex of their life with the great Sergeant Lefoko Dintwa. Their relatives can write it on their tombstones!*

He enjoyed her willingness and her softness. She was pliant. She gave in to his every desire.

When their love-making was over, she declared that she must get home or her mother would worry.

Sergeant Dintwa was very satisfied. Very satisfied indeed. He lay in the soft undergrowth and ran through his pleasant memories of the past two hours. Eventually, he fell asleep.

A few hours later, he awoke. It was dark. It took him a while to remember where he was. He thought that he must get up to his feet and return to his lodgings in Tobetsa.

Suddenly, he heard some rustling in the bushes. Very slowly, and soundlessly, he reached for his rifle. He pulled it towards him, confident that he could pull back the breach, slip the safety catch, and fire it at any attacker, in a split second. Nobody in the whole of the

143

Botswana Defence Force was quicker than him.

The rustling continued, getting closer.

*It must be robbers,* he thought. *They are about to regret tangling with the greatest soldier this country has ever known!*

In truth he was scared. He was actually trembling with fear.

He pointed his weapon at the bushes and shouted a warning.

"Halt! Who goes there?!"

The rustling stopped for a few seconds, and then continued. His attackers were getting closer.

"Halt! I am armed. One step closer and I will fire!"

Whoever was in the bush ignored his advice and stepped closer.

The bush exploded and a giant lunged towards him.

Terrified, he fired. Twice.

The giant knocked him to the ground. For a moment he thought that his life was over. But then he realised that the giant lay dead beside him. He realised that this was a hippopotamus. It could be none other than the legendary rogue hippo, Menomagolo.

He was still shaking, but he soon recovered enough to examine the body.

The only entry wound that he could find was through the hippo's eye. He had a brainwave. This was unbelievable luck. He used all of his strength to force his thumb through the eye socket and into the hippo's brain. He knew that he would be able to tell the gullible villagers that he had killed the hippo with his bare hands. With his killer thumb!

The next morning, Sergeant Lefoko Dintwa was even more of a hero than he had ever been before. The word spread, and when it reached Itlhomolomo, Thapelo was full of joy. His predictions had come true. He boasted to his family, and anyone else who would listen to him, that there had never been any doubt in his mind that the great Sergeant Lefoko Dintwa would kill Menomagolo. Furthermore, the sergeant had killed the hippo with his bare thumb! There had been no need at all for a gun, or any other weapon.

"Who else could do such a thing? He is truly the best!"

A great feast was arranged very quickly. Naturally it was in Tobetsa, the village which had been most affected over the years by the maimings and killings of the beast.

Everyone helped to prepare. A big pit was dug and filled with wood. The fire was lit. When the flames died down, the men of the village pushed the great carcase into the pit and buried it.

The women of the surrounding villages prepared lots of vegetables and other foods to go with the meat and brought them along to the feast. The women had prepared plenty of traditional beer: Mochema and Mberere.

As the buried hippo cooked, everyone sang and danced to traditional music. They all drank copious amounts of beer.

By the time they dug up the well-cooked carcass of the hippo, most of the villagers were drunk, even the children. Boi finally accepted that Sergeant Dintwa was actually a real hero. She drank some beer because it was expected of her. It was a wonderful celebration.

To add to the merriment, almost everyone who attended, from miles around, brought gifts for the sergeant who had finally ended the reign of terror of the killer hippo.

The meat and the vegetables were shared amongst everyone. There was plenty to go around.

One of the merry-makers, Gotweng, who was from Itlhomolomo, was shocked when he almost broke his teeth on something hard in his portion of meat. He was surprised, when he examined the offending item, to discover that it was a bullet!

It didn't take him long to figure out that Sergeant Lefoko Dintwa was a liar. He had not killed the beast with his bare hands after all. He has killed the beast with a bullet from his rifle.

At first, Gotweng didn't know what to do with this knowledge. He needed time to think. For the rest of the day, he didn't touch any more beer. He watched the false hero carefully.

It occurred to him that he might turn the situation to his advantage, but it would take some courage. Eventually, he judged that the sergeant was drunk enough, and happy enough, surrounded by beautiful women as he was, to approach. He sidled up to the hero of the day.

"Could we have a quiet word please Sergeant? In private?"

"No we could not! Can't you see that I am very busy with these ladies?"

"Yes. But I only need two minutes, and I think that you will agree that this is very important to both of us."

"Oh. Alright then, Gotweng. But you will regret it if you are wasting my time."

They went to a quiet place behind the nearest hut. By the time that they returned to the feast, Sergeant Dintwa had agreed to generously share his gifts with his new friend.

Gotweng was, naturally, very grateful.

# # # # #

# Eleven - Lesomenngwe

During the school holidays, Ntate, Tabansi and Nyack were able to return for a whole week.

Nyack had learnt to drive and had also worked as an apprentice mechanic in a garage in Orapa, so that he was now fully qualified to become Mister van Gils's chauffeur when Bokang retired. It would only be about four weeks after they returned to Orapa. His uniform was ready for him, and he would be living in a room in the gate-keeper's hut at the big house. He was very excited about his new job.

Boi was also excited when Nyack told her that Kagiso had given him permission to take her for a ride in his car, in return for a free service.

Even better than seeing her two elder brothers and her father, and the prospect of a ride in Kagiso's car with Nyack the chauffeur driving her, was the thrill that she felt when she unwrapped a present that they had brought for her.

"It was Nyack's idea," said Ntate. He thought that your running might improve if you had a proper pair of road shoes. Much better than bare feet or rubber tyre shoes. We all clubbed together to buy them for you.

As she ripped the paper off her parcel, she could not have been more delighted if the contents had been a handful of diamonds from the Orapa mines. They were light blue, with black and white laces: the colours of the national flag. They were so light, with tough foam soles.

She could hardly breathe as she put them on her feet and walked up and down in front of her family. Her grin threatened to split her face in two.

"I have never received such an excellent present in

all my life! Thank you Ntate. Thank you Tabansi, and thank you Nyack. I am so happy."

"Mme has been telling us about your wonderful achievements. You can be even better with these on your feet."

"I shall not disappoint you. Since I started Form Four, I have had personal coaching from Mister Way. He cycles some of the way home with me so that he can help me with my pace and my breathing. He thinks I could be a top marathon runner some day."

"I am not surprised," commented Tabansi. "The distances that you run, just to get to school and back, are probably more than most of the top athletes."

"Yes. But I still have a long way to go before I can be as good as they are. These shoes will certainly help me. Thank you! Thank you! Thank you!"

She gave them each a big hug.

The next day, she ran barefoot to school with the new running shoes in her bag. She wanted to surprise her friends when she revealed them to the world.

When she was with her best friend, she couldn't wait any longer.

"Oh Grace! I have something very exciting to show you! Come over here."

As they found a quiet corner of the playground, Grace told Boi, "I have something very exciting to tell you too, Boi! You go first though."

The shoes were duly taken from the bag and placed on the ground.

"Oooh! They are beautiful! You will surely go even faster wearing those, Boi. You will be the national champion. There is no doubt about that. And I will be there to cheer you over the finish line."

"Yes. I dream about winning big races, and receiving gold medals. I hope that I can repay Mister

Way for all his hard work in training me. To win an Olympic gold or silver medal to parade alongside his bronze triathlon medal would be a dream come true."

"I really believe that you can do it Boi. You are very, very good. And the colours. They could be made for the queen of Botswana athletics!"

"Thanks Grace. And to have you there to see it happen will make the dream complete. But what is your exciting news?"

Grace blushed.

"I am officially Moagi's girlfriend."

"Well, THAT is hardly news to me Grace. It is very obvious that you are close. You spend a lot of time with him."

"No. You don't quite get my meaning. I have joined your club. We actually did it last evening. I am no longer a virgin Boi!"

Although Boi was not particularly surprised, she was momentarily shocked by the revelation.

"Now that IS what I call news, Grace! Congratulations. Was it good?"

"Yes, it was VERY good. And some of that is down to you my sister."

"How can that be so?"

"Because of what you told me about your experiences with Kethwaahetse."

"What do you mean?"

"We were very careful. We planned everything in advance and we took it slowly. We had condoms, and we found a place where we could not be interrupted."

"Where? Where did you do it?"

"In the chicken hut in the corner of our big field. It was very comfortable, and private"

"So what happened?"

"We cuddled for a long time, and slowly undressed

each other. Even though I wanted to rip his pants off, we resisted the temptation to rush. We were touching each other, and playing, for over an hour before we actually made love."

"Wow! That is quite amazing. I don't think that Kethwaahetse and I could do that, even now, after we have been love-making for almost a year. Amazing!"

"Yes. It was Boi. I think it made the final act even better when it came."

"I am so pleased for you. I know Moagi was reluctant. How does he feel now?"

"He is very happy. He says that he loves me, and he wants us to get married."

"That is going too far, Grace. It is far too early. And you have to think that you are both caught up in the emotion of the big event."

"I know that is the truth. We both want to go to university. That is the whole point of working hard at school to obtain good results and have a career. To get married and start having children would defeat the object of why we are here. We don't want to be stuck in the usual rut of that kind of life."

"That makes sense. I feel the same. I don't want to have six children and die young. I want to be a professor at the university, or a surgeon, or a woman who can bring great benefit to the community in some other way. I know that it will happen if I keep going with my education."

"Exactly! Moagi and I discussed this. I told him that I would marry him if we were still in love when we graduate from university."

"It is good that you can agree on these things, Grace. Who knows what will happen between now and when you graduate from university? You may fall in love with another boy along the way."

151

"I know I won't. Moagi and I have known each other since we started Form One. I know that he is the right boy for me. And he feels the same way. He told me so."

"I hope it works out for you both. But won't Moagi go to the Botswana College of Agriculture. You will surely go to the University."

"Yes. We have thought of that. It is not a problem. We will both be in Gaborone for our studies. And you will be there too, Boi."

"We will all still be together. Kethwaahetse too."

It was time to go into the classroom for the start of the day's classes.

Rre Kitso, the Form Four class teacher was pleased to allow Boi the chance to show her new shoes to the rest of the class. Just as Grace had done, they expressed their genuine admiration and all hoped that Boi would be a great champion someday.

"I am sure you will be a top runner, Boi," said Rre Kitso. "I hope that you won't forget your friends back in Marekisokgomo when that day comes."

"I most certainly will NOT forget my friends, Rra. I can promise you that."

"Good! Have you shown these shoes to Mister Way yet?"

"No Rra. Not yet. We have P.E. this afternoon. I will show them to him then."

"He will be pleased."

And so it proved. When it came to the P.E. lesson, Mister Way admired the shoes.

"These are exactly what you need, Boi. They will improve your performance, and they will help you to avoid injury. Running as you do, in bare feet, gives you no cushioning at all. I always feared that the hammering that your knee and hip joints take when you run would finish your career before it had even really started. Now your family have given you a wonderful chance. You must be very happy."

"I am Rra. And I am very grateful to them too. I only hope that I can repay them someday."

"I am sure that you will, Boi. I have no doubt at all about that."

\* \* \* \* \*

It was true that Boi's running performance improved with the new shoes. Mister Way's coaching helped her too. Sometimes he would cycle all the way home to Itlhomolomo with her to ensure that she maintained a consistent pace. He also made her do tempo runs, varying the frequency of her pace, and interval training.

"It is good for you to be able to increase your speed for a relatively short distance, whenever you want to, or need to. There is an old saying, 'to run faster, you must run faster.'"

"Well, that is fairly obvious, Rra!" she laughed.

"Yes. It is. But what it means is that you must train to run faster. Your body and mind are used to running at a regular pace for long distances. You must train your body to run faster. So when your mind says to you that you need to pick up the pace, your body feels that this is natural."

"That makes a lot of sense. I'd never thought of that before."

"You have all the makings of a great marathon runner. Between us, we must make sure that you continue to travel along the right path."

"I know that I can do it with your help. I will run for Botswana in the Olympic Games one day. But that is far off."

"It is not so far off, when you think of it. You are fifteen now. There have been Olympic medal winners who have been in their late teens. Not marathon runners though. The youngest man to win at the Olympics was twenty-two. I am not sure about the youngest woman gold medallist, but she would have been a bit older than that. I think twenty-four or twenty five."

"It doesn't matter, Rra. All I want is the gold medal. I don't necessarily want to be the youngest. In fact, we will have no choice in the matter. The Olympic Games are every four years, so we would have to accept whatever age I would be when the games come around."

"That is why you are so good at your schoolwork, Boi. You are much cleverer than me to even think of that."

"Perhaps Rra. But everyone has their own God-given talents. You are the best coach, and you have already won an Olympic gold medal."

"I believe that you will achieve your dreams, Boi. But keep up with your studies too. You don't know what will happen in life. God forbid that you had a terrible accident, but if you did, you would need your qualifications to continue with your chosen career."

"That is my plan, Rra. So don't worry."

\* \* \* \* \*

Despite the serious direction of her running training, Boi kept up her series of fun aquathon races with her best friend. By the time they were getting towards the end of the third term of Form Four, the scores stood at 96-94 in Grace's favour. They were both guilty of winding each other up with taunts about who would be the first to reach the magical figure of one hundred wins.

"My side of the tree will soon have no room left for any more marks, Grace!"

"I will catch you before you get to a hundred. The momentum is with me. I have won the last three, and I will win the next six."

"We'll see!"

"Well, you won't catch me for the Form Four school prize. I am already too far ahead of you, with only two weeks left until the end of term. I'd have to score zero in every subject from now on."

"Yes. This is true. I can't catch you now."

"But your precious boyfriend is so besotted with you, that he will allow you to keep your lead over him, so you can be sure of second place."

"Now, you know that is rubbish, Grace. He would beat me if he could."

"I am only teasing. Of course he would. But you are too clever for him."

They had made it to the edge of the river where they normally swam.

"C'mon Boi. I'll race you to the other side and back. No running today, and I promise not to gloat too much when I beat you."

"One day, I will surprise you and beat you at swimming, Grace. Anything is possible, as we have seen."

They stripped naked, ready for their race. But Boi hesitated.

"What is wrong?"

"I am just looking at the water. It looks fierce today. It is much muddier than usual, and look at those whirlpools and currents. See how that log is being swept along so rapidly. I don't think it is safe. Let's have a running race instead."

"Don't worry, Boi. It is usual for the water to rise and flow faster at this time of year. The flood waters come down from the east. See! Look over there. You can see the big dark clouds on the horizon. It is still raining over there even though it is sunny here."

"I don't know, Grace. I don't think I have ever seen the river like this before."

"I am telling you, Boi. There is nothing to worry about. We are both strong swimmers. Let's go now!"

She waded to knee deep in the water, ready to swim.

"Please Grace. Please come out of the water. Let's put on our clothes and race up to our tree. It is not safe in the river today."

"Don't be such a chicken Boi. Chase me!"

With that, she dived forward and struck out at full speed for the far bank."

Boi had no choice. She followed her friend into the water, but was already twenty metres behind. Every time she raised her head above the water for a breath, she glanced ahead. She was actually gaining on Grace.

Suddenly, she could not see Grace's head where she expected to see it. She stopped swimming and looked around. She was astonished to see Grace about fifty metres downstream, in the middle of the river.

*How on Earth did she get there?*

"HELP! HELP!" she heard her friend screaming desperately.

She swam as fast as she could in Grace's direction, but the current swept her towards the bank. She was helpless. She could do nothing about it. Her feet hit the stones on the bottom, very hard.

She scrambled out of the water and ran down the side of the river as fast as she could sprint.

Grace was still screaming to her for help. Her head kept disappearing below the surface.

As she came up, she shouted, "Grab a long stick and run ahead. You can pull me ...." She went under again.

Boi continued to run. She was resisting the strong, natural urge to panic. She looked around for a suitable stick as she ran, but could see none.

She drew level with Grace.

"HELP!"

The river was in turmoil. She had never seen anything like it. She had heard of massive torrents suddenly sweeping down towards the delta in the rainy season, but these were very rare indeed. Normally, the water was quite calm. It could be deep and slow moving on the surface, with known undercurrents, but it was never like this.

There were still no long sticks in view, but at least her friend had stopped ducking under the water and was moving smoothly, but helplessly, down the river with her head above the surface.

She looked ahead for a place where she might be able to reach out and rescue Grace. Instead of a refuge, what she saw struck terror into her heart. There was white, rough water ahead. And sticking out of the water: sharp jagged rocks!

*Oh no! Please God, NO!*

"Swim this way Grace. Quickly! Swim Grace!"

Grace was heading straight for the rocks. She struck them with terrific force, bouncing off one onto another, and then another.

Her limp body floated onward, but drifted towards the shore further down.

Boi was able to wade into the calmer, shallower water and pull her friend onto dry land. She was obviously unconscious.

Boi placed her index and middle fingers on Grace's neck, just as they had been taught in first aid classes at school. At first, she feared the worst. There was no pulse!

Then: tick, tick, tick-tick, tick. A faint, irregular pulse. And Grace's chest was rising and falling. She was breathing, but only just.

Then Boi saw the blood oozing from the side of Grace's head.

She was scared. Very scared.

She needed to get help, but she couldn't leave her friend lying there, unconscious while she ran to the nearest village.

*It must be Inagolo. How far? Maybe less than two kilometres. How far have I run down the river? If it's two kilometres, that will take me about eight minutes. By the time I find somebody who can help and get back here, it is going to be at least half an hour. Every second counts. What can I do?*

Her mind raced. Grace's breathing was shallow, and her pulse was still feathery. She quickly decided that she would have to carry her friend to the village.

Boi was strong, but Grace felt heavy when she picked her up. *A dead weight. No! Don't think like that!*

She walked as fast as she could. Tears welled up into her eyes and she squeezed them away. She prayed harder than she had ever prayed before.

*Please God. Don't let my sister die. She is a GOOD person. She is too young to die. Please God. I beg you!*

She soon arrived in Inagolo and knew exactly where she should go. People were staring at her. She suddenly realised that she was still naked, and so was her friend. She didn't care. What mattered was Grace's life.

She arrived at Mma Mothoriyana's house.

"Goodness Boitumelo! What is wrong with your friend? Come in quickly. Put her on the bed."

"Give her some aloe vera Mma. You said it cures everything."

Mma Mothoriyana hopped across the room and grabbed two blankets off a shelf.

"Here. Wrap this around you. Cover yourself up. I'll get you a dress in a minute. I need to tend to Grace first."

She put the other blanket over the prostate body of the injured girl and sat on the edge of the bed, next to her.

She felt her pulse, just as Boi had done down at the riverside.

She leaned forward and put her ear next to Grace's nose and mouth. She felt for a pulse once more. Then she stood up and put her arms around Boi.

"I am sorry Boitumelo. Grace is dead," she whispered gently.

Boi broke free from the old lady's gentle embrace.

"No!" she screamed. "She cannot be dead!"

She fell to the ground next to the bed and felt for Grace's pulse. There was nothing to feel.

Boi wailed at the top of her voice.

She screamed, "NOOOOOOOO!"

Then she burst into tears.

A crowd had gathered in the doorway of Mma Mothoriyana's house. Small children and their mothers watching the scene, wide-eyed.

Mma Mothoriyana dropped to the floor beside Boi and hugged her tightly, rocking back and forth.

They stayed like that for a long time, as Boi wept.

Mma Mothoriyana beckoned to one of the boys in

the doorway. When he came close, she told him to run to Itlhomolomo and find Mma Patience Tumelo. "Tell her to come quickly to my house. If she asks what is wrong, tell her that there has been an accident. Tell her that Boitumelo is alright, but that her friend has been seriously injured. Hurry!"

The boy took off.

* * * * *

It was dark when Mma Tumelo eventually got home with Boi. She sat her on her own bed and got her to sip some water. Boi refused any food that was offered. She sat cross-legged, with her back against the wall, staring straight ahead. She cried no more. She said nothing. She made no sound, not even a whimper.

For three whole days, Boi sat in the same position. She hardly moved. She ate nothing, only taking sips of water when Mme held the cup to her lips. Occasionally, she would doze. She did not speak. The only sign of life from her would be a weak smile when her mother wrapped her arms around the girl and whispered gentle words of comfort in her ear. She said nothing in response.

Thapelo went into the school on the way to his work in Marekisokgomo, and told Rre Kitso what had happened. He had already heard about the tragedy, and told Thapelo to let his mother know that he wasn't expecting Boitumelo to come to school.

"If there is anything at all that we can do, please come here and let me know. Mma Tlotlo and I send our condolences, and so do the entire class. We are devastated, as I am sure you are Thapelo."

"Yes Rra. It is truly terrible. Grace was one of the loveliest girls you could ever wish to meet. But it is worse than that. She was as good as a sister to my own sister."

"I know Thapelo. I know." He paused. "How is she?"

"I don't know Rra. She won't speak. She just sits there like a statue."

"Give her time boy. She is strong. She will come through this. Believe me."

When Thapelo arrived home that evening, he was surprised to see Mma Mothoriyana sitting on Mme's bed next to his sister.

Boi was actually in deep conversation with the old lady.

"Come away, Thapelo. Leave them to talk," urged his mother.

They went outside.

"How did she get here Mme?"

"I sent Kagiso to get her from Inagolo. I had a feeling that, if anyone could break into Boi's shell, it would be Mma Mothoriyana. It appears that I was correct."

They waited. Twenty minutes later, Mma Mothoriyana emerged from the hut and smiled at the woman and boy.

"She will be alright. She says to tell you that she is hungry and would like some supper. I will go home with Kagiso now."

"Thank you Mma. I am sure that Boitumelo will come to see you soon."

* * * * *

The burial of Tshegofatso Grace Maphenyo was arranged by her family with the minister of the small church in Inagolo. This was the local church that the

161

villagers of both Kango and Itlhomolomo attended every Sunday. The minister had baptised the baby Grace and was now very sad that he was now called upon to conduct her funeral service.

The day before the funeral, the coffin was taken from the undertaker's to Grace's family home in Kango. It arrived at about four o'clock in the afternoon. It was taken into the house and placed on a table. The lid was removed and placed against the wall.

Relatives and friends had been gathering from far and wide for the whole two weeks since the tragic accident to pay their last respects. Prayers were being said every day, led by the minister or by the elders of the church. Some had brought tents, and others just slept in the open. Everyone had brought food, firewood and water to help out during the communal period of mourning.

The church choir sang hymns as small groups of people entered the main house to say their goodbyes to the lovely little girl who had died far too young. The mortuary staff had cleaned her and made her look very pretty in her final resting place in the coffin.

The home was far too small for all of the people. There were at least three hundred. Grace had been such a popular girl.

Nobody slept at all during that night. Some of the assembled congregation swapped places with the choir from time to time, so that the hymns could continue through the hours whilst the choristers rested.

At five o'clock in the morning, the table and coffin were moved to a position just outside the door of the house. The minister took his position in front of the table. The choir fell silent. He commenced the formal order of service with a prayer. Then he invited Grace's mother to step forward and say a few words about her daughter. The congregation were very moved by what they heard.

Another hymn was sung. Everyone joined in, although some of them could not contain their tears.

As agreed with the bereaved family, Boi was the next to be asked by the minister to speak about her best friend. She was well prepared, but when she saw her best friend's peaceful face it took her a full two minutes to compose herself. The congregation waited in respectful silence. They knew how close the two girls had been.

"Grace was my best friend, and my sister, from the day that we learned to walk. She devoted her life to helping others and she was much loved. She excelled at everything she did. We all knew her very well, so there is no need for me to tell you anything about her achievements. There is no doubt that she would have gone on to be very successful in life.

"I swear to you that Tshegofatso Grace Maphenyo will live on. The flame of the candle of her life will burn in my heart forever. For me, Grace will never die. This..." she waved her hand towards the coffin, "... is just the beautiful body which her spirit occupied. From this day forward, her spirit will live in my heart." She clutched her chest with her right hand.

"I will never forget her."

She took a deep breath looked out over the hundreds of people who had assembled to honour her friend.

Mma Mothoriyana hobbled forward on her crutches to join Boi in front of the coffin. She addressed the congregation.

"I have known both of these girls for only four of my eighty-one years. I love them both. In all the years of my long life, I have never known two friends who

163

were so close. I am extremely proud to have known them. And today, I am especially proud of Boitumelo Hope Tumelo. The words that she has just spoken to us all are the solemn truth. I know this. You should believe, as I do, that the flame of the candle of the life of Tshegofatso Grace Maphenyo will burn brightly, forever, in the heart of this young lady. From this day forth, you should look at Boi and see the spirit of Grace. These two girls are united in love, never to be separated. None of us should ever forget Grace,and we never shall, because, in the heart of Boi, Grace lives on."

The whole congregation were left in no doubt whatsoever that the words which they had just heard from Boitumelo Hope Tumelo and Mma Mothoriyana were absolutely true.

An hour later, the minister led the final prayers as Grace's closed coffin was lowered into the ground in the churchyard of Inagolo Church. Boi stepped forward and dropped the single protean flower that she had been carrying throughout the night onto the coffin of her friend. Tears streamed down her face as she sobbed silently. Her mother led her away from the grave side and took her home.

# # # # #

# Twelve - Lesomepedi

Three days after the funeral of her best friend, Boi returned to school for the final day of term. She could not find the energy, or the will, within herself to compete in any of the events in the sports day. Everyone knew that she could have taken the ten thousand metres title by just jogging around the track at her normal pace, without a thought, but they understood.

There was no way that she could accept the Form Four academic prize. Grace had already done enough to win that prize. Boi was the runner up.

*How can they possibly expect me to take the top prize because the real winner is no longer with us? The very idea is outrageous!*

She had privately expressed her concern to Rre Kitso, who had spoken with Mma Tlotlo. In turn, the headmistress had talked to Mma Maphenyo.

"The prize rightly belongs to your daughter, Mma. Boitumelo was second in class, but she refuses to take it."

"I am very proud of Grace's achievements, Mma. And I am very happy that she worked hard to come top of class this year. But you were at the funeral service. You heard what Boitumelo said to us all. My daughter lives on. Her flame shines brightly in Boitumelo's heart. Let me speak to Boi. I am sure that she will accept the prize in Grace's name. This is what I would like her to do."

And so, that is exactly what happened when it came to the prize-giving. As Boi walked back to her seat, to enormous applause, she paused to hand the little shield to Mma Maphenyo, who whispered through her tears, "Thank you, my daughter."

* * * * *

Throughout the school holidays, Boi just went through the motions. She helped with all the chores in the home and in the field. When she wanted to be alone, she went for a long run. She would join the other children when they went swimming, or fishing or hunting, but sometimes she would just sit and watch them.

She often visited Mma Maphenyo in Kango. They shared their happy memories of Grace. Such conversations made them both feel good. They would laugh a lot, and they would cry a lot. When Boi told Grace's mother about the magic dust, Mma Maphenyo could not stop laughing. Tears streamed down her face, but they were tears of genuine laughter and happiness.

"I vowed that I would pay her back for that one, but I never found the opportunity to play such a great trick on her."

"She really had you there, Boi! I can remember when you sat under that tree over there, evening after evening. It really puzzled me. Grace just told me that you were probably waiting for her to come out to play."

They both laughed at the memory. For the next few days, Mma Maphenyo teased Boi about Grace's big joke.

One day it was, "Didn't you come across on your bike today, Boi? Ha ha ha ha!"

The next, it was "What did you wish for today, Boi? Fresh air? Ha ha ha ha!"

On Sundays, they would visit Grace's grave together after church.

Mma Maphenyo burst into tears on one of those Sundays, when Boi stood in front of the mound and sang a song for her friend that they had learned in primary school. Boi stopped singing immediately.

"Oh. Sorry Mma. I just suddenly felt the need to sing that song to Grace. Sorry."

"No. Don't be sorry. Please sing that song. It brings back such happy memories of you both when you were little girls."

Boi started the song again from the beginning.

*Modimo o Mogolo ke yo o dirileng*
*Tse di molemo tsotlhe le tse di phatshimang.*
*Letsatsi la go tlhaba le bo le phirima*
*Ngwedi le dinaledi tse di benyabenyan.*
*A re supeng Tebogo a re itumeleng*
*Re ise Malebogo go Rara mo pakong.*

As the last note died away, Mma Maphenyo said, "You are such a lovely girl, Boi. And Grace's light really does shine from deep inside you."

"I feel her every minute of every day, Mma."

They hugged each other in a loving embrace.

* * * * *

Even though Boi's greatest passion had long been her education, she had never been more eager to return to school to start her final year. She was determined to work harder than ever before. Her Form Five results would count for two people, so she would put in proportionate effort. She would set off on her run to school even earlier than usual, and continue working after school hours for as long as she could.

Of course, she would also find time to continue her romance with Kethwaahetse. She loved him.

Her running would not be neglected either. Grace would be with her, and be proud of her, when she won the big race. She realised that her academic studies and her running training would require equal amounts of dedication. Apart from her boyfriend, the rest of her life would have to take a back seat for ten months.

Mma Lesedi, the Form Five class teacher, soon noticed that Boi was putting in many extra hours after school. Pupils who worked hard always scored highly in Mma Lesedi's estimations, and deserved extra investment of her own time. She stayed with Boi, and coached her in history, her own subject. She was also able to provide plenty of advice on many other subjects. She loved Boi's attitude.

Mma Tlotlo was also more than happy to help Boi out with her Additional Maths. By half way through the first term, Boi had worked through all of the exercises in all of the Form Five text books, so setting homework for her was very difficult. The head teacher knew exactly what to do. She challenged Boi to come up with three questions which were similar to the ones at the end of the chapter on which the rest of the class were currently working. When Boi had written up her questions, and the answers, Mma Tlotlo sat with her till late in the evening to improve the quality.

It was very encouraging that Mma Tlotlo would often use one of Boi's questions as homework for the class. By this stage, not only was Boi tutoring Moagi, but she was giving the same benefits to the rest of the class.

Poor Moagi had let the sudden death of Grace get to him in a big way. He was suffering, and was naturally down-hearted. Boi knew, better than anyone else, why it had hit Moagi so hard. But that was a secret between her and her best friend. Nobody else would ever know. Even Moagi would never know that Boi knew about what had happened between her two friends.

By the end of the first term, Boi was, unsurprisingly, top of class in every single subject. She had been tireless in her application, and it had paid off.

Her running was improving too. As there was no official marathon event in the national school championships, Mister Way had decided to concentrate her efforts on the 10,000 metres. He taught her how to run the perfect race. The length of her pace never varied. He enlisted the help of the music teacher, Mma Reetsang, to embed tunes in Boi's head with the exact rhythm and beat that he wanted her to replicate with her feet. He worked on her breathing until it was always synchronised with the tempo of her pace.

Boi's mental approach to the distance was perfected. She could ignore everything that was happening around her, and maintain her stride length, cadence and breathing until she was 600 metres from home. Then she would build it up gradually over the next 200 metres, and really stretch it out over the final lap. During that final lap, she would only take twelve breaths. Nobody would be able to catch her with that strategy.

Mister Way told her that she must stick with it, even if her rivals pulled thirty or forty metres clear in the middle of the race. There wasn't the slightest possibility that any of them would be able to maintain that pace to the end of ten kilometres on the track.

"Trust me, Boitumelo. I know!"

She did trust him, but it took some discipline. During training, he would use some of the school's other track athletes to run segments of the distance alongside Boi to try to distract her. She learned good discipline very quickly.

Mister Way registered her entry into the 10,000 metres event in the Botswana national school championships. He persuaded Mma Tlotlo to invest some of the P.E. budget into equipment for Boi. She was provided with two sets of shirts, shorts and socks, all in the school colours. Best of all, she was given a new pair of running shoes. The ones which her father and brother had clubbed together to buy were still alright for running to and from school, but the cushioning had gone and they would not be good enough for the race that Mister Way and Boi had in their minds.

When the shoes arrived, Mister Way made Boi promise that she would only use them on the track. They were NOT to be used on the road. In fact, they were not to be taken home. They could live in Mr Way's office in the school gym.

Kethwaahetse happily spent much of his spare time at the track, watching his girlfriend run around the field. He knew how important this race was to her. Her dedication was unquestionable, and he could only marvel at how Boi could demonstrate such devotion to her running training, whilst continuing to achieve outstanding results in every subject of her academic work. One hundred percent in any given homework was an unremarkable mark these days for Boi. Although two or three of their less generous classmates would say that it was hardly surprising, when she was actually setting some of the homework questions, most agreed that her achievements were the result of her terrific efforts. Furthermore, she was also helping them to achieve better results.

Boitumelo was already one of the most inspirational characters at Marekisokgomo Integrated

Secondary School.

* * * * *

The day of the national school championships finally arrived. It was to be Boi's big day. It would also be the big day for another seven school athletes who went with Mister Way to the Marekisokgomo bus station on Friday morning. It was an eight hour drive to Serowe. They slept on the bus and arrived in the evening.

Kethwaahetse and Moagi both came to wave goodbye to Boi and to wish her luck. Moagi had become more attached to Boi since Grace's death. He knew that she was Kethwaahetse's girlfriend. That much was obvious to everyone. But he felt very close to Boi, and she enjoyed his friendship.

It was a long journey, but Serowe had been chosen as a central location for the school championships. It evened out the distances that school teams had to travel from around the country. The capital city would make it very difficult for schools from the north and west of the country.

When they arrived in Serowe, they had a thirty minute walk up to the Serowe Sports Complex where the games would take place. The town was very proud of its sports venue, and it was much more suitable for the national school games than the sports fields of the Swaneng Hill School.

Boi had hoped that they might pass the barracks of the Botswana Defence Force and catch a glimpse of the legendary Sergeant Lefoko Dintwa. Or perhaps they might visit the statue of the national hero, Sir Seretse Khama. It was clear to Boi which one of these two was more deserving of her adoration. Unfortunately, there

171

was no time for sight-seeing. They saw neither.

Overnight, children from all over Botswana camped in and around the complex. The team from Marekisokgomo had brought some food with them for the evening. In the morning, Mister Way took them down the hill and treated them all to breakfast at a cafe that he'd spotted on the walk from the bus rank. They were a happy bunch, chatting about their expectations for the day. All of them had high hopes.

The events commenced at 10:30 am on Saturday morning. Mister Way had told Boi that the 10,000 metres wasn't scheduled to start until just after 2 o'clock. They all knew that they wouldn't be back in Marekisokgomo until very almost midnight, but camp beds had been set up in the gym back at the school. They wouldn't be expected to go home, and their parents had been forewarned that they would be sleeping at the school.

Their hopes were that when they returned, they would be celebrating the team's success. Mister Way had ingrained in them the ethos that any individual's success was a success for the whole school team. They were all very excited.

The first event involving anyone from Marekisokgomo was the semi-final of the boys' 110 metres hurdles. The whole team, including Mister Way, cheered on Mogotsi as he qualified with ease for the final. They were so proud of the brand new school shirts and shorts that they were all wearing. To see one of their team-mates flying across the finish line, wearing the shirt, was a joy to all.

Next was the girls' long jump. Baboloki was a very tall and wiry. Every sinew of her legs was clearly defined. Boi loved to watch her as she powered down the runway and sprung high into the air off the board

172

like a gazelle. It was poetry in motion. Her feet planted into the sand, and she pitched forward to land with elegance. The amount of practice that she had put in with Mister Way, to perfect her technique, had certainly paid off. There was only one other girl who jumped anywhere near her distance in the first round. A girl from Gaborone had jumped further, but had received a red flag for a no jump. Mister Way thought that this girl would be the biggest threat.

Being at the championships was very exciting for all of the children from Marekisokgomo. They had never had the chance to mix with so many other athletically talented children before. Although the competition was fierce, they were making lots of new friends.

Mister Way was ensuring that all of his team were drinking lots of water. Most of them were too nervous to eat.

As the time for Boi's race drew nearer, she found a quiet place where she could sit, with her eyes closed, and focus on how she would run. In her head, she sang the rhythmic songs that Mma Reetsang had been teaching her to help her with her pace tempo. She visualised every lap of the race. She'd already walked across to the 200 metre mark, which would be 600 metres from home on the penultimate lap, and placed a small white pebble at the side of the track. Even without that, she would know the distance, but attention to detail was very comforting.

About half past one, Mister Way shook her shoulder.

"Boi. You need to loosen up. And you must pay a visit to the toilet. You know exactly what I mean. Once you start running ..."

"Yes, yes. I do. Thank you, Sir. I must get ready

now. I am totally in the zone, as you say."

"I am glad to hear that, Boi. You know exactly what you must do. There is nobody on that track but you. Just run the disciplined race that we have planned and rehearsed. Ignore the other runners completely."

"See you after the race, Sir."

"I'll be there. Good luck, Boi. Run the race of your life!"

A few minutes later, Boi stepped up to the line, staring straight ahead. She closed her eyes and listened for the starter's order. She was already singing the rhythm in her head. The noise of the crowd of children was completely blanked from her mind.

"Set!"

BANG!

*Modimo o Mogolo ke yo o dirileng*
*Tse di molemo tsotlhe le tse di phatshimang...*
*(God almighty is the one who has done*
*All things holy and shining...)*

By the time they had run half of the first lap, Boi was at the back of the field. She didn't panic at all. She just kept her rhythm going.

*Letsatsi la go tlhaba le bo le phirima*
*Ngwedi le dinaledi tse di benyabenyang...*
*(The sun that rises and sets*
*The moon and stars that twinkle so bright...)*

Even when she was at the back of the main pack, a few laps further into the race, she had no fear. Three girls had already dropped a significant distance away from the main pack. Two girls had broken away and were fifty metres ahead of the rest.

*They are either idiots or they are the fastest runners in Botswana. Stop thinking, Boi, and sing!*

In her mind, she sang.

*A re supeng Tebogo a re itumeleng*
*Re ise Malebogo go Rara mo pakong*
*(Let's show our appreciation, let's rejoice.*
*Let's give thanks to the Lord in praise)*

Lap after lap, she kept her unchanging cadence, her stride length and her synchronised breathing. Gradually, she worked her way through the field. One of the early front runners pulled out of the race. The other drifted backwards from the sixth lap onward. Her legs could give her no more.

Before they reached the half way mark, Boi was lapping a few stragglers. By the time she reached 6,000 metres, she was about 20 metres ahead of her nearest rival. Still, she kept her rhythm. But she was oblivious to where the rest of the girls were in relation to her. She just kept on running. She just kept on singing in her head. Her feet pounded the track. She just kept on breathing in time to her metronomic pace. And she kept on passing other runners.

By the time she passed the 8,000 metre mark, twenty laps, she had lapped all of the other girls, some of them twice.

She was relentless. She just kept on running her race.

Two laps from home, she ran the outward bend and watched the side of the track until she saw her little white stone.

She stepped up the pace. There was absolutely no need for her to step up the pace. She could have walked from that point to the finish, and she would still have won the race.

Striding out. Stretching. Knees high. Hardly breathing.

The bell.

Stretch. Count. *One-two-three-four, one-two-three-four...*

Into the final straight. Almost sprinting. Through the tape. Arms raised. Over the line. Into the arms of Mister Way.

"Well done Boi! The perfect race. You did it. I have NEVER seen anything like it. You are the best!"

"Thank you, Sir. Thank you very much. You got me to this point."

"No Boi. YOU got you to this point. You worked hard, and you did everything I asked of you. Now forget the analysis. Enjoy the moment. Go and see your friends over there. See how they are cheering for you."

It was a moment of pure exultation. The peak of joyfulness. An individual and a Team Marekisokgomo victory. She was loving every moment. And she deserved to. She definitely deserved to enjoy every moment. She had earned that right.

As she celebrated with the rest of the team, Mister Way approached the group accompanied by a very tall, distinguished looking gentleman whom Boi had noticed several times in the day. He seemed to be greatly respected by all of the teachers and the Serowe town dignitaries. She wondered who he was. She was soon to find out.

"Children. Allow me to introduce Rre Bonolo Gosego, the head coach of the Botswana national athletics team."

"Good afternoon. I am very pleased to meet you all. A formidable team from Marekisokgomo. I am not surprised. You have a magnificent coach. Steve, erm, Mister Way, and I have had many a battle in the water and on the roads in the past. Please tell me your names."

He spent some time conversing with each of them,

176

genuinely interested in their events and their enthusiasm.

He deliberately left Boi until last.

"My name is Boitumelo Hope Tumelo, Rra. I am here to run in the 10,000 metres."

"Not just run, Boitumelo. You won that race in style! How old are you?"

"I am fifteen, Rra. Almost sixteen."

"I have never seen such a dominant performance at your level. You show great promise." He turned to Mister Way. "She runs the 10,000 metres like a marathon runner, Steve. Do you think that you could work on her strength and stamina so that she could race over that distance?"

Mister Way burst into helpless laughter. It took him a while to recover. Even Boi could not suppress her smile. Some of the other children were smiling too. Rre Bonolo Gosego was extremely puzzled.

"Oh Bono! You are so funny!"

"I wasn't joking Steve. This young lady has huge potential. It won't be long before she is in my national team."

"I KNOW you weren't joking, Bono. What YOU don't know, is that this young lady runs eighteen kilometres to school EVERY day. She studies harder than any other student. She attends training. Sometimes she will rehearse a complete 10,000 metre race. THEN she will run the eighteen kilometre road home. NOW you can understand why I laugh when you ask such a question. Running a marathon is an everyday occurrence for Boitumelo Hope Tumelo."

"I am amazed! Is this true, Boitumelo?"

"Yes Rra. But sometimes I take a break on the way home to go for a swim, or go fishing."

"I don't know where you get your energy from."

"I don't know either, Rra. I used to walk to school when I started at Junior Secondary School, but I soon decided to run so that I would have more time for other things in my life."

"I see. And you sometimes go swimming?"

"Yes Rra. I used to race against my best friend, but she tragically died."

"Oh. I am sorry to hear that. But you say that you raced with your friend?"

"Yes. She was a brilliant swimmer. Much better than me. We used to regularly race each other on our own aquathon course. That' swimming and ..."

"Yes, I know what aquathon is. Are you seriously telling me that you run 36 kilometres each day, and THEN do your athletics training AND race against your friend?"

"Yes Rra. An education is very important to any Motswana who wants to make something of her life. The school is eleven miles from my village, and I decided that running, rather than walking, would give me more time to do other things."

"You are awesome! I swear, you are the most remarkable child I have ever met in my entire life! And I have met many remarkable young people. Steve, we need a serious chat."

"OK. I just want to talk to the team. We have two events left. I'll come and find you in a few minutes, Bono."

"Make sure you do Steve. If you don't, I'll come looking for you."

The pair hugged each other, like the old friends they were.

By the end of the day, before Mister Way led his

squad back to the bus rank, he had agreed to Rre Bonolo Gosego's suggestion that they should enter her into the forthcoming Durban marathon. Boitumelo would wear the national colours of Botswana!

#####

# Thirteen - Lesometharo

Over the school holiday, Boi did a lot of extra reading and school work. Going in to her final term, she was very determined to achieve the best possible results in her forthcoming BGCSE exams. And, even though there was no need, she continued to clock up the miles in her effort to be ready for the Mandela Marathon in Durban.

Mister Way had been out to visit Mma Patience Tumelo, to seek her approval. As luck would have it, his visit coincided with one of Rre Mompati Tumelo's trips home, so he was able to meet with them both.

They were immensely proud of their daughter, and had no hesitation at all in granting approval. They were also happy to excuse her from most of her usual chores in the home and in the field, until her exams and her big race were over.

"We don't have much money though, Mister Way. I don't know how we can afford to pay for her to go all the way to Durban and stay in a hotel or hostel for two or three nights."

"You don't need to worry about that. The BAA have said that they will contribute something towards the expenses, and Mma Tlotlo has agreed that the school will pay the rest. You won't have to pay anything."

"The BAA?"

"Yes. The Botswana Athletic Association."

"That is wonderful, Mister Way!" exclaimed Mma Tumelo.

"It is. But you didn't see how pleased Rre Bonolo Gosego, the national coach was when he saw Boitumelo win that 10,000 metres race. I always expected her to win, but for a girl who is not yet sixteen years old to run that distance in less than 45 minutes is truly remarkable. It is a new national schools record by a big margin. Bono would do anything to have her in the Botswana team."

"Of course, we are delighted that she has been picked to run for her country, but I do have one concern."

"Oh? What is your concern, Mma?"

"I don't want her to go on such a big journey without a chaperone."

"I see. You are quite right, of course. I will be going along, but do you have somebody in mind from your family? One of her brothers, perhaps?"

"Yes. I have the ideal person in mind, if he will agree. My husband's brother. He lives in Phuthadit\u0161haba. His name is Rre Tsholofelo Poifo. He can help you, because he was once a very good athlete himself. You may have heard of him?"

"No, Mme. I am sorry I have never heard of your brother-in-law. Did he compete for Botswana?"

"No. He didn't compete for Botswana, but he was very well known in these parts for his long jump and his one hundred metre sprint. Just like Carl Lewis," she joked.

"I really only know Batswana athletes who competed internationally in my era. That's why I know Bono, Bonolo Gosego, so well. He was a top long distance runner when I was competing at international level in the triathlon. We used to hang out together at meets all over the world. He is fun to be with, but is very serious about his training. That is why he is such a good coach."

"It doesn't matter. I am sure that my brother will agree if he is available at the time of the marathon," interjected Mompati.

Boi was slightly irritated. They were talking about her as if she was not there. *Doesn't my opinion matter in this?*

"But, Ntate, I don't really even know Uncle Tsholofelo. How can you and Mme decide that he will be my chaperone without asking my opinion?"

"We have chosen him for good reasons, Boi. He will be going to Durban with you."

She appealed to her mother.

"He doesn't listen to me, Mme. I told him that I do not know Uncle Tsholofelo!"

"Rubbish child! He came to the big family party when you graduated from primary school. I am sure that you remember him."

Boi laughed loudly. "You are joking, Mme! That was nearly five years ago. There were lots of people here, and much has happened since that time. How can you expect me to remember somebody from that party?"

"You remember lots of things, Boi. You are very clever. You have a better memory than an elephant!"

"Pah!"

There was silence for a while. Mister Way sipped his water and thought that it would be better to keep his nose out of family affairs.

Eventually, Boi's father broke the tension.

"It has been decided, Boitumelo. We will not discuss this matter any further. Unless you would rather not go to Durban?"

"Yes, Ntate. I will go to Durban with Uncle Tsholofelo and Mister Way."

"Good! That's settled then."

By continuing to arrive very early at school, and by staying until long after everyone else had departed, Boi established an unassailable lead in every single subject in her final year at Marekisokgomo Integrated Secondary School. She was quite pleased with that achievement, but it didn't matter to her as much as her final exams. If she hadn't felt confident about those, she would not have gone to Durban for the Mandela Marathon, even though she was very excited about the race. She would not let a single athletics event impact her academic ambitions now that she was so close.

It was encouraging that Mma Tlotlo and Mma Lesedi were also very positive about Boi's prospects.

Mister Way had worked on Boi's marathon tactics. They were not too different from her perfect 10,000 metres tactics. The main differences were that she would actually have to pay some attention to what the other runners were doing, especially in the latter stages of the race.

"If they want to run off into the distance early on, let them. But you can't afford to let a big gap to develop in the last eight kilometres. You can maintain your race pace and let them get four or five hundred metres ahead, but no more. You just need to increase your stride length for a while until you close the gap."

They practised this. Mister Way start riding his bike along the road about four hundred metres ahead of Boi and allow her to gradually catch him up.

The other major difference would be that she would need to start increasing her pace, in stages, from much further out.

"Instead of 600 metres from the finish, you will have to step it up from FIVE KILOMETRES from the tape!"

Boi almost staggered backwards at this news. Her jaw dropped, literally, so that her mouth hung open.

He laughed.

"Don't worry. I am not asking you to run at that last-lap-and-a-half pace for five kilometres. It would kill you. Well, not quite.

"No. You will quicken your pace ever so slightly at first. We are going to work out the points on the course where you will change up a gear. It will only be in the last five hundred metres that you will push your pace to the limit. It takes good planning, and great discipline, to be able to sprint over the line at the end of a marathon. But you can do it.

"Bono agrees. And he is the boss."

"It makes sense to me, Mister Way. I can do it, but I obviously need your help."

"You CAN do it. But there is something else we need to change."

Boi was anxious about what was coming next. He saw that. He had prepared a little, personal speech in his head."

"You are sixteen now. You are almost at the end of your secondary school days. You will soon go to university with top grades in your BGCSEs. You are a member of the Botswana athletics team. People will give you the respect that you have earned, and so richly deserve. The hotel staff and the race officials will call you Mma. I think that it's about time you started calling me 'Steve', don't you?"

"Yes Sir. I mean, yes Steve."

"Good! Call me Steve outside of school, including while we're training. You'd better call me 'Sir' and 'Mister Way' when we're in school. Is that okay with you?"

"Yes Steve."

"Right. Let's get started on working out our pace intervals. It would be a good idea if we can work with Mma Reetsang on some more songs to match your new, quicker rhythms towards the end of your race."

"That would be wonderful. It is really helpful. And we all know that it works. Or it worked at Serowe, anyway. This will be different though. I am not running against schoolgirls. I'll be running against international athletes from all over the world."

"That is true. There will be thousands of ordinary people running too. But you will be in the elite field starting at the front. And you will be wearing the blue, black and white of Botswana! That already makes you feel like a winner!"

It was Boi's turn to laugh.

"We both know that I won't win, Steve!"

"I agree that it is very unlikely, although anything is possible. Especially in the world of sport. Start every race believing that you can win it. At the age of sixteen, you can be very proud of yourself, as I shall be, if you finish in the first one hundred."

\* \* \* \* \*

After a long overnight bus and train journey, Boitumelo, Mister Way and Uncle Tsholofelo arrived in Gaborone. They were to meet Bonolo Gosego at the airport. Boi had never seen aeroplanes at such close quarters. To her, they had just been vapour trails or, at best, little dots high in the sky. She was thrilled to see how big they were.

"You wait till you see the 'planes at Johannesburg,

185

Boi. They are much bigger than this. You are not scared are you?"

"No Steve. I can't wait to get on board and up in the air. This is so exciting!"

Bonolo approached them with a lady that Boi had never seen before. She was obviously older than Boi, but was about the same height, and she appeared to be quite skinny.

"Hi Steve. Hello Boitumelo. And you must be the famous Uncle Tsholofelo?" He hugged Steve and shook hands with Boi and her uncle.

"Yes. I am Tsholofelo. I am very pleased, and honoured, to meet you Rre Gosego."

"Please call me Bono. Everyone else does." He smiled warmly.

"Allow me to introduce Moreetsi Mothatego. She has been running marathons for Botswana since she was nineteen." Boi judged her to be in her late twenties or early thirties. *She must be very experienced. I should watch her and learn from her.*

Moreetsi smiled as she shook hands with each of them.

"Bono has been telling me all about you, Boitumelo. I am very pleased to meet you at last. Welcome to the team. I hope that we will be running together for many years."

"Thank you. It is a pleasure to meet you too Moreetsi."

They arrived in Durban in the middle of the afternoon, having had a two hour stop in Johannesburg. Boi marvelled at the size and shininess of both airports. As Steve had promised, even the planes were much bigger than the ones she'd first set eyes upon at Gaborone airport. What fascinated Boi most was that there was smooth marble everywhere. Even the floors

186

were marble. In Johannesburg, she had crouched down and smoothed her hand over the surface. It was incredible!

They registered the two Botswana runners for the race on the way to the small hotel which had been booked in advance. There was time to relax, but it was not a sightseeing tour. Steve and Bono took Boi and Moreetsi for a five kilometre jog at slow pace. Boi found this much more relaxing than sitting about, or lying on her bed in the hotel room, which she shared with her new team mate.

After a small supper, which provided another new experience for Boi, spaghetti alla carbonara, Bono took her aside for a one-to-one chat.

"I know that you have been through this a million times with your coach, but I want you to talk me through your race plan. Ideally, I would have had some time on the road with you by the time you came to your first race for the country, but that hasn't been possible. Just tell me what you are thinking about tomorrow's race."

Boi told him about the songs that she and Steve had worked on with Mma Reetsang to dictate her race rhythm. Bono was impressed. She told him about how she would maintain a regular cadence over such a distance; about her breathing and her stride length. How they had practised until it had all come together perfectly. She told him about their plan for a gradual, staged increase in pace over the last five kilometres, and how she would use the distance markers to keep her on track with the plan. And she told him about how she would blinker herself to the other runners and stick to her race plan no matter what they did, except, as she had discussed with Steve, if the leaders got too far ahead in the final third of the race."

"That is an exceptional plan, Boi. I am extremely impressed by both you and your coach. And, having seen you run in the school championships, I am very confident that you can execute this plan."

"Well, as Steve tells me, the plan is the plan!"

"You will do well. But don't be disappointed if you come well down the field. You are against some very experienced athletes. Moreetsi has ten years of international experience over you, for example. There are Moroccans and other African runners who have even more experience than that. If you come in the top one hundred, I will be very pleased with you."

"Good! That's almost exactly what Steve told me."

"He is a great coach, Boi. You have been in good hands."

Later that evening, it was early to bed for Steve, Moreetsi and Boi.

The two young ladies didn't get to sleep until almost midnight. They found so much to chat about. Moreetsi was also a village girl, from the south-eastern Kgalagadi district, which was even hotter and more arid than the verdant Okavango Delta.. They quickly became friends and found much in common, and much to laugh about.

Uncle Tsholofelo opted to spend his evening in the bar, bragging about his niece. Unsurprisingly, although almost everyone was in town for the big event, including some journalists, nobody had ever heard of Boitumelo Hope Tumelo.

"You will all know of her soon enough. She will be Botswana's greatest athlete. You mark my words. Write it down that I, Tsholofelo Poifo, told you on this day."

Not many of his audience paid much attention to his prediction. Most of them had soon broken away into little conversation groups of their own, or gone off to find themselves some supper. However, one man stayed. He appeared to enjoy the Tsholofelo's company.

"Do you really think that she will do so well?"

"Yes. I do. Maybe not tomorrow, but eventually she will be world famous. I really do believe that."

"Will she be amongst the money prizes tomorrow?"

"What do you mean?"

"Will she be in the first ten females to finish?"

"I doubt it, but I suppose it is possible. Why?"

"Well, there are money prizes for the first ten places. The top prize is about quarter of a million Rands. Even tenth place yields ten thousand Rands."

"Really?!"

"Yes. There are other marathons around the world which pay out even bigger prizes than that. Your niece could be worth a fortune."

That statement set Uncle Tsholofelo's mind whirring. A plan had started to formulate inside his head.

\* \* \* \* \*

The next morning they assembled very early for a light breakfast prior to the departure of Steve and Boi on the shuttle bus to the start area. Uncle Tsholofelo would make his way to the finish area. Before they split up, Tsholofelo took the opportunity to discretely ask Steve about the prize money.

"It is very unlikely that Boitumelo will finish in a position which would win a prize, but it has already been agreed that any possible prize money will go into the school's development fund. Your brother and sister-in-law have signed a written agreement, and your niece is very happy with this."

*I can't believe that Mompati could be so stupid!*

"I am sure that there will be many more chances for her to win more prizes in the future though."

"Of that, there can be no doubt, Tsholofelo."

"She will need good management. I am a businessman as well as a relative. I will volunteer my services to my brother's family."

\* \* \* \* \*

A few hours later, as the leading runners approached the finish, a running commentary boomed out over the speakers. Most of the leaders were very familiar to commentator, but he was struggling with one of them.

"And next, in the national colours of Botswana, we have ... erm ... runner number one-four-five-eight, who is ..."

There was a pause while he rifled through the sheets of paper on the desk before him.

"... Boitumelo Hope Tumelo, from Itlhomolomo in the Okavango Delta in Northern Botswana. She is only sixteen years old! Let's hear it for Boitumelo!"

The noise of the crowd was deafening, but Boi heard none of it. All she heard, in her head, were the words and the tune and the rhythm of Mma Reetsang's song for the final straight.

With a finisher's medal around her neck, and the customary tin foil poncho over her shoulders, Boi made her way to the assembly area under the sign for athletes with surnames starting with the letters 'S-V'. Mister Way and Uncle Tsholofelo were there waiting to greet her with big smiles and hugs.

"Ninth Boi! You came ninth! I am so very proud of you! Exclaimed her uncle.

"You are amazing! You have beaten some of the top runners in South Africa, Lesotho and Zimbabwe! You even beat the top female runner from England. The eight runners who beat you are world famous stars from Ethiopia, Morocco, Kenya, USA and Japan. You are truly amongst the best runners in the world. And they all have ten years of experience on you. Unbelievable!"

"All I did was run my race exactly to our plan," she replied modestly.

"I think that there were dozens of women ahead of me at one stage. I didn't count how many I passed. I wasn't interested. I just concentrated on all of the things that we talked about, and practised over the last year."

"This is true, Boi. But it really does take a great athlete to run such a disciplined race, especially in this atmosphere. Well done. Well done, indeed!"

"Can we go and get some lunch, Steve? I am starving!"

"Anything you want today, Boi. Anything! Isn't that right, Uncle Tsholofelo?"

"It certainly is, Mister Way." He turned to his niece. "It will be a great honour for both of us to dine with Botswana's leading lady!"

They were soon joined by Bono and Moreetsi. Both of them were bubbling over with happiness and compliments for Boi's running. Boi already counted Moreetsi as a friend. They had lain awake, chatting, in their shared room at the hotel, for a few hours the previous evening.

"I could see you up ahead of me all the time, Boi.But every time I pushed myself to catch you, you seemed to accelerate too. I never got to within a hundred metres of you."

"What position did you come, Moreetsi?"

"I was twenty-second, Boi. I am fairly happy with that amongst such a distinguished field. But you have done fantastically well. I can't believe that you achieved ninth place! I am so happy for you!"

She gave Boi a big hug.

"Thanks Moreetsi. That means a lot to me. I hope that one day I can win a marathon."

"I hope so too, Boi. I will be there to see it. I don't think that I am going to have to wait very long for that day to come."

# # # # #

# Fourteen - Lesomenne

Back at school on the following Monday, Mma Tlotlo invited Boi on to the platform. Her Botswana running vest was held up for all of the pupils to admire.

"We are all very proud that Boitumelo Hope Tumelo has represented the school, and the nation, in the Mandela Marathon in Durban. She was up against some of the world's best women athletes."

She paused and looked around the sea of faces in front of her.

"In that esteemed field, having run 42 kilometres, Boitumelo crossed the line in NINTH place!"

Mma Tlotlo took a step back and applauded her star pupil.

The whole school applauded and cheered. They rose to their feet. A standing ovation! Boi was embarrassed, but she raised her arms towards them in grateful acknowledgement.

Even at that moment, she thought, *I can do better!*

When the applause died down, and the pupils and teachers had retaken their seats. Mma Tlotlo stepped forward to make a further announcement.

"Boitumelo's magnificent achievement is not the end of this story. In gaining ninth place, she also gained twelve-thousand-five-hundred Pula for the school sports fund. This will benefit us all. Thank you again, Boitumelo.

There was more applause as Boi made her way back to her seat in the front row.

The song that had been chosen by Mma Reetsang for assembly was *Modimo o Mogolo ke yo o dirileng (God almighty is the one who has done)*. Very few of the people in the hall new of the real significance of

193

that song. Boi tapped her feet to the familiar rhythm.

* * * * *

After assembly, the head teacher took Boi to one side.

"I am very proud of you Boitumelo. Over all of the years that I have been teaching, you are one of the best pupils that I have ever had the pleasure to teach. Not only do you work as hard as you can to achieve excellent results at everything that you turn your hand to, but you have continually helped others who are not as talented as yourself. For me, that attitude to life is even more commendable than your personal achievements."

Boi was wondering where all this was leading.

"You had to take a few days off from school to go and compete in the marathon. I don't have any problem with that, because you are so far ahead in every subject, anyway. But I need hardly tell you that your exams start in two weeks from now. Until those exams are over, I want you to forget your sport altogether, and concentrate entirely on your revision for academic subjects. Mister Way agrees with me, and he will not be expecting you to turn up for training. Promise me that you will do this."

*She only told me to forget my sport. She didn't say anything about enjoying the company of Kethwaahetse!*

Boi saw nothing wrong with sneaking away for some mutual pleasure with her long-term boyfriend. Distracting their minds from their studies could do no harm, and it made them both very happy as well. The risk had also gone out of their relationship since Ntate had recently guessed that they were going out together. Surprisingly, he had seemed pleased with the

194

revelation.

"Yes Mma. I promise you."

"I could always see the brightness in you from your first day at Junior Secondary School. A big part of your cleverness though, was realising that your brains are not enough. You understood, from early on, that you would only succeed if you worked hard. Now is the time for that final push. I am sure that you will put everything into it."

"I shall Mma." *With a little bit of fun on the side!*

As expected, Boi sailed through her exams. The rule was that, if you finished your paper more than 15 minutes before the end of the allotted time, and you had reviewed your answers to your complete satisfaction, you could quietly leave the room taking care not to disturb the other students. Boi left every single exam early.

After the final exam, which was the second English Literature paper, she waited for the rest of the class to emerge from the hall. There was great joy amongst most of her friends. They were all eager to get home.

Boi took Kethwaahetse by the hand.

"Let's go for a walk by the river."

When she got home, many hours later, it was already dark. She was surprised to see Uncle Tsholofelo sitting outside their home, drinking tea.

"You are very late. I suppose you were celebrating your last exam with your friends. How did it go?"

"I feel that it went very well, Mme. The questions were as I expected, almost exactly as Rre Kitso had predicted."

"That is good, Boi."

"You must be very relieved that it is all over?"

"Yes Uncle. It is good to get the exams finished. We have to wait until February for our results now."

"That is a long time. Over three months!"

"Yes. I will be able to help Mme around the house and the field, and I will find a job somewhere so that I can save some money towards my university fees and living costs."

"When will you start university?"

"Not until the end of next August. But I have secured my place at the University of Botswana, subject to getting good results in my exams."

"That is nearly a year away. That is a very long time."

"Uncle Tsholofelo has been discussing an idea with me. I am sceptical about it, but it is only fair that you should hear what he has to say."

Boi sat down on the ground, waiting for his uncle to expound his 'idea.'

"You are an excellent runner, Boi. You have already been selected for the Botswana athletics team, and you enjoyed amazing success in Durban.

"I am sure that you could make a lot of money by entering prize races. You could win enough between now and next August to pay for all your university education, and send plenty home to your family. And you are good enough to attract sponsorship. I have already approached Safari-ade, the energy drinks company in Gaborone. They will sponsor you, as a trial, for one race: the Marrakesh Marathon in January."

Boi couldn't believe what she was hearing. *How dare he make these arrangements without even asking her opinion!*

Mme could see that she was shocked.

"I knew that you wouldn't like the idea, Boi. I told

your uncle that..."

"Yes Mme. You are right. I don't like this. I am surprised that my uncle has gone so far before saying anything, but I'd like to hear what else he has found out before I give my opinion."

"I told you. She is a very clever girl, Patience. You should let her hear me out."

"Alright. Tell her about it. She is old enough to make her own decisions."

"Tell me about it Uncle Tsholofelo."

"Safari-ade have agreed to pay for all your kit, plus your travel and accommodations expenses, PLUS mine, as your manager, if you run in the Marrakesh Marathon in January. You get to keep 100% of your prize money. All you have to do is wear their branded shirt and shorts, and put on their branded baseball cap at the end of the race. The winner of the women's race gets ten thousand US dollars. There are good prizes for the first six.

"But that's not all. Even if you don't win any prize money, they will pay you two thousand dollars in what they call 'additional expenses.' If you come in the top ten, they will offer you a one year sponsorship deal. I worked out that, if we enter you into eight races between now and when you go to university, you easily could pick up twenty or thirty thousand dollars. Think what you could do with that sort of money."

"It all sounds too good to be true, uncle. Mma Tlotlo says that if anything ever sounds too good to be true, it usually is. My immediate question is, what's in it for you, uncle?"

"Boi! Don't be so cheeky!"

"No Patience. She is quite right to ask. I just want to use my own talents and experience to help a very talented member of my own family. Ten percent of any

197

prize money would not be too much to ask for. I won't make a living out of that, but I will feel good about helping you along your way."

"Hmmm. That actually sounds quite reasonable. Let me think about this for a few minutes." She stood up and walked out of the compound.

It wasn't long before she was back. She sat down in her previous position. Her mother and uncle awaited her verdict.

"It sounds like a good idea. It is worth a one-off trial in Morocco. If it worked out, I could think about carrying on. To have all my university expense covered in advance would be a tremendous weight off my mind. And, if I can help the family out at the same time, that would be brilliant. We have lived close to the bone, occasionally, and it would be nice to eliminate those worries. Just to always have enough food to eat, would make our lives easier."

"You have made a good decision, Boi. I'll call the sponsors tomorrow, and I'll set up a joint bank account for your winnings so that I can manage it for you."

"Wait a minute. I was just saying that it seemed like a really good idea. I haven't made a decision yet."

"Oh. What else do you need to know?"

"Nothing. I just want to discuss this with Mister Way. I value his advice."

"I suppose that makes sense. But you know that you can trust me."

"Yes. I know, Uncle Tsholofelo. It won't take me long though. I will go to see him tomorrow."

"Okay. I'll come back tomorrow evening."

# # # # #

198

# Fifteen - Lesometlhano

The next morning, Boi set off at her normal time for school. Mister Way was surprised to see her walk in to the gym at eight o'clock, but was happy to listen to her proposal, and to offer his advice. She was home before the sun reached its zenith.

Mme was very pleased to see her. As any wise mother would, she waited until Boi was ready to open up to her. That happened in the middle of the afternoon.

"Mister Way offered me some good advice, Mme. And he agreed to my suggestions."

Mme waited.

"As you know, I can think clearly as I run along."

Mme nodded.

"I have decided that I will go with Uncle Tsholofelo's plan, and run in the Marrakesh marathon in January. I stand a good chance of doing well enough to win some money because Mister Way has agreed to be my coach. He doesn't need to come with us to Morocco. He just needs to help me with my race preparation."

"That sounds good. I believe that you can do very well."

"That's not all, Mme. I have decided that, after I have given Uncle Tsholofelo his ten percent, and I have given you twenty percent and saved twenty percent for my university costs, I would like to use the other fifty percent for a very special purpose."

"That sounds interesting. What have you in mind?"

"I would like to build a fund to buy a school bus to take children from Itlhomolomo, Kango and Inagolo, and other villages along the way, to Marekisokgomo so that they have better access to education than we ever had. More young people will have a chance to make

199

something of their lives."

Mma Patience Tumelo was stunned. She was filled to the brim with emotion.

"Oh Boi. I am so proud of you. You are such a lovely girl. What a beautiful thought. It is typical of you. You will use your talent to bring benefits to others. You are so kind."

"I hope I can make life better for future generations of children in these villages, Mme. I am sure that some very clever children do not get on in life, because they don't have access to education. I want to change that."

Patience Tumelo's eyes filled with tears, as she realised that her little girl had become a woman of substance.

"You have a good soul, my daughter."

\* \* \* \* \*


That evening, Boi was so excited that she waited on the edge of the village to greet her uncle. It was difficult to keep her decision to herself until they reached the house, and waited Mme to put a mug of hot tea in his hands. When they all were sitting comfortably, Boi started to explain the background that had led her to make such a big decision. She wanted it all to be clear to her uncle: where it had come from, and what it would most certainly lead to.

Before she started, she requested that he should kindly keep quiet, and listen, until she had finished. But that she knew he would love the final outcome. Mme confirmed this with a wide smile.

She told him a lot of things that he already knew. She told him all about her family's poverty, and that many other village families were in the same position.

Often, this would mean that they could not afford for their children to extend their education beyond the end of primary school, especially the girls.

"So many very clever children are not as lucky as me. They do not go to secondary school, or on to university.

"I was very lucky indeed. Ntatemogolo worked at the lodge, and sent a lot of what he earned to pay school fees for me and Thapelo. Ntate and Tabansi sent money home from their mining jobs in Orapa. Everyone in the family contributed in some way: whatever they could manage.

"The other big problem is that the secondary school is so far away from the villages. Not everyone can stick to walking several miles each day, for five whole years, just so that they can study to gain their BGCSEs."

"It has been difficult, even for me, some days. When there is no food left for breakfast, or even a little snack, before I set off for school, I have felt like staying at home and helping Mme with the chores all day. But I made myself go because I knew that I must if I wanted to achieve my dreams.

"In all my five years at Marekisokgomo Integrated Secondary School, I have only missed five days of lessons. One was in Form Two, when I was sent home for being late. The other four were when my best friend was tragically killed and my mind went for a walk in the wilderness for a few days."

"Yes. Yes. I know all this. But what about the Marrakesh marathon, Boi? What about the sponsorship? What about ...?"

Boi held up her hand, palm towards her uncle.

"Please, Uncle Tsholofelo. I promise that I will come to that very soon."

Patience chuckled deep inside. Her baby was taking total control of a discussion with a grown man who was used to being the one in charge. It was incongruous and very funny.

"My luck continued. I had brilliant teachers at my school, who have helped me to get to a position where I am sure I will get top grades so that I can go to the University of Botswana in Gaborone and study for my degree.

"One of those brilliant teachers was my P.E. teacher, Mister Steve Way, who you know very well. How lucky can a girl get? To have an Olympic medal winner coaching me for five years! You have seen the results. Rre Bonolo Gosego has picked me for the national team. I was the youngest ever athlete, male or female, to wear a Botswana shirt in an international marathon.

"And I am lucky to have you on my side too. You are an experienced businessman, so you will be a great manager for me."

Uncle Tsholofelo beamed and was about to interrupt when Boi held up her hand again.

She started to tell her uncle about her visit to Mister Way, and the thoughts that had occurred to her as she ran home. As she told him about her plans for any prize money that she earned, his anger rose. All his dreams of making big money out of his niece's running talent were evaporating as she spoke. By the time she had finished, her mother was bursting with pride, and her uncle was exploding with rage. He was fuming!

He leapt to his feet, shouting.

"This is an outrageous conspiracy! You two have cooked this up today to steal the small amount of money from me that I could make by taking Boi to races all over the world!"

Of course, he had been thinking about the money he could make from big sponsorship deals, once she was successful, as well as a larger cut than the ten percent that he had mentioned.

"Besides, if these kids really want an education, they will do exactly what you did and walk to school. They are just lazy! Their families should work harder to pay the fees too. Buying them a bus will just make them soft!

"I swear, you two are crazy! This is NOT going to happen! If you want to be successful, you will need my experience. You have no idea how to manage you schedule, or your finances, or the logistics involved. You have not the slightest experience of ..."

"Brother!" Patience Tumelo shouted her brother-in-law down. "She has said that she wants you to be her manager. Last night, you said that you wanted just a ten percent cut, and that you would feel good about helping a family member."

"Yes. But can't you see, she just wants to throw the money away!"

Eventually, Patience and Boi managed to settle him down. As he supped a second mug of tea, and agreed, out loud, to Boi's plan, his thoughts were turning to alternative ways of making personal gains out of the situation. *There are many other roads down which those funds can be diverted.*

\* \* \* \* \*

Over the next few weeks, as Boi prepared for her trip to Morocco, and helped her mother as much as possible, she also had time to spend with her friends down by the river. There was nobody to race against, but she would often run and swim the old aquathon

203

course. Each time she made it back to the tree, she would add a mark to the bark, alternating sides, so that her friend would always keep up with her.

She sometimes cried as she made a mark, and sometimes she smiled.

She also had time to sit chatting with the villagers in Itlhomolomo and Inagolo. It was always enjoyable to sit listening to Mma Mothoriyana's stories of days gone by. Of her adventures as a child, and her travels to other parts of the country and even further afield.

In her own village, she had become quite a celebrity. Her Botswana running vest was something that everyone wanted to see, and to touch. One hour later, she was sitting under a tree, having a conversation with Gotweng, and she had shown him her famous shirt, when he told her that he had something to show to her.

He went to his hut and brought out a beautiful carving of a palm tree, complete with a bunch of coconuts. In its branches sat an owl. The intricate detail was superb

Boi was surprised that somebody who just worked as a casual labourer, in the fields and on the roads, could own such an expensive looking carving.

"If you don't mind me asking, where did you get such a wonderful carving? It is so beautiful, and it doesn't look as if it came from anywhere around here."

"You are correct, Boi. It is from Angola. Sergeant Lefoko Dintwa brought it back from a detachment up there, and gave it to me as a present. He is a very generous man, as well as being a national hero."

"Yes. He is definitely a big hero. My brother worships the ground he walks on, especially since he killed Menomagolo. I have noticed that he is a good friend of yours. Thapelo is quite jealous of you. He always comes to see you when he is home. Did you go to school together?"

"No. Nothing like that. He is about five years older than me. He just likes me a lot."

"There must be a bit more to it than that, Gotweng. The only other people I notice him being so kind to are the girls who chase him from bar to bar. Forgive me, but you are hardly in their league!" She laughed.

"Perhaps he just likes to sit talking with me for some reason. He will always buy me beers, and he has given me many good presents. Even the gifts he received from everyone for killing the monster were too much for him, so he gave many of them to me. I don't know why."

*You DO know why. There must be more to it than that,* thought Boi. *I am determined to find out for myself.*

There could be no escape for Gotweng. Once Boi was fixated on a goal, there was no way that she would ever let it go. She sat under the tree, talking with Gotweng, for almost three hours before she cracked him. She turned the conversation in many directions, so that Gotweng was enthusiastically opening up to her about all sorts of events in his life.

When they were talking about the feast that followed the slaying of the rogue hippo, she had a strong feeling that she was getting close. And when she expressed her amazement that a man, even such a man as the great soldier, could kill a massive, vicious hippo with his thumb, he looked embarrassed.

*Ah! He is hiding a secret! I have found it!*

After that, it took only a few minutes before the secret of the bullet was revealed.

"But please don't tell anyone, Boitumelo. He would kill me if he found out that I told you. Please promise that you won't tell."

"I promise you Gotweng. I will not get you into trouble."

*This is a very useful piece of information. I will store it for future use. There will come a time when Sergeant Lefoko Dintwa can help me. Now I know that, when that time comes, there is no doubt that he WILL help me!*

# # # # #

# Sixteen - Lesomethataro

The Marrakesh marathon was a different prospect to the Durban marathon. Once again, some of the top athletes in the world would be there, but the climate would be quite different. Contrary to the impression that Boitumelo had formed of Morocco during her geography lessons, she was told that it would be relatively cool. Compared to northern Botswana and the South African coast at that time of year, Marrakesh would be about fifteen degrees cooler than Durban. Furthermore, there was a small chance that it might rain.

Steve was cycling out towards Itlhomolomo to take Boi on training runs. They talked as she ran. He told her that the weather on the day of the race would be perfect for long distance running.

"I used to love racing in light drizzle. It keeps you at a really comfortable temperature. You have always been used to running in the hot Botswana sun, so you had an advantage over many of the European and American runners when it was over thirty degrees in Durban in November. In Marrakesh they will be running in familiar conditions, so they will have an advantage over you. There is no way that we can acclimatise for that. I have a feeling that it will actually suit your running style though."

"There's only one way to find out! I'll let you know when I get back."

"Well, I don't think that you could be much better prepared for the race. I wish that I could be there, but you know I have to stay here and work at the school. Your uncle will look after you though."

"Yes. We have made our peace now. He is even

207

going to help me with buying the bus. If I win enough money at this race, I will buy a second hand bus that can be used until we can afford a really good one that will last. I have heard that you can get a reasonable one for thirty thousand Pula. The top prize in this race is over thirty thousand Pula."

"It is unlike you to get carried away, Boi. I don't want to discourage you, because you should always believe that you can win, but don't bank on it."

"I won't Steve. It may take me a few races to buy the first bus. And I have to put money aside for other things."

"I am sure you will get there, Boi. Just think of your race."

* * * * *

It was a very long journey to Marrakesh. Even after taking almost a whole day to get to Johannesburg, they still had a further twenty-four hours of flights to go, with a stop in Amsterdam. Boi had looked it all up on maps, and couldn't believe what she found. It looked like they were going half way around the world.

She was very grateful that Uncle Tsholofelo had set up the sponsorship with Safari-ade. The trip would not have been affordable without their money. She was also very happy that her uncle was with her. The aeroplanes and the airports, and the taxis and hotels were all very daunting. She wasn't sure that she could have coped without him.

Boi was delighted when Moreetsi joined them at Johannesburg. Moreetsi was equally delighted, as she had been travelling on her own and hadn't expected to see Boi. During their time in Durban they had become quite good friends, and they immediately picked up where they'd left off. Uncle Tsholofelo managed to swap seats with Moreetsi, so that the two runners could sit together and chat, while he was able to watch the in-flight films in peace.

Despite the description that Moreetsi had given her on the plane, Boi was awestruck by the sheer size of the shopping mall in Schiphol airport. It seemed to be as big as a town. When she thought about that, she convinced herself that it was even bigger than Marekisokgomo. And the variety of goods that were on sale!

She walked around with Moreetsi for three hours, while Uncle Tsholofelo sat in the bar, nursing a beer. He'd suggested that they join him, but they had had enough to eat and drink on the long flight from Johannesburg. Although they came from a diamond producing nation, they were dazzled by the jewellery that they saw on display. Boi could only dream of the day when she might be able to afford such expensive rings and necklaces.

Boi had no money, but she was enjoying her tour of the shops. There was such a variety. In one shop that sold bathing costume, shorts, t-shirts and hoodies, a t-shirt caught her eye. It bore a cartoon of a yellow school bus wearing a big, cheesy grin. The caption underneath the bus read, "Driving towards a great education."

"Oh! I've got to have that t-shirt, Moreetsi. It is my dream on a shirt! How much is it?" She examined the label. "Twenty-five Euros. How much is that?"

"I'm no good at arithmetic, Boi. All I know is that one Euro is roughly eleven Pula."

In a flash, Boi had the answer. "That's two-hundred-and-seventy-five Pula. I wonder if Uncle Tsholofelo will lend me the money. He's convinced I'll win a prize in Marrakesh, so he could take it out of my winnings. Let's go and find him."

Her uncle smiled when she told him about the t-shirt. "It is your birthday on Sunday. I have been wondering what to get you. Here. Take this and buy the shirt."

Boi almost skipped back to the shop. She was absolutely delighted with the t-shirt. It was perfect.

\* \* \* \* \*

The taxi ride in from Ménara International Airport to the centre of Marrakesh was yet another new experience for Boi. The sights and sounds and smells of this bustling city, possibly the busiest in the whole of Africa, captivated Boi from the start. She thought that the red sandstone walls were just wonderful. They were steeped in history. She lost count of the number of mosques that they passed. And there were market stalls, selling foods and spices, everywhere she looked. The city seemed to be one huge market.

Arriving on Friday evening would give them the Saturday to register for the race and spend the rest of the day exploring the city centre at their leisure. Uncle Tsholofelo had promised his sister-in-law that he would take his job of chaperoning his niece very seriously, so he would go with them to the Medina. He didn't mind though. This was quite an experience for him too.

Having checked into the hotel, they all retreated to their rooms to rest. Two days of travelling had tired all three of them out.

In the morning, Boi and Moreetsi were keen to go for a gentle jog to loosen up. They were advised to wear tracksuits and stick to the main thoroughfares. For young ladies to run through the city with bare arms and legs would be acceptable the following morning, during the race, but was definitely NOT acceptable at any other time.

When they returned to the hotel, Boi observed that Mister Way's advice regarding the climate had been spot on.

"He said that it would be cooler, but that I would enjoy running in these conditions, and he could not have been more right. I feel totally ready for this race tomorrow, Moreetsi. I cannot wait!"

After showering, they joined Uncle Tsholofelo for a light breakfast before making for the Medina. There were several other athletes staying in the same hotel. Moreetsi knew a few of them and pointed them out to Boi.

"The best one I have seen, so far, is that blonde lady over there in the corner. She is called Tatiana something. I can't remember her second name. Russian names are so difficult."

Tatiana saw them looking in her direction and gave a little wave and a smile. They exchanged brief greetings on the way out of the dining room.

On the short walk to the city centre, Boi and Moreetsi were able to call in at the registration for their race. Seeing the date on the forms reminded Boi that it would be her birthday. She knew in her heart that her seventeenth would be one that she would never forget.

They spent several hour wandering around the Medina. All three of them found much that was interesting. Boi loved the smell of the spices. Her uncle had given her a few Dirhams to spend, but the only purchase that Boi made was a large bag of olives. They were delicious, and Boi happily shared them with her companions. She was very tempted to buy some of the spices that were on display everywhere. The aromas were heavenly.

Uncle Tsholofelo dissuaded her though. He told her that there were sometimes problems with airport authorities when carrying such goods in one's baggage.

"If you wish to buy some spices for your mother, it is probably safest to buy them when we are back in our own country, Boi."

"Yes. But I have never smelled such beautiful spices in any market anywhere near our home."

"I agree, but if the customs officers in Amsterdam or Johannesburg decide to confiscate them, you would be wasting your money."

It made sense. She gave up.

On the way back to the hotel, they were looking for an Italian restaurant so that they could take on some carbohydrates on the eve of the race. Boi was hoping to repeat Durban's spaghetti alla carbonara experience.

They were out of luck. There seemed to be a lack of Italian restaurants in Marrakesh. However, Moreetsi spotted a local restaurant that was serving couscous.

"That could be even better, Boi. Couscous is one of the healthiest carbohydrates. It is packed with protein and calcium, and is very low in fat."

"Let's try it then," enthused Boi.

When she'd enjoyed her fill of a dish of couscous and roasted vegetables, Boi was glad to make it back to the hotel where she could relax and plan for an early night.

Moreetsi invited her to sit in the bar and try the mint tea. Boi loved it. She was happy to sit chatting to her relatively new friend for a couple of hours and to help her polish off three or four pots of the refreshing tea.

\* \* \* \* \*

When they arrived at the start in the morning, radio and TV presenters were milling around amongst the elite athletes, snatching quick interviews where they could. Boi was not surprised that none of them wanted to speak with her. They didn't even recognise her.

Two and a half hours later, it was a very different story. Everyone wanted to interview Boi, the winner of the Marrakesh Marathon!

Initially, she hadn't really believed it herself. She had just focused on her race, as usual, ignoring all other runners. As she'd run down the home straight, following several male runners, the race marshals had leapt across her path with a finishing tape. Puzzled, she had just run through it. The cheers were deafening as she was welcomed by more race officials with water and a space blanket. She was taken to a resting area to await the medal ceremony.

She was quickly followed by Tatiana and an Ethiopian runner, both of whom congratulated her warmly.

"We could not catch you. You did amazingly well!"

"Yes. You are a phenomenal runner. Especially for one so young. Well done!"

"Did I really win the women's race?"

"Yes. You did. Is it really your seventeenth birthday today?"

"Yes."

"Well, happy birthday Boitumelo! You are the youngest ever winner. All the TV stations want to speak with you."

Uncle Tsholofelo appeared in the tent.

"Well done Boi! You won!"

Suddenly, Boitumelo Hope Tumelo was a name that was famous right around the world. She had sprung from total obscurity to global fame in just three hours.

* * * * *

On the long journey back to Botswana, Moreetsi was full of encouragement for Boi. She kept telling her about the coaching prowess of Bonolo Gosego, and how bright her future would be with the national athletics team.

"You could be the most successful Batswana athlete ever, Boi!"

"Let's not get carried away. But I am starting to think that my uncle is correct. If I delay my first year at university, I could earn a lot of money. That would pay my way through my degree course, and it would make my family very comfortable. Most of all, I might be able to actually buy more than one school bus to bring children in to Marekisokgomo from the surrounding villages. I can't tell you how passionate I am about making that happen."

"I know you are Boi. I think that it is a wonderful ambition. You are such a generous soul. God will bless you."

"I already have enough from Marrakesh to make a start. Uncle Tsholofelo is going to come with me to buy a second-hand bus next week."

"That is great. But I would advise you against taking a year out from university."

"Why?"

"Think about it. You could travel the world with your uncle, taking in races like yesterday's, and make a lot of money."

"That's exactly the idea, Moreetsi."

"I know. But there are two reasons that I am giving you this advice. The first is that, if you get seriously injured, you will waste a year of your education and you won't win any races with your feet up."

"And the second?"

"The second reason is that, if you take up your place at University of Botswana, you will be based in Gaborone. Guess what? Bonolo Gosego, and his coaching staff are also in Gaborone. So are many of the national athletics team. You will have continuous access to the best training in the country, and you will have the highest visibility. If you continue to run the way that you have raced so far, your name will be first on the team sheet for every international competition."

"I hadn't thought of it like that Moreetsi. This is good advice. Thank you."

"You are welcome, sister. You will still have the chance to win some good prize money to fund all of your ventures."

"You have convinced me. This is definitely the right way for me to go."

"Good. I am pleased. I am sure that you are making the correct decision. And it also means that I will see more of you. I hope that I still have a few more years in the Botswana team. We are already good friends."

"Yes. We are. I like being your friend. I like it very much."

At Gaborone, Moreetsi said her farewells to Boi and Uncle Tsholofelo.

Boi accompanied her uncle to the bank where they deposited the cheque for $10,000.

215

"It will take at least four days to clear, so I suggest that we agree a time to meet up at the garage in Marekisokgomo, where you saw that bus, a week from tomorrow. If he wanted thirty thousand Pula for it, I am sure that we could knock him down to nearer twenty-five."

"That would be very good. I don't mind waiting till next week. Nyack is going to be home. He can come with me. He is an expert mechanic and driver now. He is the chauffeur to Mister van Gils in Orapa, you know."

"I know, Boi. You have told me several times. Remind me of the name of the garage."

"It is called Kemnai Motors. It is on the main road leading to Serowe. Do you know it?"

"Yes. I know it very well. He has a good reputation. I will meet you there at noon next Wednesday."

Boi was dreading telling Uncle Tsholofelo about her decision to take up her place at the University of Botswana as originally planned. She knew that he would be furious. She waited until about fifteen minutes before their bus was due to arrive in Marekisokgomo.

Strangely, her uncle was not perturbed at all. He just accepted it, and didn't even ask her why she had changed her mind. Perhaps he had already thought it through and come to the same conclusions as Moreetsi.

\* \* \* \* \*

The following Wednesday, Nyack was able to borrow Kasigo's old car so that he could drive his sister to Kemnai Motors. They arrived just after eleven o'clock. The school bus that Boi had seen was still

216

there. She was delighted. She was even happier when she saw that the price had been reduced to BWP 28,000.

They told the owner of the garage that their uncle would be coming with the cash in about one hour, and asked if they could take a look at the bus. He readily agreed and even offered them a test drive.

The test drive went very well. Nyack thought that it was worth more than the asking price, but he might be able to get a reduction if she let him do the talking.

As they waited for Uncle Tsholofelo to turn up with the money, Nyack made sure that the owner was within earshot before telling his sister that the rear axle was making a bit of a worrying noise, and that the front tyres were nearing the end of their life.

"But the engine is in very good condition. It has been well looked after and probably has many more miles left in it yet. The bodywork needs a bit of attention, but that is normal for a vehicle of this age. There is nothing that I can't put right with a bit of filler and a few coats of paint. We could soon have her looking like new."

Boi could hardly contain her excitement, but had promised her brother that she would do so. He winked at her. They would not say any more until their uncle arrived.

Uncle Tsholofelo was not there at noon. They were still waiting at one o'clock. Boi was restless.

"He will be here, Boi. Don't worry. Let's go across to that cafe and get a cup of tea. We will see him arrive from there.

When the hands of the clock turned past two o'clock, Boi had a feeling that their uncle had forgotten about their appointment, or perhaps he had been diverted by an important business appointment and been unable to get word to them. She suggested that they should go to the bank and withdraw the money to buy the bus.

"It is a joint account, so I can take the money out. Uncle Tsholofelo notified them that we would need thirty thousand Pula today, so they won't be surprised."

Nyack drove her to the bank and went in with her.

When she told the teller that she wanted to withdraw a significant amount from her account, the teller looked very worried.

"I will have to get the manager, Mma."

"That's okay. We don't mind waiting."

The teller was back with the manager within seconds.

"Please come into my office, Mma."

He led the way. Nyack followed.

"Please sit down."

They sat.

"This is a little embarrassing, Mma. Rre Tsholofelo Poifo withdrew the money last Friday, as soon as your cheque cleared."

"Oh. Don't worry. That is not a problem. I presume that he took the money that we need for the school bus that we are going to buy from Kemnai Motors. He was going to meet us there, but he is an important businessman. He probably has some emergency to deal with and forgot to tell us."

"No. You misunderstand me, Mma. He has withdrawn all of the funds and closed the account."

"What?! There must be some mistake."

"I can assure you, there is no mistake, Mma. Look here." He pointed to his computer screen. It showed a withdrawal of BWP 92,080.97 and a balance of zero. The next line of the statement read, "ACCOUNT

218

CLOSED".

Boi was stunned.

"I ... I don't understand."

"I am very sorry Mma. Perhaps your uncle can explain it to you. He must have his reasons."

Recovering quickly, Boi replied, "Yes. You are quite right. Thank you Rra. You have been very helpful."

She turned to her brother. "Come on Nyack. We must go immediately to Phuthaditšhaba and ask Uncle Tsholofelo what he is up to."

Twenty minutes later they arrived at their uncle's house. He was not in.

His next door neighbour approached and asked them if they were looking for Rre Poifo.

"Yes. We are. I am Boitumelo Hope Tumelo, and this is my brother Nyack. We are his niece and nephew from Itlhomolomo."

"Oh. Didn't he tell you? He left on Friday on a business trip to New York. He told me that he wouldn't be back for several months."

This time, Boi was more than stunned. She was shocked. As she realised what had happened, she was furious. Her world had suddenly collapsed around her. From the heights of optimism, she had suddenly plummeted into the depths of despair. Her despicable uncle had stolen her money! Not just her money, but her family's money and the money that would have made such a difference to the lives of the children of her village!

"NO! How could he do this! He is a thief!"

She burst into tears. She sobbed.

Nyack put his arms around his little sister. He couldn't believe it either. He had never liked Uncle Tsholofelo, but this was beyond the limit. *How could he do this!*

"Get back in the car. We need to go and tell Mme about this immediately."

Boi was still crying when they got home. Nyack had to explain the situation, as Boi was far too distraught to speak about it. She was so upset that she went straight to her bed even though it was only late afternoon.

Mme couldn't believe that her brother-in-law had double-crossed them either. She blamed herself for insisting that he should become Boi's chaperone in the first place. And then she had agreed to Tsholofelo becoming her manager with full control over their joint bank account. *How foolish have I been?*

She looked across at her daughter. *I have betrayed her. She needs my help.*

Boi was still crying. She was supposed to go and fetch some water, but one of the boys could deal with that.

Mme decided to leave her until she was ready to speak. She offered her some food and water, but Boi just rolled over closer to the wall of the hut.

The next morning, Boi rose when the cockerel crowed and went to sit on the ground outside the hut. Her mother joined her.

"Oh Mme. I am very upset. Uncle Tsholofelo has stolen the money that I won, by beating the best marathon runners in the world, and run off to New York. He will never come back. He has betrayed me. That money was mine, not his. I had plans for it. It was more money than we have ever had before."

"I know Boi. He will never be welcome in this house again, even if he does ever come back. Ntatemogolo already knows about this. He is very angry. He will tell all of our relatives that Uncle Tsholofelo Poifo will never be welcomed in ANY of our family homes."

"I swear that I will find him one day. He will pay for this."

"The minister would preach forgiveness, but it will be difficult for any of us to forgive him for this. Will you kneel down and pray with me."

As the sun came up, Boi and her mother knelt on the ground and prayed that "His will be done." Boi prayed that God would meet out justice. That Uncle Tsholofelo would receive his rightful punishment, and that He would help her to give access to education to the village children.

They prayed and knelt in silence for almost an hour.

Boi went to fetch some water, but told Mme that she was not going to do anything else that day. Her mother accepted that. She didn't expect Boi to do any chores in the circumstances.

"Don't worry Boi. If God doesn't punish Uncle Tsholofelo for his sins, I am sure that Saturn will. And Saturn's wrath is well known for being fiery. He will burn from now until eternity."

"Not if I catch him first Mme!"

\* \* \* \* \*

By the time that the BGCSE results were published in the last week in February, Boi had calmed down and decided that she had no other choice than to put her uncle's appalling behaviour down to experience and move on. She had learnt a painful lesson and would never be tricked in such a way again.

However, she would not forget. One day, she would find Uncle Tsholofelo and make him pay. Unless, of course, Saturn beat her to it.

Two or three of her classmates had mobile phones and were able to discover their results via new SMS messaging service, without having to go to the school. Boi was one of the many who could not afford such luxuries. They assembled around the school notice boards at 8 am on the 22nd of February. There was great excitement, and some trepidation as Mma Tlotlo pinned up the sheets of paper that she'd received in the post that morning.

Boi was very happy to see Kethwaahetse. She hadn't seen him since the day before she'd departed for Morocco. She hadn't really been in the mood.

"How did you get on?"

"I am pleased. I got six A's, a B and two C's. Have you seen yours yet?"

"No. I will look now."

"There is no need. I saw that you got ten grade A's, as everyone expected. But you deserved it. You worked twice as hard as any of the rest of us."

"That's brilliant! I still want to see it with my own eyes though."

Boi returned to Kethwaahetse's side a few minutes later, looking glum.

"What's wrong?"

"You didn't look properly at my results. I got nine A's and a B."

"Oops. Sorry. I just thought I saw all A's."

"That's okay. Don't worry. My results are still pretty good. Easily good enough to take up my place at university."

"Pretty good? Achieving nine A's is more than pretty good, Boi. Don't be so modest. It is brilliant!"

"Yes. As usual, you are right. But I am annoyed with myself about the B."

"Which subject was it in?"

"English Literature. I remember that Paper 2 was the last exam. I must have allowed my concentration to slip. I should know by now that I need to focus right up to the last second. That's what I do when I am running, so I must do it in all things."

"Don't be so harsh on yourself, Boi. Smile!"

She smiled.

"You did well too. We will be at university together. I see than Moagi got very good results. He will be able to go to

Agriculture College in Gaborone. We will all be together."

"We will have some great times in the coming years. But it is so long, six months, until the term starts."

"Never mind that, Kethwaahetse. I think that we should go and celebrate. Let's go for a walk into the countryside. We can find somewhere private to use the supplies that I have in my pocket. It has been far too long."

Kethwaahetse needed no second asking.

"Let's go!"

# # # # #

# Seventeen - Lesomesupa

In the six months before she started her first year at university, Boi had been steeled by the awful experience following the Marrakesh marathon. Her mother and her boyfriend had comforted her, and Steve Way had offered her many wise words of counsel.

She had decided to take care of her own destiny. She knew that she was clever enough, and strong enough, both physically and mentally. She had proved that from a very early age.

She had entered three more marathons with prize money potential, but had not been as successful as in that venture to Morocco. Her total winnings had amounted to less than six thousand US dollars.

As Moreetsi had predicted, Boi had been invited to join the national athletics team as soon as she arrived at the University of Botswana. Bono had been delighted that she would be studying in the capital city for the next four years. The two young women soon became very close friends. They would run for miles together, and Boi always welcomed Moreetsi's advice.

At the beginning of the following year, the Botswana team was announced for the forthcoming Olympic Games in Buenos Aires. It came as no surprise to anyone except for Boi herself, that she was selected to run the marathon. Moreetsi's performance had recently improved, and she was relieved when she was also chosen to join the team. Although Boi was now friendly with many of the regular team, she was pleased that her friend would be travelling to South America with her. They immediately made it known to the rest of the team that they would buddy-up and be room-mates in Buenos Aires.

As July approached, the training got more

intense. Boi was also studying hard for her Part One exams.

Bono's approach to race training was very similar to Steve's. By the time the team boarded the flight from Johannesburg to Buenos Aires, Boi and Moreetsi were laser-focused on their race plans, which were slightly different. Boi still maintained her metronomic rhythm by silently singing the songs that she had honed with Mma Reetsang and Steve Way. Moreetsi was used to running her race in stages, and would tune her running to the behaviour of the leading pack. This was a risky strategy, but it had proved successful for her in the past.

This was Moreetsi's third visit to South America, and she was full of enthusiasm. Her excitement rubbed off on Boi as they sat together on the flight across the South Atlantic. They were not disappointed. The city was every bit as vibrant as they had expected. There were Olympic Games posters and paraphernalia everywhere. Even the buses and trains were painted with logos and mascots.

The Olympic Village on the edge of the city was something else again. There were athletes from almost two hundred participant nations. Boi wanted to meet them all, and was soon making plenty of new friends. Unlike her experience in Marrakesh, she already enjoyed some fame. Her victory over some of the world's best had made news headlines all around the planet.

The camaraderie in the Botswana team was amazing. In the evenings they sang and danced for their own enjoyment and self-entertainment. Members of other teams would visit their area of the Village to enjoy the culture of Botswana.

Two days after their arrival, a fleet of buses

transported the athletes to the main stadium where they assembled outside, ready for the Opening Ceremony. Excitement levels were very high. The teams marched into the arena in alphabetical order, so Botswana were one of the first. The impressively huge hammer thrower, Mooketsi Simanyana, led the team on to the track. He carried the blue, black and white flag in one hand. The rest of the team danced behind him. A few of them carried cameras and took photographs of the big occasion. It was a long night. Boi was in awe.

*I cannot believe the difference between this and an evening in Itlhomolomo, wishing that the wild dogs would be quiet. How far have I travelled?*

During the following eight days leading up to the women's marathon, Bonolo made sure that they remained disciplined in both their training and their diet. He also made sure that they relaxed and supported each other in their events. The marathon started in the main stadium at exactly eleven o'clock.

The streets of Buenos Aires were lined with cheering spectators, solidly, for the full forty two kilometres. There were drink stations, and flags, and balloons, and bands along the way. Despite all of these distractions, Boi ran her normal, focused race. Moreetsi was influenced by her younger team mate, and ran much of the race with her. As Boi's pace picked up over the final five kilometres, Moreetsi dropped back slightly.

The stadium was packed with a capacity crowd. Boi entered, with three other African runners. They were about seventy metres behind the leader. Boi knew that it was now or never. She dug in and gave it her all, sprinting around the final lap as if her life depended upon it. She was gaining all the way, but crossed the line fifty metres behind the American, Mary-Jane

Deakin.

She was overjoyed, as was the whole of her nation. There were a two or three hundred Batswana inside the stadium, but almost everyone in Botswana who could get close to a television set was watching back at home. Most of her family had travelled in to Marekisokgomo from Itlhomolomo and surrounding villages to watch. Her father and two elder brothers were watching in Orapa.

Somebody in the crowd ran down to the front and handed her a Botswana flag. She accompanied Mary-Jane Deakin on her lap of honour. They were joined by Tiki Debaba, the bronze medalist from Ethiopia.

It suddenly occurred to Boi that she was taking the applause with the gold and silver medalists. *What does this make me? I am really the silver medalist? Yes! YES I am!*

Moreetsi and Bonolo were waiting for her as she completed her lap of honour. Moreetsi had run in to a very credible sixth place.

"Boi! You were brilliant!" enthused Bono. "Do you realise what you have done? You are by far the youngest ever medalist in the Olympic women's marathon. You are incredible. I am so happy! I am so happy for YOU!"

Moreetsi hugged her. "Well done Boi. You are a national heroine! Botswana loves you!"

Mary-Jane was walking past. She stopped to hug Boi once more. They exchanged congratulations. Boi felt extremely proud, and rightly so.

Three hours later, as she stood on the podium listening to "The Stars and Stripes", and watching her national flag being raised alongside the flags of USA and Ethiopia, she cried. She cried with happiness. *Is this really happening? How did I get here?*

\* \* \* \* \*

On her return to Botswana, Boi had intended to go straight home to Itlhomolomo to spend some time with her family and friends before commencing her second year at university in Gaborone. She hadn't taken into account the impact of her new-found fame. As Moreetsi had predicted, she had become an overnight heroine in her own country.

All of the TV and radio stations wanted to interview her. The Mayor of Gaborone held a civic reception for the returning athletes. The team was invited to an even grander reception at the Presidential Palace.

The President made a big speech, which was broadcast on national TV. For Botswana, the Buenos Aires had been the most successful ever, with one silver and two bronze medals. The President was delighted with the performance, and promised that there would be more government investment in sports in the future. He spent several minutes talking to Boi and Bonolo about the achievements and their experiences in Argentina.

So it was almost a week later that Boi finally made it back to Itlhomolomo. Nyack had met her at Marekisokgomo with Kasigo's car, so there'd been no need to hitch a ride on the back of a truck.

As they drove back to their village, Nyack turned to Boi and told her that there would have been plenty of volunteers to drive her home if he hadn't been there.

"You really are a big local celebrity now, sister."

"Yes. That's what I am afraid of. I really don't

want to be a celebrity. I've had enough of it over the past few days in Gaborone."

"Well, you are about to get some more when we get home. Sorry! Mme has invited everyone in the area to a big feast in the village. The party had already started when I left. They've all brought food and beer with them. Your old friend, Mma Mothoriyana is taking the place of honour, and helping Mme with the cooking. Imagine! At her age!"

"I will be pleased to see my family and my dear old friend from Inagolo, of course. And it will be nice to be welcomed by everyone. It will all die down and return to normal in a few days. I hope so, anyway."

"I am sure that it will. But it's your fault, Boi. You're the one who went off and won a silver medal in the Olympics," he teased.

"Yes. Imagine what it's going to be like when I bring back a gold from Paris in four years' time!"

\* \* \* \* \*

Boi really didn't want all of the fuss, but she was delighted to see all her family and friends who had descended upon Itlhomolomo from all of the surrounding villages. They all wanted to see and touch her silver medal. She was only the second Batswana to bring one home.

Mma Mothoriyana had baked her a celebratory cake. It tasted of lemons. The memories of her first day at secondary school came flooding back as she tasted the delicious sponge. A time when she had sat in Mma Mothoriyana's hut with Thapelo and Grace listening to the story of the amputation of the old lady's leg.

In a rather sweet reversal, Sergeant Dintwa Lefoko publicly expressed his admiration for Boi, who he called "a national icon." Boi enjoyed the moment and had a few thoughts about what she might say to him about bullets and thumbs if they had a moment alone. She was happy to bide her time. He would pay for his deception.

The celebrations went on through the night. There was much singing and dancing. The sun was already rising when Boi finally got to bed. She was very tired, and very happy.

By the time she was up and about in the afternoon, most of the guests had dispersed. Boi was able to enjoy some time with her mother.

"I know how well your running is going. The whole of Botswana knows about that. But how are your studies going?"

"Really well, Mme. Thanks for asking. It seems that all people are interested in these days is my running."

"It is natural. You are the best this country has ever seen."

"I am looking forward to my second year. I've forgotten all the ideas about being a professor. I think I can do more good by becoming a top doctor or surgeon. And I have to think beyond my running career. That won't go on forever."

"You are very wise, my daughter. I don't know where you get it from."

"I get much of it from you, Mme."

"That's good of you to say, Boi, but I am sure that you are much wiser than me."

"Well, I have seen my friend Moreetsi. She has been a great runner in her time, but she realises that her international running days will be over in a year or two. She says I should make the most of what I have while I still have it. That is why I have entered the New York

City Marathon."

"I don't understand. What do you mean?"

"I still want to buy a school bus. If I could win that race, I could afford two! The first prize is fifty thousand dollars. Even second or third prize will buy a bus and leave a huge amount for you and the family, and for my university fees."

"When is it?"

"In November. I'll have to take a few days out of my studies, but I can soon catch it up, and the Dean is very supportive. He just loves having one of his students winning Olympic medals. He'll do anything for me.

"That sounds good to me, Boi. And once you have bought this bus, it will clean away the foul stench of your uncle's dastardly deeds."

"Yes. It will. And if I go to New York a couple of days early, I can find Uncle Tsholofelo and sort him out."

"Sort him out? What will you do to him?"

"I don't know yet. I'll think about that."

"The important thing is that you win the money for the bus. Forget your rotten uncle. He's not worth it."

"Maybe you're right, Mme, but I'm going to have to think about it for a while. One thing that I can be absolutely sure about is where the money will go this time. I am the only person who can access my bank account."

"That's good, Boi. Can you afford to go to New York though?"

"Yes. I was going to approach Safari-ade for sponsorship, but I didn't need to. When I got back from Buenos Aires, they came to me. I won't have any worries at all in paying my way to New York. And they'll put me in a very nice hotel too."

"You have landed on your feet."

Boi laughed. "Yes! My feet! These are the feet that got me here!"

\* \* \* \* \*

# Eighteen - Lesomerobedi

Boi arrived in New York four days before the race. This time she was all alone, as Moreetsi wasn't competing. This was her first trip outside Botswana without a travelling companion, but she was quite confident in her ability to cope. Safari-ade had booked her into the Library Hotel, which was not too far from Central Park where the race would finish on Sunday. The receptionist was most welcoming.

"I am honoured to meet you Miss Tumelo. There are several other top marathon runners staying in our hotel for the weekend. You are the only Olympic medalist amongst our guests though."

"Thank you. I shall look forward to meeting them."

Boi was thrilled that she was recognised in New York. *They know me in The Big Apple!*

She wondered if she would be able to find her uncle. She had no plan other than to confront him and hope that her appearance would give him a heart attack. She dipped into the side pocket of her rucksack and produced the only photo she had of her evil uncle.

"Have you ever seen this man? He is my uncle, Tsholofelo Poifo. He came to New York over a year ago."

"Did he stay at this hotel madam?"

"I shouldn't think so. I don't know where he stayed. He left no forwarding address."

"I don't think I have ever seen him. This is a very big city. Haven't you heard from him since he arrived in New York?"

"No. And I don't think that I will. He stole ten thousand dollars from me before he left Botswana in a hurry."

The receptionist was so shocked that she stepped back from the desk with her mouth hanging open in stunned surprise.

"Wow! He robbed you?"

"Yes. He took everything I had. It was my first ever prize money from a big race, and I had plans for it."

"You must be really mad at him, madam."

"Yes. You can say that again. I'd really like to find him but, as you say, this is a huge city. I don't know where to start. The only thought I have in my mind is to show every New Yorker I meet this photo."

"If you don't mind me saying so, madam, I believe you may well be wasting your time with that approach. I have an idea though."

"Really? Anything you can suggest to help would be welcome."

"This is a real long shot, but your uncle is a criminal, so he may be known to the police."

"That is possible, I suppose."

"My boyfriend is a traffic cop with the NYPD. He has a friend who is a detective at the Central Park Precinct. Perhaps his friend could look your uncle up on the national crime database."

"Yes. He might be there. But only if he's been caught for committing a crime since he's been in your city. The American police wouldn't know that he stole my money."

"Okay. I'll mention this to my boyfriend when he meets me after work. I'll try to arrange an introduction to his detective friend."

"Thanks. You are very kind. I don't hold out much hope though. I am out of my depth with this. I should really concentrate on my race. That's what I am here for. I don't want searching for my uncle to distract me too much."

"I'll leave you a message when I find out what he can do. Here is your room key, madam. You are in room 2147 on the twenty-first floor. The elevators are right behind you. I hope you enjoy your stay."

\* \* \* \* \*

Boi met the detective the following morning. He was a huge sports fan and was very excited that he had the chance to meet a genuine Olympic medal winner.

"I remember watching the Olympic marathon live on TV. As an American, I was real happy that Mary-Jane Deakin won the gold, but you were gaining on her. Another two laps of that track, and I think you'd have caught her."

"Maybe. But the marathon is twenty-six point two miles, forty-two kilometres. My job is to run my race so that I complete that distance faster than any of the other runners."

"I am sure that you'll do it someday. Maybe this coming Sunday!"

"That would be great if I could do that. To win the New York City Marathon would be almost as good as winning Olympic gold. That is my ultimate ambition."

"Well good luck with that Miss Tumelo."

"Thank you. So what do you think the chances of finding my uncle are?"

"To be completely honest with you, very small, but we can try. Just give me as much detail as you can and leave it to me. There is very little point in you trawling the streets of this city looking for this schmuck. There are millions of people here. You won't find him and you'll stress yourself out. If I can find him for you, I will."

"I am very grateful to you, Sir."

"It is not a problem. To help an Olympic star out would be a dream come true for me. It's what detective work is all about. The reward is doing what I do. Will you be going back home straight after the marathon, or staying over?"

"My flight is on Monday evening, so I will still be here until three o'clock on Monday afternoon."

"Great! I will stop by and update you Monday morning."

For the next hour, Boi drank her favourite tea, mint flavour, and Detective Johnson drank strong black coffee while he collected information about Uncle Tsholofelo.

\* \* \* \* \*

Over the next three days, Boi spent a lot of her time in the nearby Bryant Park. She sat and watched the world go by, thinking deeply about how she would run the race on Sunday. It had been very easy for her to visit parts of the course. She'd walked the length of First Avenue, across Willis Avenue Bridge, through part of the Bronx, and then across Madison Avenue Bridge and down Fifth Avenue until she came to Central Park. She had strolled around the huge park, and lingered around West Avenue, where the finish line was already set up. She'd tried to imagine what it would be like to run up there on Sunday morning with huge crowds lining the route.

Back in the hotel, she had met several other runners from a variety of backgrounds. There were only a couple of elite runners, and quite a few who were club runners or enthusiastic first-timers. She didn't recognise anyone, but plenty of them recognised her. It was slightly embarrassing at first, but she was flattered that so many people knew of her achievements.

*I am still not nineteen years old, and I appear to be world famous. At least in New York!*

Many of the people she met asked the same question: "Do you think you can win it on Sunday?"

Her answer never varied. "That has always been my intention."

\* \* \* \* \*

On the day of the race, Boi was in the start area on Staten Island by eight o'clock. She had over an hour to go before the elite women's start time. During that waiting time, a few of the runners that she had competed against in Buenos Aires came over and greeted her, including Mary-Jane Deakin. It was good to see them and they were all genuinely happy to meet her.

In good time, she made her way to the start and started to really focus on the race ahead of her. In place of numbers, the elite runners had their names pinned to their vests. She looked down at hers: "BOITUMELO". The crowds might call her name, but it would just be background noise. She would be hearing the old songs of her homeland beating out the rhythm in her head.

Boi deliberately took up a position alongside her fiercest rival. Although they had already greeted each other in the assembly area, they shook hands. They both knew that this signified the end of their friendship. At least for the next two-and-a-half hours. Then they could be friends once more.

Boi turned to stare across the windswept Staten

Island Bridge. Her mind was already running down the other side towards the two mile marker in Brooklyn. She closed her eyes, fast forwarding through the whole course, into Central Park and up to the finish line.

The starter called them to order. The gun was fired and the first steps of many were taken.

> *Modimo o Mogolo ke yo o dirileng*
> *Tse di molemo tsotlhe le tse di phatshimang*
>
> *Letsatsi la go tlhaba le bo le phirima*
> *Ngwedi le dinaledi tse di benyabenyang*
>
> *A re supeng Tebogo a re itumeleng*
> *Re ise Malebogo go Rara mo pakong*

As they ran down 5th Avenue, approaching the entrance to Central Park, Boi was in the tight-packed leading group. She was still running her own race, to her own cadence and stride length, when she was clipped by the Ethiopian runner alongside her. She fell heavily to the ground. By the time she'd recovered, the pack was already entering the park, some two hundred metres ahead of her. She quickly re-planned the last four kilometres of her race, and struck for home. She knew that she could still win. Just!

**Excerpt from the end of race commentary on ASNTV**

*As they come around the final bend with three hundred yards to go, the gold and silver medalists from the Buenos Aires Olympics are battling it out once more. They have left the rest of the runners in their wake. This is a phenomenal performance by the African teenager. Three miles out, it looked as if her day was over when she was tripped and crashed to the ground. To come back from that to challenge at the end is nothing short of heroic.*

*Has she got enough to take the extra two or three yards out of Mary-Jane Deakin in the final straight? Maybe she has. She is still gaining.*

*They are pushing each other to the line. It will be a new world record for one of them, for sure. This is incredible running folks! How can they sprint like this at the end of twenty six miles?*

*The crowd is roaring. They know this is special.*

*There is nothing between Deakin and Tumelo as they come to the line. Tumelo lunges for the tape, and I think she got it!*

*I really don't know. We'll have to wait for the official result. It's a photo finish to a marathon. I have never seen the like of this in my life!*

*Deakin is on her knees. Now she has rolled over onto her back. Tumelo is pumping her fists in the air and leaping for joy. These two runners know who won.*

*Tumelo is helping Deakin to her feet. They are hugging each other. They must be exhausted.*

*Deakin has grabbed Tumelo's wrist and is holding the African's arm aloft.*

*The winner of this year's New York City Marathon, and the new world record holder, is the eighteen year-old Boitumelo Hope Tumelo. A girl from a remote village in Botswana.*

*One year ago, you had never heard of her. Now she is the Olympic silver medalist, the winner of the New York City Marathon and the holder of the women's world record for the marathon distance of twenty-six point two miles.*

*WHAT an athlete!*

* * * * *

Before Boi left the hotel the following morning, having had not very much sleep, Detective Johnson appeared. As expected, he had no news on the whereabouts of Uncle Tsholofelo. Boi really didn't care anymore, but she would pray for God's vengeance. She hoped that her uncle had been able to watch her performance in the marathon. Perhaps that would be enough punishment for him. Had he been honest, he could have shared her success.

Detective Johnson really wasn't too interested in discussing the star's uncle either. He was just thrilled to be having a conversation with one of the world's greatest athletes and to be receiving her warm gratitude for his efforts.

* * * * *

A few days later, Nyack helped her to buy a brand new school bus in Marekisokgomo, and to place an order for a second. He had resigned from his job as Mister van Gils's chauffeur, at Boi's request. She would employ him, and pay him. He was now the driver and mechanic of the first ever Itlhomolomo school bus.

Boi had carefully calculated a business plan for the bus. Its primary purpose would be to give greater access to secondary education to the children from the villages. It would be much better than making the long walk into the town, or the unreliable option of hitching a ride on any passing truck.

It would also be used as a community bus in the area, which would earn a little extra income for the bus's budget.

She met with her old headmistress, Mma Tlotlo, to arrange a date and time for the formal presentation of the bus to the school. The business would be owned by Boi, but the presentation would make it clear to everyone that the purpose of the bus was to serve the school and its pupils. The local media would be in attendance.

Two days before the presentation, Nyack took the vehicle to a local sign-painter, so that the name of the bus could be painted, to Boi's exact specification, on the front of the bus in big, bold, colourful lettering. The name was top secret; known only to Boi, Nyack and the artist. When it was completely dry, it was covered with a large piece of cardboard that was taped all around its perimeter so that nobody could get a sneak preview.

On the eve of the presentation, Boi and Nyack slept on the bus outside their family home. It was a security measure. The ceremony could not take place if the wheels went missing overnight.

Early the next morning, three children boarded the bus in Itlhomolomo. They picked up a further two from Kango and four from Inagolo before making their way to the front of the Marekisokgomo Integrated Secondary School. A crowd had already assembled. Mma Tlotlo greeted Boi and Nyack heartily, and made a very short speech before handing over the proceedings to Boi.

Boi made a brief speech of her own, just to make absolutely sure that everybody clearly understood why she was standing there with a bus. Then she stepped up to the front of the bus.

Boi gripped the corner of the tape where she had already peeled it away slightly from the surface of the bus.

"It gives me the greatest of pleasure to name this

bus..."

In one swift movement she ripped away the rectangle of cardboard that had been concealing the hand-painted name on the front of the bus.

"Grace!"

Mma Tlotlo audibly gasped. She spread her arms wide. A tear welled up into her eye, and a broad smile lit up her face.

"Beautiful! Just beautiful!"

## THE END

# # # # #

# Epilogue

Mma Tlotlo stood up and walked forward to the edge of the small stage. Before her was a sea of smiling faces. She smiled silently back at them. Each person in the audience shared the impression that Mma Tlotlo was smiling solely at them; picking them out as individuals.

The headmistress could not possibly have felt any prouder than she did at that moment. She could feel her ample chest swelling with pride. Even in the normal heat of the Botswana day, she felt hotter. But it was a marvellous feeling.

"Boys and girls, ladies and gentlemen, mothers and fathers, family members, and, of course, honoured guests..."

She paused and turned to nod a respectful acknowledgement to the honoured guests.

"It gives me the greatest of pleasure to stand here, before you all; at the culmination of what has been a truly momentous, and historic, year for our school.

"You will remember well, the Christmas concert, when our school orchestra and choir welcomed back one of our most famous former pupils, the world famous soprano, Katy Motowana. Her singing that evening was a wonder to behold. Most of the teaching staff could recall her first day at this school and some of her achievements whilst she was studying here.

"Our sporting achievements, as a school, over the past year have also been tremendous. Our netball team won the national schools championship. Our football team and our cricket team were both runners up in the respective national championships. Three of our athletes represented Botswana in the African Junior Games in Nairobi in June.

243

"No less than FOURTEEN of our form five students have been accepted to study for their Bachelor degrees in various universities in Botswana and South Africa.

"One of the most joyous occasions was when yet another of our world famous former pupils, Boitumelo Hope Tumelo, returned to present us with a bus to bring pupils from surrounding villages to school in the morning and to return them to their homes in the afternoon. That bus was generously donated using money which she has earned as the number one marathon runner in the world. We are all extremely grateful to you, Boitumelo, for your magnificent generosity."

Mma Tlotlo turned around and smiled her acknowledgement to the number one guest.

"I am sure that I speak for us all when I say that we feel honoured by the presence of Boitumelo Hope Tumelo at our sports day and presentation ceremony today. What a way to end the school year!

"Boitumelo has agreed to present the prizes, both academic and sporting, today. Before she does so, she would like to address you all.

"Please join me in giving Boitumelo Hope Tumelo a huge Marekisokgomo Integrated Secondary School welcome."

Mma Tlotlo stepped aside as the whole school and the occupants of the stage rose to their feet, clapping and whooping.

Boitumelo walked slowly to the front of the stage, arms aloft. The standing ovation lasted for several minutes, despite her repeated signals to them to resume their seats. Of course, she enjoyed the recognition, but she felt that the day was not about her. It was all about the pupils who sat before her.

When the furore had died down, and everyone was seated, Boi began to deliver the speech which had been forming in her mind for many weeks.

"Thank you all so much for such a lovely welcome.

"And special thanks to you, Mma Tlotlo Mothale, for inviting me to present the prizes today. It is a great honour for me to be here today, and to have received the personal invitation of the headmistress, for many reasons.

"Firstly, to receive the invitation from your esteemed headmistress was a great thrill for me. Aside from my mother, Mma Tlotlo has had the greatest positive influence on my life of any living woman. Over the years, literally hundreds of pupils at this school have benefited from her great wisdom. I know very well that many of you sitting here before me today will benefit from her wisdom throughout the rest of your lives.

"Secondly, it gives me a great opportunity to shake hands with, and to congratulate, the deserving winners of the sporting and academic prizes. Believe me, this is as much a thrill for me as it is for each of the recipients.

"But, most of all, I have the chance to speak to all of you about your own, individual achievements and what you can achieve in the future.

"I remember my first day at this school. I was scared. I don't mind telling you that. Just like me, most of you come from little villages scattered throughout the countryside around Marekisokgomo. Like me, many of you will have walked to school every day, worked hard all day, and then walked home in the evening. It is very tiring. And when you get home, your family expect you to do your chores before you eat or play or go to sleep.

245

"You have to admit that it is quite scary to come to a big school, with lots of pupils, not knowing what to expect.

"But I was excited too. I wanted to learn. I wanted to learn a lot of things. I knew that a good education could be my path to greater things. I did not know what at that stage, but I was certain that my life would be better with a good education. You know that too. That is why you are prepared to walk to school, to work hard, to walk home, and to do your chores to help your family.

"And, like me, the first person who made an impression on you on the first day was Mma Tlotlo. She stood in front of you and gave you a big, warm welcome to Marekisokgomo Integrated Secondary School. She introduced you to all of the teachers, and to the head girl and the head boy. She told you about some of the subjects that you would be learning, and she told you about the standards and values of this school and how she expected you to behave.

"I remember feeling proud to be part of this school, and I am still proud to this day that I studied here. This school not only provided me with a good academic grounding, but it helped me to become an athlete representing Botswana on the world stage. It helped me to believe in myself, and to believe in what I could achieve. It also taught me how I should treat my fellow humans, with kindness and compassion. You are all already benefiting from being part of this great establishment.

"One of the most valuable lessons that Mma Tlotlo taught me was not in mathematics, or in English, or in physics, or home economics. She taught me to visualise my objectives.

"Whatever you want to achieve, you must imagine

yourself actually accomplishing that goal. Just close your eyes and picture yourself as you reach the final point of that particular goal. I'll give you an example.

"You already know that I am the world champion and Olympic silver medalist of marathon running, and I hold the world record, so I am not being immodest when I claim to be the best in the world. I really am the best in the world. And you know that I used my prize money from the New York City Marathon to buy the first school bus which now stands proudly outside the school gates. In winning that race, I broke the world record. But you may not know how I achieved that feat.

"When I lined up with the other competitors at the start line on Staten Island, I knew that the biggest threat to my success was the famous American athlete, Mary-Jane Deakin. She had already beaten me in the marathon at the Buenos Aires Olympics. I deliberately stood alongside her. When we are not racing, we are actually quite good friends. I shook her hand and gave her a cordial greeting, which she returned. Then I turned to face down the street where we were about to run.

"Mary-Jane was standing upright, with one foot slightly in front of the other. I adopted the same stance, but leaning slightly forward. Although our feet were level, my head and shoulders were slightly ahead of her chest. I kept my head pointing towards the huge bridge across which we would soon be running. But as we waited for the race to begin, I was looking at Mary-Jane out of the corners of my eyes. As I did so, I imagined that we were not on the start line, but on the finish line. I was visualising myself crossing the finish line inches ahead of her. At that moment, I really believed that this is what would happen. I closed my eyes. In my mind, the roars of the crowd around the start line became the

247

sound that I would hear as I won the race. I KNEW that I was going to win that race!

"The starter's gun fired, and we were off. I kept to my usual regular, metronome-like pace. In my head, I was singing a song that Mma Reetsang taught to me when I was here at this school.

"The number of runners in our leading group gradually diminished until there were only five of us. As we approached the water station at the thirty-eight kilometre mark, the Ethiopian runner who was just ahead of me suddenly diverted across my path to grab her drink. I touched her heel and tripped. I tumbled to the ground, hurting both of my knees on the hard surface of the road. By the time I recovered and re-established my pace, the four leading runners were almost 200 metres ahead of me.

"Simple arithmetic will tell you that, with only four kilometres to run, I needed to make up at least 50 metres in every kilometre if I were to beat those girls to the finish line. I wanted to maintain my comfortable cadence. My body metronome is always very important to me as I run. I need my rhythm. So I worked out that I needed to stretch my pace length to compensate. It was a big challenge, but I believed that I could do it.

"When I passed the thirty-nine kilometre point, I knew that I was on track to catch them. I was less than 150 metres behind the leaders. I knew that they were at my mercy. They stood no chance of beating me!

"As we rounded the final bend in Central Park, the finish line came into view. I was less than two metres behind Mary-Jane with three hundred metres to run. The other three girls had dropped back behind us and were no longer a threat. It was me against her. I could almost smell Mary-Jane's fear. She already knew that I would beat her. Her legs were gone, and she had nothing more to give.

"The two of us ran in unison over the last fifty metres of the race. Two strides from the line, I dipped my body forward as Mary-Jane remained almost upright. The scene was EXACTLY as I had visualised on the start line.

"I had won the race. I had broken the world record. I was very happy, but I had known for over two hours that it was going to happen this way. In fact, I had known for many weeks that I would win that race.

"So, whatever it is that you want to achieve in your life, take Mma Tlotlo's advice, and mine, and visualise your goal."

There was a long pause before Boi continued.

"Before I begin to present the prizes, I just want to ask you one question. Don't answer me. Just think about it.

"What are you worth?"

Boitumelo paused to let the question sink in.

"That is my question to you. Exactly what are you worth?"

Boitumelo paused again. She paused for a long time. She looked around at all of the enraptured faces. None of the children were fidgeting or being distracted in any other way. They were all staring at her, without exception, and she could feel that they were thinking very hard about her question.

Eventually, she broke the silence.

"I will tell you.

"Each one of you is a diamond.

"Do you know how much a diamond is worth?

"What is a diamond? It is hard. It is shiny. It is priceless.

"Each one of you is priceless.

"You can be what you want to be. You can achieve whatever you want to achieve.

"Whatever your dream is, it can come true. Whether you want to be an athlete, or a scientist, or an artist, or a farmer, or a writer, or a driver, or a builder, or a tour guide, or a film star, or anything else at all that is popping into your mind right now: with a lot of hard work and dedication, and a strong belief in your own ability, you can be the best.

"Every single one of you can be the best in the world!

"Like a diamond, you must be hard. Like a diamond, you will shine. And, like a diamond, you will become priceless.

"Always believe that you will achieve your dream. And always work hard at achieving your dream. Never, ever, give up on your dream.

"Dreams are free. So dream on, because dreams DO come true!"

#####